THE SECRET SELF

The first time she pulled sheer nylon hose over freshly shaven legs, she had experienced a truly shocking sexual thrill, a gasp of fierce pleasure exploding from her mouth, and for a brief moment she had felt as if she would pass out from the almost overwhelming impact of this ever fascinating and endlessly erotic material on her smooth, ultra-sensitised skin. And even now, as she checks her bronzed, perfectly shaped legs for even the tiniest speck of hair, she is filled with a teasing anticipation at the thought of their impending envelopment in soft, endlessly caressing hose.

THE SECRET SELF

Christina Shelly

The LAST
WORD *in*
FETISH

enthusiast

First published in 2006 by
Nexus Enthusiast
Nexus
Thames Wharf Studios
Rainville Rd
London W6 9HA

www.nexus-books.co.uk

Typeset by TW Typesetting, Plymouth, Devon

ISBN 978 0 352 34069 6

Penguin Random House is committed to a sustainable future for
our business, our readers and our planet. This book is made from
Forest Stewardship Council® certified paper.

MIX
Paper | Supporting
responsible forestry
FSC® C018179

Printed and bound in Great Britain by Clays Ltd, Elcograf S.p.A.

Contents

1

A Different Centre of Gravity

Eve is finally ready for her debut. She steps with a gasp of nervous excitement into the crisp evening air and feels an electric shock of fear and arousal course through her carefully prepared body. It is early winter and already the night-shrouded streets are bathed in the unsettling glow of an orange electric light. She feels her heart pound against her chest and hears her high heels strike the tarmac of the driveway. Everything sounds and appears louder and clearer; her senses are heightened. Her mind is flooded with tension and desire. She is in a world of beautiful, anxious clarity.

She points a key at her modest red Peugeot 206 and presses a black button set into its hard body. The car's head and taillights flash brightly and briefly. A sharp mechanical click echoes down the quiet street. She opens the driver's door and looks down into the dark interior. Then she looks up and around, suddenly aware of potential others. She imagines people staring from curtained windows, armed with cameras and phones. Any second she will be exposed not as beautiful, graceful Eve, but as her other self – as Adam.

She climbs into the car, taking care to lower her bottom on to the driver's seat first and then carefully and slowly pull her black nylon-sheathed legs, held modestly and elegantly together, into the dark space beneath the steering wheel. Even so, the short skirt rises up to reveal her shapely thighs and a hint of red panties. She cannot resist a gasp of pleasure at her own feminine beauty and its erotic revelation. Her long legs are momentarily revealed in all their lithe geometric perfection beneath the street lighting – legs, wrapped lovingly in soft, expensive nylon, that stretch down to feet held beautiful captive by a pair of black patent leather, stiletto-heeled court shoes. She has deliberately chosen the three-inch heels tonight: nothing too spectacular for the challenge of the interview.

She straightens the black-and-white check mini-skirt and runs her hot hands over her nylon-sealed thighs. She feels her sex, her paradoxical male desire, stretch angrily beneath the body-shaper and fails to suppress a moan of almost painful arousal.

'Oh God,' she mutters, her eyes closed, her hands slipping beneath the skirt and pressing against the warm gusset of the panties.

Yes, she never imagined it would be like this. Within a few minutes, she is lost in angry sexual excitement, overwhelmed by her first foray into the world outside her modest, three-bedroom house. She lowers the window and lets cool evening air flood the car, gasping down deep breaths and trying desperately to bring her arousal under control. She grasps the steering wheel and stares down at her surprisingly small hands – hands whose long, false nails have been painted the same cherry-red as her lips. She breathes in the rose-tinted aroma of the subtle French perfume purchased especially for this evening and tries to find an element of balance, of poise.

'You can do this,' she whispers. 'You *can*.'

She removes a shaking hand from the steering wheel and inserts the key into the ignition slot to start the motor. She feels the slight, even vibrations of the new engine pass through her body and the rush of need and panic slowly passes. She presses the soles of the court shoes against the control pedals, creating a counter-pressure against the heels as they press into rubber matting. A few days before, she had driven to work as Adam, in business suit and tie, but once in the car, she had slipped into the shoes she wore

2

now, a trial run with heels to ensure that tonight would not be undermined by a mere technicality.

She drives the car out on to the street. A few minutes brings her to the main road that leads through the city to the nightclub. She finds herself becoming more confident, more relaxed. The terror of the last few hours finally begins to pass. Now on the move, she is making real the thing she has so long wanted to happen. And it is this simple fact that fuels her confidence. As she drives through the busy city on this cool October evening, she experiences the sense of achievement that has been lacking for so long. Suddenly, Eve is shockingly real: the beautiful alter-ego, previously locked tightly within the confines of the house, and before that in the London flat, has been released. The she-male genie has been summoned from the lamp.

She had taken the afternoon off work and slept little that night. At work in the morning, it had been impossible to concentrate, inspiring looks of concern from her handsome, maternal secretary, Angela. By two p.m., she had been standing before the full-length mirror in her bedroom facing Adam, the male reflection, the self presented to the world as her authentic being, the self she had known for many years as a lie, a construct forced upon her by the values of an oppressive and deeply flawed society.

Then she had begun the ritual of transformation from male to female that had become an inescapable and marvellous fact of her double life, a ritual she had practised for twelve years, a ritual whose fuel was desire and the events of a rain-soaked evening two weeks before her sixteenth birthday.

As she negotiates the city traffic, Eve contemplates her past and her future. She feels the teasing embrace of the gorgeous red satin blouse against her silken arms, a blouse that tightly covers the full, perfectly formed bosom provided by the erotic genius of the body shaper. Once again the image of Aunt Debra enters her tormented mind. She switches on the CD player. The exquisite, sensual music of Antony and the Johnsons fills the car. 'One day I'll grow up and be a beautiful woman.' The haunting,

3

haunted falsetto inspires more memories of a very special dressing.

It has taken just over three hours to create the look she needs, the look she is sure will impress Priscilla Rouge, the club's chairperson, and thus guarantee her admission to the Crème de la Crème; the look already demonstrated in the portfolio of images she presented as part of her formal application to join the country's most famous transvestite club – an application rooted in her terrible desire to escape the loneliness of her private dressings following her recent move from London. Now it is time to change everything. She is twenty-eight years old and overwhelmed by fear. Her life as a man, as Adam, is an elaborate deceit sustained through her time at university and through her career as a junior manager in one of the country's largest financial corporations. She, as he, agreed to move to a better job in the new national headquarters because he knew the lie and the fear it disguised could not be prolonged further. And now it is time to face this fear head-on.

Earlier, she had stared into the mirror and felt a terribly familiar and still very powerful thrill. Eve revealed. Eve created. The masterpiece of herself. A disturbingly real creation, made more so by naturally feminine features and a slender physique. How easy, she thought, to walk the streets like this, to 'pass' in the public universe of others. Yet also, how hard. For it wasn't just a matter of looking real: it was a matter of *feeling* real, of having the confidence to announce herself without doubt or fear as Eve. No more secrets. No more lies. Only dazzling, gorgeous truth.

She had looked at herself in the mirror and felt pride and desire. 'I am this beautiful woman,' she had whispered.

Adam's deliberately short, dark hair had been hidden beneath a blonde wig, a cascade of elegant, erotic Monroe waves that brought Eve's large, crystal-blue eyes alive in a way far removed from the effect of her naturally dark hair. Make-up had been applied sparingly: she had nurtured her skin very carefully since Eve's birth and become expert at removing every trace of facial hair. There was no need for the layers of melodramatic cake favoured by so many cross-dressers; a little light foundation, a touch of pale-blue eye shadow, a hint of blusher and a striking cherry-red lipstick that matched her nails and the shimmering, sexy blouse. This was all she needed to create a strikingly believable illusion.

The neck of the blouse had been tied with an elegant fifties-style bow. The blouse had been carefully and seamlessly tucked into the check mini-skirt and sealed in place by a thick black leather belt fitted with a diamond-shaped buckle. The skirt reached no further than the middle of her shapely thighs and allowed a complete view of her perfect model's legs. Her legs: wrapped, as always when Eve, in the sheerest of nylon hose. Tonight, a pair of expensive Falke tights, 20 denier nylon – jet black. Tights that teased her very sensitive, silken skin with soft fetish kisses every time she moved. Tights that inspired more furiously erotic memories of the original encounter that had exposed the truth of Eve.

As she had so very carefully drawn the shimmering, ultra-delicate material up her freshly shaven legs, she remembered the first time she had experienced the incredible pleasure of pulling sheer hose over exposed and aroused skin, a moment that had ensured her lifetime addiction to the gentle pleasures of femininity. And as she recalled her dreadful, terror-streaked arousal at this first contact, she remembered the smile of Aunt Debra, the beautiful, loving woman who had encouraged her to dress. Indeed, the tights she had used on that fateful afternoon had been her aunt's, taken from a drawer in the bedroom soon after Adam had been discovered exploring the secrets of her underwear drawer and the large wardrobe that contained her dresses and shoes.

Yes, Eve had always been there, deep within Adam, hiding, waiting for the right moment. And it had taken the intervention of a sympathetic woman, of a thirty-five-year-old divorcee, to ensure her first, startling revelation.

Yet the traces of Eve had been in him, in Adam, even before this first true revelation – in his slender build, in his

5

elegant movements and gentle personality. At school, he had found himself drawn to the company of girls and was immediately labelled a sissy by boys eager to hide their own doubts in the rituals of nascent masculinity. But this deliberate and hypocritical contempt never spilled over into violence or the other, less overt forms of bullying. For despite his strangely feminine character, Adam quickly proved himself a fine athlete and an academic high achiever. He held the school record for the 1500 metres and, by the time he was fourteen, was a member of the county swimming team. This evidence of the more 'male' virtues secured a certain degree of safety from bullies, but did little to prevent him being excluded from male society and quietly mocked by his male classmates. Yet this had never upset him. The girls loved him in a totally unsexual way. He was a very special boy who seemed to understand and respect them: handsome and gentle, yet often painfully shy. A number of the girls had tried to move beyond friendship, to something more intimate and sexual. But, despite his obvious heterosexual interest, he had backed away, frightened in some indefinable way, as he was to remain frightened for the next twelve years.

Then there had been the strange, profound encounter with Aunt Debra, the moment that had changed everything, that had exploited his helpless interest in the details of girls, particularly their dress, their movement, their physical engagement with the world, and transformed it into a new reality: the reality of Eve.

Debra was ten years younger than his mother, who was already ill with the disease that would kill her before his sixteenth birthday. Indeed, he had been sent to spend the Easter holidays with his aunt after his mother had gone into hospital for the first exploratory operation.

At the time, it had been regarded as a relatively minor matter and the journey to Aunt Debra's country cottage as something of an adventure. Yet the anticipation Adam had felt was more than that of a youth undertaking a special journey: at the heart of his excitement was an inescapable sexual thrill. For Aunt Debra was a true beauty, a striking brunette in her mid-thirties with a mysterious past and present, who now lived in a beautiful, sleepy village. She had visited the family home in London perhaps twice a year and, since his early teens, these visits had been events of an increasingly heightened, eroticised reality. As his male desire emerged from the initial rapids of puberty, one of the first, and perhaps the most powerful, sexual attractions he had felt had been towards his gorgeous aunt. Like his mother, she was a buxom woman, yet she held her ample form within a strange halo of sexual beauty and physical grace. Added to this was a striking style in dress and appearance that made her appear truly gorgeous and deeply elegant. Poor Adam was hooked by the time he was thirteen, a fact his aunt clearly recognised and exploited with teasing remarks and a general flirtatiousness that he had tried to laugh off, but which always left him with a painful erection and the furious, almost irresistible urge to masturbate. Indeed, his first, very powerful wet dream was fuelled by haunting images of Aunt Debra, images that had teased his conscious and unconscious mind for over fifteen years.

In the image of Aunt Debra he had found a very pure expression of the contradictory forces that struggled deep within his increasingly powerful and will-destroying sexuality: the desire for the female and the desire to become feminine; a heterosexual orientation combined with a deeply feminine personality and a deep, burning sexual attraction towards everything associated with the feminine. Much as he found himself drawn to her stunning, plump form, he also found himself fascinated and intensely aroused by the trappings of her elegant, scrupulous femininity, particularly her clothes and the delicate intricacies of her make-up. In itself, this fascination was nothing new: the girls at school provided the same source of endless interest. Yet with Aunt Debra, this interest was framed and very effectively fuelled by a powerful sexual desire, and this was the catalyst for Eve – the water that fell upon the tormented ground of his soul and helped to ensure the growth of a helplessly beautiful she-male.

Then he had found himself alone with Aunt Debra in her isolated home, willingly trapped in a tiny bit of paradise. And it was here that his aunt had inspired the first true revelation of Eve.

It had been a few days into his visit. During the daytime his aunt worked, her exact employment always unclear and certainly never discussed in any detail. Thus he was left to explore the striking, ancient house and the beautiful grounds, including a large private wood that surrounded most of the house. Yet, even after just a few days, he found himself too tormented to appreciate his impressive sur-roundings. To be near Aunt Debra so consistently was just too distracting. At first, he had been very nervous and, to a certain extent, embarrassed. She was even more beautiful than he had remembered, and also very pleasant and constantly attentive. To make things worse, she seemed intent on firing up his helpless sexual interest by wearing the most delightful and intricately feminine attire. He found himself confronted by tight, often surprisingly short skirts showing off her large, yet strikingly shapely bottom and very long, firm legs, legs that were always wrapped in various shades of soft, shimmering nylon, and very clearly and deliberately on display, proclaiming their beauty and perfection in daring, fetishistic detail, and always perfectly completed by a variety of high-heeled shoes, normally of black patent leather, and always verging towards the deceptively soft edge of the sado-erotic.

As she sat before him in the large, yet cosy living room and questioned him about his day, he would fight the helpless need to stare brazenly at her long, crossed, teasingly hosed legs and feel his sex – hard, hot and angry – press desperately and uncomfortably against the zipper of his trousers. To stand was to confess all, and so he had stayed seated as if tied tightly in place, paralysed by dark desire and a strangely pleasant humiliation.

His eyes had explored her with a helplessly frank sexual desire and, although he didn't fully realise it, another type of desire: to imitate. Despite his embarrassment and nervous fear, his gaze would travel up her nylon-sealed legs, over the smooth second skin of a satin or silk blouse, a blouse always tight enough to stress and celebrate her large yet firm breasts, and up to her full, heart-shaped face, a face given dazzling beauty by full, cherry-red lips and sensual, honey-brown eyes. And she had gazed back, observing his desire, a teasing curiosity in her smouldering eyes, an ironic smile shaping her gorgeous, glistening mouth.

As she had crossed her legs, her skirt would rustle restlessly against nylon-wrapped thighs and his heart would beat faster. Then a weird, debilitating giddiness would possess his consciousness. He would taste animal desire in his dry mouth and swallow back a mixture of aggression and blind sex terror. Yet nothing had happened between them, and nothing would. His fear ensured an absolute immobility of action.

In his bed at night, in the absolute dark and quiet ensured by the country location, he had thought of nothing but her, of his gorgeous aunt and her costumes of elegant beauty. He had masturbated with an addict's reckless abandon and faced each morning with a bleary desperation. Then it had all become too much for him. On the third day of his visit it had rained heavily and he had been trapped alone indoors. Without the casual diversions of fresh air and nature, his mind focused quickly on his aunt and her sensual attire. The first thoughts of exploring her bedroom had been rebuffed with a weakly imposed moral outrage, a defence mechanism that had been broken down by a flood of dark sex hunger. Then he had been at her door, his sweating, shaking hand gripping its brass handle with a terror-fuelled tightness. He had opened the door expecting to discover his aunt standing before him, a look of anger and betrayal filling her gorgeous eyes. But the room was empty; and as he stepped into it no alarm sounded, no trap-door opened to send him hurtling into a sinner's abyss. Instead, there had been the pristine, perfectly ordered space occupied by a very beautiful, elegant woman.

He had walked to the centre of the room as rain pounded against large, lace curtained French windows

9

opening out on to a small balcony, which provided a striking view of the surrounding woodland. His shoes sank into thick, pale-blue carpeting. A smell of fresh roses filled the room. A large, ornate chest of drawers dominated one corner. This was positioned close to a walk-in closet. On top of the drawers was a beautiful crystal-glass vase filled with the roses that released a strong, teasing scent.

A striking, equally ornate dressing table was positioned against the opposite wall, its large oval mirror providing a strange illusion of additional size, almost like a portal through to another room exact in every detail but perfectly inverted. On the table-top was a vast array of perfumes and make-up, and Adam had soon found himself picking up exotically shaped and named bottles and letting their sensual fragrances fill his flaring nostrils.

Then he had moved towards the bed, a large double bed covered in cream coloured silk sheets and matching pillows, its headboard and frame made from a beautifully crafted white mahogany. Directly above the headboard had been a strange picture, an almost photographic representation of a beautiful, dark-skinned woman dressed in a long, silk nightgown, her coal-black eyes fired by desire. It was a provocative and deliberately erotic picture that added highly inflammable petrol to the fire already burning in Adam's tormented loins.

He ran his hands over the electric softness of the sheets and stifled a moan of helpless, mind-bending pleasure. He longed to feel these sheets against his own naked skin, his own silky smooth, feminine skin. A wave of femininity washed over him, a sense of absolute entrancement that he would come to feel every time he was close to becoming Eve. Here, he had begun to experience the shocking truth of his most secret self.

By now he was overwhelmed. He moved from the bed towards the chest of drawers. He noticed more pictures on the walls, walls that had been covered in a strange, cream-silk wallpaper, its colour almost exactly the same as the elegant bedclothes. There was a picture of another woman, clearly by the same painter, this of a striking

Negress, kneeling, naked except for a thick leather slave collar, her position one of absolute submission, arms covering her breasts, eyes filled not with desire but with embarrassment and fear – a shocking and furiously erotic image that instantly made his aunt an even more mysterious and sexually alluring individual.

Then he opened the large top drawer and entered the world of his darkest, most intense dreams. A gasp of shocked pleasure escaped his mouth as he found himself looking down at row upon row of neatly folded silk panties, a rainbow explosion of his aunt's intimate underwear that stopped his heart and stiffened his prick.

'Oh God,' he whispered, plunging his hands deep into this sea of secret delights.

The panties were all of silk, very fine, very expensive silk. So soft they were almost liquid. He pulled out one cherry-red pair and pressed them against his cheek. It was like lowering his face into a cool pond of scented water, a pond from which Eve, in her earliest incarnation, had begun to rise.

He placed the panties on the top of the chest and then pulled open the second drawer. Here he discovered even greater pleasures: a vast and neatly ordered array of hose: tights and stockings, again in a wide variety of colours. He remembered the teasing displays before the fire each evening, remembered his eyes crawling over the shimmering surface of her perfectly formed legs and how he had longed to feel this sheer, teasing nylon film against his own skin.

Extracting a pair of almost black tights, he placed them next to the panties. He opened the third drawer, to discover brassieres, again neatly folded and arranged, a cornucopia of feminine support. He held a black silk model up before his chest and burst into nervous laughter. His aunt was, despite her ample proportions, not that much taller than himself, and he had been surprised how close her undies were to fitting his own body size. Then the desire that had driven him to his aunt's room and drawn him since puberty to all things feminine, that had spurred

11

his admiration of women and their special, elegant world, drove him to the next stage of transformation. Cracks were appearing in the eggshell and Eve was beginning to emerge.

He had undressed slowly, nervously, yet also with a terrible, inescapable determination. He was filled with new purpose, possessed of certainty and clarity. As he ran his warm hands over the cool feminine fabrics, over his aunt's most intimate attire, he felt a new force inside him. In a few minutes he had stood naked before the chest of drawers, his heart pounding, a low-level quiver of fear and sex hunger rippling across his slender form, his sex a rigid pole of merciless arousal.

He had pulled the soft silk panties up his long, feminine legs and felt a dreadful, stunning sexual shock. As the soft, electric silk material had touched his skin, a larger crack had split the egg and Eve moved further towards the light. He found his movements slowing, becoming more careful, more graceful. As he pulled the panties up over his thighs and then against his furiously erect penis, the levels of fear and hunger began to subside. A sudden feeling of peace washed over his body. Yes, this was right – this was the healing moment. The confusion and unease of the last few years began to pass. Eve had then stepped forth into the strange reality of everyday life.

Once the panties had been snugly positioned, everything else seemed shockingly simple and inevitable. He had taken the tights from the chest of drawers and run his calmer, cooler hands through the sheer, intensely erotic fabric. How many times had he looked at the shapely legs of so many women and wished his own could be sealed tightly yet softly in shimmering, sheer nylon? How many times had he envied them this simple, feminine pleasure? Yet, while the panties at least resembled underpants in terms of the mechanics of dressing, the tights were a totally new challenge. Clearly he would be unable to slip his legs into them while standing. He walked to the bed, each step new and strange, each step shorter and slower, each accompanied by a slight wiggle of the hips. It was almost as if he were suddenly inside a new body.

He had sat on the soft silk sheets and felt his body sink slowly into the erotically forgiving fabric. Holding the tights before him, he gazed into the shady film of sheer nylon with a renewed sexual attraction. The confusion over the dressing passed – it would be simple. He gently bunched up the left leg and created a wide bowl. He then leant forward and slipped his outstretched foot, with its toes elegantly and femininely pointed, into the bowl, and began to draw it over the foot and up his leg.

The sensation had been instantly overwhelming. He had fought a cry of powerful and utterly irresistible pleasure as the soft, teasing fabric kissed and caressed his already very feminine legs. Never had he experienced such pure and immediate tactile delight. The image of Eve had become suddenly clearer as he wrapped his legs in the startling, sheer nylon. The feminine sensibility that had haunted every waking minute of his teenage life was now revealed at its strongest and simplest. He had stepped into the strange space between male and female, a smile of quiet ecstasy lighting up his face.

He had pulled the tights up over his thighs and the tender embrace of the silk panties, his very stiff sex outlined like a totem of ambiguous desire against the soft, shiny fabric.

He was about to study the effect of the tights on his legs in the dressing-table mirror when, to his utter horror, the bedroom door opened and he had found himself facing Aunt Debra.

Trapped in the powerful light of her astonished gaze, he had been frozen to the spot, his heart pounding with a profound animal fear and a bottomless, sickening humili-ation. He had been sure this was the end of everything: he would be shipped back to his mother, his secret perversions exposed. He would be a laughing-stock. He would be sent to a psychiatrist. Perhaps the police would be involved. The possibilities were endless and appalling.

'What on earth are you up to?' his aunt had snapped.

He had been struck down by terror and embarrassment. Tears filled his large, girlish eyes. He had felt a tear run down his left cheek and a sudden, violent dizziness had

washed over him. He fell back on to the bed and his aunt
had rushed over to him.

'Are you OK, Adam?'

Then there had been blackness.

He had awoken only a few minutes later, laid out on the
bed, still in the tights and panties, with his beautiful aunt
looking down at him, her look of shock replaced by one of
genuine concern. Strangely, he had felt much better. The
fear and humiliation had, at least temporarily, passed.

'I'm sorry,' he whispered. 'I don't know what happened.
Got carried away. All got a bit too much for me . . .'

She had smiled at him then, a smile that had changed
everything instantly and forever.

'Yes . . . I can see that.'

He tried to pull himself up, but she had placed a gentle
yet firm hand on his naked chest.

'Don't move yet.'

He had obeyed her command, his eyes meeting hers and
finding something very odd: an interest, even a fascination.

Then she had stepped back and studied his prone,
semi-feminised form, her smile widening.

'You've got lovely legs, Adam. The tights really set them
off. But I suppose you know that.'

Her words had astonished and aroused in equal
measure. His mouth had fallen open. Now he was dumb-
struck for a very different reason.

He had looked up at her and felt a renewed desire. She
was dressed in a very tight black sweater, a white-and-
black check skirt and black nylon tights. With the usual
added touch of three-inch stiletto-heeled court shoes, she
looked absolutely fantastic. His sex had tightened against
the soft panty prison and a look of dark irony had entered
her sparkling eyes.

'Is this just teenage curiosity or something more . . .
developed?'

His face had darkened. A dark crimson stain of embarrassment crossed his cheeks.

'You can tell me, Adam. I've seen the way you look at
me. I know what you've been thinking. But this . . . well,

it's not exactly what I expected. But then again, it doesn't really surprise me. The way you are. The way you hold yourself. The things you're interested in. It all makes sense, really.'

'It's something more . . . serious, more . . . developed,' he had spluttered, suddenly aware of how exposed he was, of how ridiculous he looked.

'So you want to be a girl? I don't think so. Not a real girl. No . . . not from what I've seen. I mean, you don't like boys, do you?'

He had been outraged by this, sitting up and shaking his head, snapping 'No, of course not!'

She had laughed and told him to calm down. 'But you want to be a pretty boy . . . a feminine boy. A boy who can look and act like a girl. Who can experience and express his feminine side. His other self. Is that it?'

Adam had been astonished by this abrupt and exact insight and had found himself nodding helplessly.

'Yes, that's it . . . exactly.'

'Don't look so shocked, Adam,' she continued. 'I know more than you might think about men and their needs.'

He had averted her gaze and felt the crimson confession spread further across his face. She had told him to get up. There had been a strange moment of hesitation, their gazes locked, his heart speeding up once again. Then he had pulled himself off the bed and faced her – his gorgeous, imperious aunt – dressed in her tights and panties, his cock a dreadful and helpless betrayal of his true needs.

'You should have told me,' she had said. 'There was no need for this. If you want to dress up . . . let me help you.'

It had been difficult for him to comprehend fully the true love in her words, a love that would allow Eve to be born and would support him throughout the years that followed. She had smiled and held out a long, elegant hand and he had taken it willingly, even desperately. Never had he felt more helpless and needy than at that moment of absolute confession and surrender. And never, as his beautiful, generous aunt led him back to the dressing table, had he felt happier.

It had been before the dressing table that she had created the first clear image of Eve. The impossible truth of his long-hidden but constantly present femininity was told for the first time before the oval mirror. She sat him down on a white leather-backed stool and they had faced each other through the mirror – together and apart. He had looked at her and at himself. Her sexual beauty had been so terribly apparent at that moment. The smell of her perfume had seemed to induce a shimmer of desire, a film of sex mist that hung before reality and its strange reflection. She had rested a hand on his naked shoulder and a bolt of life-creating electricity had pulsed through his body.

'Let's start with the rest of the clothes.'

She had left him facing his reflection to disappear into the walk-in closet. He had stared at the strange image of his semi-naked self, his heart still pounding, his mouth desert-dry with desire and an impossible anticipation. It was hard to believe that he was in this strange, highly erotic situation with this beautiful woman. Ever since her earliest visits to his mother's home, there had been a dark, sensual fire in her eyes and a teasing nature hidden behind a soft wall of silk charm. All along he had been helplessly attracted to her, entrapped by her personality and appearance, by her naughty words and elegant gestures. She was his model of femininity, an image of classic womanly grace and poise that stood as his first true sex object. And then, in her isolated country home on a wet, windy and dark afternoon, the process of objectification had been inverted. As he had stared at his ambiguous reflection, he had stared at the beginning of a new object of desire, the creature who was soon to become Eve.

His aunt had returned laden with feminine attire, the magical source of the new Eve's physical being. Now he found himself watching her with even more care, the way she moved, the way each step was an erotic gesture that rippled across her marvellous, buxom form like a flirtatious smile. He had noted the careful, yet totally relaxed way she placed one high-heeled foot directly in front of the other, a physical mechanics of counterbalance based on a highly sexual rhythm producing a delightful wiggle of the hips and backside and a merry bounce of her substantial bosom. He had been hypnotised by her female design in a way that echoed his previous helpless infatuation, but this was now informed by a more instrumental purpose: preparation for imitation.

She had placed the clothes on the dressing table and faced him with an encouraging smile.

'Now, let's start with that naughty little bulge.'

His eyes widened in utter terror and she had laughed.

'Don't worry, Adam . . . it's just a panty girdle. The best way, I think, of hiding your rather obvious manhood.'

She had held up a rather pretty, white satin-panelled, elastane-reinforced panty girdle, its smooth, shiny front decorated with lovely silk flowers. He had beheld it with tormented, hungry eyes.

She had told him to stand up and then helped him step into the frilled legs of the girdle, before pulling it gently up his nylon-sheathed legs. She had been so close, inches from his teased body, her bosom brushing against his thighs as she leaned forward. As she had hauled the tight stomach- and sex-flattening device up over his waist and positioned it carefully around his slender stomach, he had stifled a moan of terrible, heart-stopping pleasure.

'There,' she had whispered, 'much better.'

And she had been right: although the rigid outline of his angry, deeply tormented sex remained visible, it was now held fast and upright and would not be noticeable beneath a skirt.

The next item of feminine attire had not been a skirt, however, but a pretty lace-edged silk slip with slender shoulder straps. It had reached barely to the tops of his nylon-sheathed thighs, yet as Aunt Debra slipped it over his head and it fell against his body, he felt smothered in the essence of femininity.

As soon as the slip was in place, his aunt had picked up a bottle of golden-coloured perfume from the dressing table and drowned his torso in a mysterious, sensual cloud of rose-scented mist. She had laughed as he coughed and

17

staggered backwards against the stool. Then she had produced a silver-coloured silk blouse.

'The slip is a little small, and I suspect the blouse will be too, but we can get you some new, proper-fitting outfits tomorrow.'

He had looked at her with questioning, desire-tormented eyes.

'Yes,' she had said, responding to his gaze. 'We definitely need to go shopping. It'll be fun.'

The fear in his eyes had betrayed a darker thought and again she had laughed.

'Don't worry, you can come dressed as a boy. We'll think about taking you out *en femme* later on.'

En femme. Mysterious then, fundamental now. A phrase betraying an understanding of transvestism and its milieu much deeper than he could have imagined. The words ring down the years as street lights fill the car and reveal Eve. Suddenly, he is she and back in the present, driving to the Crème de la Crème, the club recommended to her in a letter from Aunt Debra a month ago.

'All of this because of you,' she whispers, a willing prisoner of primal memories. But soon she is back again, as Adam, in that beautiful, elegant room, being helped into the ultra-soft blouse, experiencing the most intense sexual thrill of his young and inexperienced life, setting a course that is to lead him to addictive, desperate and beloved transvestism, and thus to Eve.

He had secured the cream-coloured pearl buttons and been surprised: the blouse was a perfect fit. It had a high neck which was used to support two strips of matching silver silk. His aunt had quickly tied the strips into a tight, fat bow. Then she had stood back to review her handiwork and a wider, so terribly sexy smile had crossed her face.

'Perfect,' she had whispered, before returning to the dressing table to retrieve the skirt. The skirt: after the sheer nylon tights, the most powerful symbol of his transformation and of helpless femininity, made of rich cotton and jet black. Like all Aunt Debra's skirts, it was short, very clearly a mini-skirt with a handy elastic waistband that

18

allowed it to mould perfectly to his slender waist. She had helped him step into it and then pulled it up his legs, before carefully tucking the blouse into the waistband and then turning back to the closet. He had seen his disturbingly shapely legs in the oval dressing-table mirror and felt a terrible sting of pride and desire. How *real* he looked; or rather, how real his black nylon-enveloped legs looked.

She returned with a striking pair of shoes and a further mystery.

'I'm afraid there are four areas where we'll never be able to disguise totally the biological facts: your hands, your sex, your voice . . . and your feet.'

Her words had been brutal, frank and quite shocking. 'Your sex'. His 'manhood', encased in silk and nylon and held firm by the tender but sure grasp of the panty girdle.

The shoes had been at least two sizes larger than her own feet and their presence in her closet had posed a profound and teasing question: whose were they?

'These should fit.'

She had held the shoes before him, before Adam transforming slowly but surely into Eve. They were black patent-leather court shoes with frightening three-inch heels. He had looked at her, fear and surprise filling his wide eyes, desire filling his heart.

'I'm sure you want to try these, Adam. What's the point otherwise?'

He had mumbled a sex-drenched 'yes' and watched soft electric light sparkle in the depth of the gleaming leather. 'But who do they belong to?'

She had smiled and averted her gaze in a surprisingly coy manner. 'Well . . . that would be telling.'

There had been no further explanation. Instead, she had knelt down at his feet and told him to sit down on the stool. As she knelt, the sexy check mini-skirt had climbed up her shapely, black nylon-sheathed thighs and poor Adam's eyes had nearly popped out of his head. He had fought a squeal of pleasure and she had suddenly looked up at him, her gaze more severe, more dominant.

19

'Point your toes forward, like an arrow; in the feminine way.'

He had nodded weakly, excited and very nervous. In a strange way, this single physical gesture said all that needed to be said.

Then he had allowed her very gently to slip the elegant, sexy shoe over his hosed foot. The sound of his heavy, deeply aroused breathing had filled the anticipatory silence that suddenly hung over the room. As the second shoe was positioned, his legs seemed to take on an even more feminine form. His sex had stiffened and his heartbeat had increased. He was on the verge of experiencing a true and startling transformation.

'Very good. Now stand up.'

He had looked at her with worried eyes and a softer, maternal smile graced her lovely face.

'Don't worry, I'll help you.'

To confirm this she had taken his right, silk-sheathed arm. He had then placed his high-heeled feet on the floor and pushed himself upward.

The immediate sensation had been of sudden and disorienting elevation. His balance was instantly questioned, tested, made deeply and disturbingly problematic.

'You have to adjust your body weight,' his aunt had said, watching his legs and feet carefully, her gleaming eyes filled with the intense concentration of a trainer.

'It's all about finding a slightly different centre of gravity.'

A different centre of gravity. Another phrase that echoes down the years. A perfect metaphor for Eve: the new point of refocus and balance that was his nascent feminine self. Eventually, Aunt Debra had realised her grip and Adam found himself swaying precariously, fighting the urge to stagger forward, to grab his aunt or some solid fixed point that represented safety, a security that supported the self he had, up to this particular point, been. But there had been nothing to grab hold of, only the person he was becoming, only the future of this new self. And after a few minutes of unsteadiness, he had begun to feel the new balance, the firmer, stronger centre of gravity that was at the heart of his new, distinctly feminine self.

'There,' his aunt had said, her body relaxing, standing back to consider a more confident Adam. 'That's much better. Now take a step.'

He had looked at her again with frightened, girlish eyes and she had nodded, her own eyes filled with aroused enthusiasm.

'A small step,' she added. 'The shoes demand careful, small steps.'

And his first step had been small, but also, in another sense, giant, for as he carefully shifted his weight to retain his balance, he had felt his hips move in a certain and strangely natural way. His hips and bottom. And this had not really been a step, but a mince, a small, elegant mince modelled on the erotic semi-steps of his sexy, buxom aunt, steps that were part of a ballet of graceful, erotic movement.

And this first step quickly became two, and then three. His confidence had increased. The final embarrassment had passed. He had wiggle-minced before his aunt with a sense of genuine pride, experiencing a new mechanics of body movement. Indeed, it was as if this was a new body – the body of Eve.

His aunt had remained silent, her smile fading slightly, but her gaze became more fixed, more intent. She had seen something in his delicate imitation.

'You're a natural,' she had whispered.

As he had moved before her, he felt his nylon-sheathed thighs rub gently together to create an electric and highly erotic surge that shot teasingly into his sex, a charge which was like an astonishing shock of life helping to bring substance to Eve. Soon he was mincing before his gorgeous aunt with a grace and fluency that turned her gaze from one of concentration and observation to one of amused excitement.

'You really do have the way,' she had whispered. 'Are you sure you've never done this before?'

He had smiled shyly, modestly, and let the waves of feminine pleasure wash over his carefully, if only provisionally, transformed being.

21

'And this is only the beginning, Adam,' she had continued. 'A few more days and nobody will be able to tell you're really a boy.'

He had stopped and looked at her. 'Really? You can really do that?'

'With a subject like you . . . no problem. I guarantee it. We'll go shopping in the morning and by tomorrow afternoon you won't be Adam any more, my love.'

A nervous smile had crossed his slender, girlish face.

'Then who will I be?' he had asked, a teasing innocence cutting across his voice.

Her smile had broadened and she laughed at his coy presumption. 'You'll be Eve, of course!'

His aunt, his splendid, sexy Aunt Debra, had named him and immediately created her: the new Eve, the new self.

'But why? Why are you helping me like this? Why aren't you ringing my dad up and telling him to come and take me home?'

This had been a reasonable and logical question, one that she had avoided with a slight smile and a barely perceptible shake of her beautiful head.

'My own reasons . . . Eve. Reasons you don't need to know about now. Just thank your lucky stars it was me that caught you and not your mother. The shock would have been far too much for her. Especially after . . .'

Her voice had trailed away, followed by a pause. In his aunt's gorgeous honey-brown eyes he had seen regret, sadness . . . loss. Then she had seemed to shake herself back into a more positive mood. She insisted that Adam – now so obviously Eve – sit back down on the stool before the dressing table and face the oval mirror.

This time, his reflection had produced a gasp of immediate and very powerful shock. Now the nature of Eve was clear. The blouse emphasised a simple fact: he had a very feminine face, with soft features dominated by large, blue eyes. His short hair had managed, in a somewhat paradoxical manner, to make him appear even more feminine than he might have been with long hair. His slight shoulders and perfectly flat chest seemed to increase this sense of a beautiful young woman. It was as if he was beholding himself and another instantaneously. This was, perhaps, the most mystifying and erotic aspect of the identity he would develop over the next ten years or so. When he became she, when Adam disappeared into Eve, he stepped into a strange blurred space between male and female which produced both a sense of intense femininity and a very male sexual attraction to this femininity. He became, becomes – is – his own object of desire.

His aunt had applied minimal make-up with an artist's care. A mere touch of foundation, light peach lipstick, a hint of pale-blue eye shadow, even a hint of peach rouge on each cheek, enough to give his face feminine colour and emphasise its naturally soft, distinctly female shape. He had watched this gradual, expert transformation with hungry and startled eyes, still amazed by the reality of Eve, by the authenticity of this new self.

Aunt Debra had continued to express her satisfaction as if this was the latest and most successful in a line of transformations. As she worked on his face, her warm, elegantly attired, almost unbearably sensual body had pressed against his. Her perfume had tortured him, her soft, large, tightly restrained breasts had rested only inches from his carefully painted lips. The erotic spectacle of transformation had also been an erotic ritual of display and casual caress. His sex burned deep in its nylon and silk prison, a bound, helpless and hungry prisoner.

Then his aunt had stepped back, as if pulling a veil from the face of Adam, to reveal, in her true, stunning glory, Eve. His secret self and true being.

'She was there all the time,' she whispered. 'Beautiful Eve.'

She. Yes, at this point, *she* had looked at *her* reflection and gasped. A very pretty, short-haired young girl stared back. She (it would always be she from now on) was so very happy and so very horny!

Then Aunt Debra had taken Eve, her lovely niece, by the hand and led her from the bedroom. As Eve had followed this stunning, graceful, deeply erotic woman, she had watched each elegant, high-heeled step with an intensely analytical eye, eager to reproduce exactly the sensual, careful rhythm of that body movement in her own increasingly feminine deportment. And with each step taken, the stronger Eve had become. By the time she entered the living room, her pretty girl's eyes pinned to her aunt's plump, shapely, inviting backside as it swayed teasingly in the tight fetish prison of her mini-skirt, she was surely Eve much more than Adam.

It had been early evening. Electric light was necessary to escape the tense and claustrophobic winterish gloom. Aunt Debra had been so very keen to instruct Eve in every gesture and movement required to live in heels and hose. How to walk, how to sit, how to stand, how to manage objects, how to cook and clean. It was almost as if she had given birth to a new version of herself: the creator with her work of living art. And Eve had loved every second of it. This new feminine self was a gateway to a stronger, clearer perception and a more immediate and clearly focused reality. To become Eve was to enter the real world; to be Adam was to be locked in a universe of distortion and deceit.

They had stayed together until nearly midnight. Her aunt had spent hours talking about the feminine and its creation. Perhaps more interestingly, she had stressed that Eve was beginning a great journey through the illusions of the limited patriarchal social order.

'Eve is the opportunity to see a new world. This is the beginning of an amazing adventure for you. An adventure we can share.'

She had sat directly opposite her new niece, her long, black nylon-wrapped legs crossed tightly, her mini-skirt riding up her shapely, carefully trained thighs. Eve's wide, dark eyes had feasted on this highly erotic display and she had instinctively crossed her own long, finely hosed and very feminine legs. Noticing this imitation, her aunt had smiled and whispered a teasing 'Exactly'.

Then she had stood and taken her pretty, doe-eyed niece by the hand and led her from the living room, upstairs into the bedroom Adam had slept in for the past three nights.

24

As they climbed the stairs, Eve's eyes had continued to submerse themselves in the ocean of feminine delight that was her Aunt's plump, gently swaying behind and her long, elegantly hosed legs.

In the bedroom, Aunt Debra had turned to face Eve and told her to undress.

'It's late and you need your beauty sleep. You can wear one of my nightdresses. I expect to see you naked when I return.'

Eve had watched Aunt Debra leave the room with a startled gaze. Her voice had been surprisingly firm. This had been an order, an erotic command, a command Eve knew she would obey without question. She remembered this harsher tone when the gorgeous shoes were being fitted. A tone that aroused her, that inspired a strange, submissive delight.

She had slipped nervously out of the layers of pretty, so dreadfully arousing feminine attire, her heart pounding, her hands shaking. As she wiggled out of the soft prison of the panty girdle, her hard, hot sex had slipped against the teasing wall of the silk panties and she was again revealed as a strange middle space between male and female.

She had very gently, carefully (and regretfully) slipped her legs out of the tights and removed the panties. Then she had stood naked, arms at her side, facing the door, her sex riding up before her like some terrible, arrogant and angry reaffirmation of a maleness that was becoming increasingly alien yet also utterly inescapable.

Aunt Debra had re-entered the room carrying more feminine attire and when her eyes had fallen upon Eve's exposed, slender, intensely girlish form, a flame of arousal had ignited in each dark honey-brown orb.

Eve had blushed, more embarrassed as a boy naked than a girl clothed, and her hands had tried to cover the furious erection.

'A man is doomed to be obvious,' Aunt Debra had whispered, throwing the new clothing on to the bed, her eyes never leaving Eve's granite sex.

'Your desire betrays you every time.'

There had been a change in her manner, a subtle, erotic shift. And as she walked towards her niece, as Eve bathed in the glorious sexual beauty of her aunt's buxom, carefully displayed figure, the newly formed she-male had noticed that Debra was holding a very fine, black nylon stocking in her right hand.

'I think we need to wrap your little stiffy up nice and tightly before we get your bedclothes on.'

Eve's eyes had widened, as had Debra's smile. Her aunt stopped a few inches from Eve's naked, shaking form. The edge of her lovely mini-skirt brushed against her new niece's agonised sex and Eve released a moan of almost unbearable pleasure.

'Please,' Eve had mumbled. 'Oh please . . .'

Aunt Debra had chuckled and knelt before Eve's tumescent sex. Her incredible, substantial breasts brushed against Eve's naked upper thighs and then, to Eve's astonishment and dark delight, her aunt proceeded very slowly to slip the stocking over the bulging, boiling head of her undeniable manhood. Eve had squealed with a shocked ecstasy and begged her aunt to release her from the torment of male desire. She had been told in a much harsher tone to keep still, and this had only served to excite her even more. Aunt Debra had pulled the stocking tightly over Eve's bulging balls and then tied it in place with a length of pink silk ribbon in a fat sissy bow. A cruel joke, perhaps; but it had left Eve in a state of utter physical transcendence, the pleasure like nothing she had ever experienced.

Debra had stood up and looked down upon her niece with loving, amused eyes.

'You poor thing. I think we need to get you into bed as quickly as possible.'

Pondering these promising words, Eve had allowed herself to be led over to the bed and presented with the latest feminine attire.

On the bed were a pair of pink silk panties and a rather spectacular baby-doll nightdress made from a very fine, almost transparent silk, plus a pair of white nylon, self-supporting stockings.

'I haven't worn this baby-doll for nearly ten years,' her aunt had mused, holding it up before a hungry-eyed, terribly aroused Eve. 'Put the panties and stockings on first.'

Eve had obeyed her aunt with almost a curtsey and the older woman's beautiful smile had darkened. 'Good girl,' she had whispered, her mind filling with possibilities. 'Very good.'

Eve had wiggled prettily into the panties and then, carefully aided by her lovely aunt, had slipped the sheer, cool, helplessly caressing stockings up her long, elegant and virtually hairless legs. Aunt Debra had watched this erotic display with obvious pleasure, taking a strange pride in her new niece's graceful, careful movements. As Eve had pulled the stockings up to her thighs, the ingenious elasticated tops had ensured a tight, seamless fit and supplanted the need for suspenders or garters. And once she had managed to pull them firmly into position, the lovely she-male had climbed to her feet and taken up the elegant, intricate and desperately sexy baby-doll. A feeling of arousal mixed with a deep inner peace had washed over her as she had carefully pulled the frilled neck of the baby-doll over her head. It was a feeling close to the one experienced as she had dressed for her aunt earlier, a feeling of certainty and serenity. Suddenly, there had been purpose and meaning: by revealing Eve, she was revealing her true self and giving her life a new and dazzling significance.

She had pulled the baby-doll into place and allowed herself to be truly, utterly submerged in the dainty trappings of femininity. I am free, she thought. For the first time, I am truly free.

Aunt Debra had then pulled back the bedclothes and helped her niece to settle down for her first night in her new feminine identity. By now, the poor she-male was shaking, her body gripped by the destabilising tremors of a furious, merciless desire.

'I don't think you'll get much sleep in this state,' her beautiful, imperial aunt had whispered.

Eve had looked up at her aunt with pleading, starved eyes. Her need was unlimited and nerve-shattering. An evening of carefully sculpted femininity had left her in a state of sexual exhaustion. Yet this was an over-tiredness, a physical draining that produced only more desire, more need, more wearying hunger.

Then her aunt had slowly pulled back the heavily frilled and very short skirt of the baby-doll to reveal Eve's sensual stocking tops and the shimmering panties so well stretched by her new niece's angry tumescence.

'Dear me,' she had whispered, a cruel, teasing smile running across her voluptuous, blood-red mouth. 'We will have to do something about this.'

Then, to Eve's astonishment, Debra had gently pulled back the panties to expose fully her stocking-encased, ultra-rigid sex.

'It looks so lovely in its little stocking prison.'

Tears of vital, savage animal need had begun to trickle from Eve's pretty eyes, eyes that had suddenly widened as Aunt Debra leant forward and took the nylon-sheathed shaft between her right thumb and forefinger and started very gently to massage it.

Eve had gasped and moaned. Aunt Debra was masturbating her. And within a few seconds, the combination of Debra's expert ministration and the teasing caress of the stocking produced a very violent and disturbing orgasm. Eve had found herself screaming uncontrollably, screaming a high-pitched wail of utter delight, as her thick, creamy semen flooded into the stocking. Her body jerked and bucked, so much so that Aunt Debra had been forced to place a surprisingly powerful restraining hand on Eve's hot, slender chest to hold her in place.

'There, there,' she had whispered, as if addressing a baby. 'It's all over, lovely. Now you can sleep and tomorrow we can really start work on Eve.'

Eve had looked up at her aunt with stunned, loving eyes. Debra had then carefully removed the stocking and wiped her flaccid sex with a damp cloth, before repositioning the panties and pulling the bedclothes over her niece's delicately feminised form.

She had then placed a gentle kiss on Eve's forehead and left the room, switching off the light and plunging the newborn she-male into darkness. And in this darkness, Eve had considered the amazing events of the day that was closing, events that she ponders once more twelve years later as she drives to the next stage in the development of Eve, events she has considered so often since, and which can be said truly to haunt her mind, to structure her imagination, to drive her ever further forward into the dark and beautiful realms of a carefully adopted and endlessly arousing femininity.

2

En Femme

Eve parks the car some three hundred yards from the building that houses the Crème de la Crème club. This is the second major test, and perhaps the most terrifying: she must reveal herself as Eve on the streets of the city – she must expose herself in a way that she has never done before.

She sits in the dark silence of the car and watches her hot, nervous breath form small clouds of transparent mist. She hears her fast, anxious breathing and her heart pounding with an arousal-tinged fear.

The morning after her startling and life-altering adventure with Aunt Debra, everything had changed again. There had been an early phone call from Adam's father. The situation with his mother was worse than originally thought. He was to return home immediately. His aunt had clearly been both appalled by the news of her sister's serious illness and the fact that she would not, after all, be able to create the strange ambiguity that was Eve. Instead, she had driven Adam (for now, once again, Eve was hidden, secret, and she was surely a he) to the station. Here they had embraced and there had been a long, terribly exciting kiss. He had been rock-hard in seconds and she had pressed her hand against his erection before saying a tearful and abrupt farewell.

And he had never seen her again.

Yet over the following months and years there had been letters, so many, so very important letters. These were the letters not of a concerned and loving relative, but of a co-conspirator and, in some ways, a lover. Letters that had openly encouraged him to continue to discover and develop the delightful secrets of Eve. Letters that had provided advice and guidance, and which had provoked with their continually erotic tone and left him helplessly and furiously masturbating and begging her to return to his tormented, confused life. But this had never happened. Indeed, a few months after that fateful encounter, she had left the country, taking up a lucrative but deliberately unexplained job in America. Yet still the letters had come, letters bearing exotic American stamps, letters always addressed 'Dearest Eve' or 'My Darling Eve'. Letters that sometimes contained photographs, beautifully staged, erotic photographs of his aunt in a splendid gown or – on one or two heart-stopping occasions – ultra-sexy under-wear. Letters to which he had replied with an addictive passion, letters expressing his fantasies of Eve, how desper-ately he wanted to turn them into reality, and how desperately he wanted to do this with his aunt – in her company, as her beautiful, loving niece.

Then he had left home to attend university and finally found the opportunity to become Eve once again, to release his true she-male self. Driven by a plan designed in correspondence with his aunt, he had found a rather plush flat in a building on the edge of a small town a few miles from the university campus. This was far beyond his means, but his aunt had ensured money was never a problem: a generous sum was transferred at the end of each month from an American bank into his own account. There was always enough to pay the rent, his general maintenance and to fund the development of Eve.

Magazines began to arrive at this new, secluded, very private address. High-quality American transvestite and fetish magazines. He began to be drawn into a new, wider world and to understand that he was far from alone. It appeared that many males shared his love of the feminine and quietly (and not so quietly) nurtured secret selves.

In his relatively spacious flat he had set to work on Eve. Buying clothes and make-up via mail-order catalogues recommended by Aunt Debra; buying wigs and shoes from specialist suppliers who advertised in the magazines; spending his aunt's money carefully. By day, he was a diligent student studying Management and Accountancy, a course his aunt had insisted he follow to keep his father happy and thus create an effective smoke-screen behind which to hide Eve. And by night, he became Eve. As the other students enjoyed the busy and complex social lives of the young and free, he spent as much time as possible creating Eve. This was his true life work, his artistic self-perfection.

Eventually, his aunt counselled him to control his increasingly obsessive impulses. Without a proper and honest revelation, there was only controlled deceit. She told him to use Adam to survive and to learn social skills. And so he had begun, quite easily, to make friends, especially with girls. This led to an almost immediate problem. Girls found him very attractive, just as they had at school; but now, the sexual interest they expressed was far more obvious and aggressive. Nor was there any doubt in his mind that he was attracted to them. And it was at this point, having been led into the realm of young, desiring women by his aunt's always guiding but never seen hand, that she tormented him with a simple order: never become involved physically. Her rationale seemed straightforward enough: you are inescapably Eve; if you get too close to a real girl, you will have at some awkward point to reveal your secret self. The consequences of this could be potentially catastrophic. And, despite his frustration, he had known she was right. Yet behind her advice was something else, something he couldn't quite put his finger on. A strange, almost cruel controlling impulse framed by a hint of jealousy.

So there had been plenty of friends, yet no real girlfriends. This confused those who wanted him. At first they thought he was gay; but then there was his obviously interested gaze, his clear male hunger, a hunger he had seemed to struggle with, to deny. And for three years, he had managed to deal with the complexities of being both Adam and Eve. He had graduated with a first-class honours degree and been snapped up by a major UK finance house. Soon, he had a bigger flat in the centre of a bigger city. Here, in this new, elegant privacy, Eve truly came into vibrant, erotic being. He had quickly transformed the spacious area into the home of a beautiful young woman, paying a discreet interior designer to oversee a highly feminine, but also deeply tasteful decoration. He had bought a beautiful antique dressing table, two large, white wooden wardrobes – both Victorian antiques – and a large double bed that was smothered in pink and white silk sheets.

Despite the opportunities provided by work, there had been no real relationships. Aided by the emerging Internet, he had entered a different social universe – a virtual community of fellow cross-dressers. He quickly formed a series of strong, deeply satisfying relationships on the Net with other TVs. Pictures were exchanged, every aspect of the TV world discussed in graphic and often erotic detail. His early pictures of Eve – clumsy, taken with a timed camera in bad light – were poor, but her beauty and reality were undeniable. He was frankly disappointed by most photos of other TVs. He wasn't arrogant, but he knew in a simple and inescapable way that none of her new virtual friends were even half as convincing as Eve. And so did they. Eve quickly became a highly popular pen-pal. Many wanted to take the friendships further, to meet, to get her to come to their societies and clubs – to become involved in a real version of the sexual fantasies exchanged with the abandon of those who know they have the absolute freedom of total anonymity.

His aunt had begun to communicate by e-mail, first on a weekly basis, and then every other day. He had taken photography classes and learned how to photograph Eve properly. This had become a fascinating and arousing hobby, and very soon he was sending Aunt Debra photographs over the Net. By this time, Eve was fully formed, shockingly convincing – stunning. His aunt was amazed and delighted. Debra returned her own photographs for his masturbatory pleasure. Now, more than ever, their relationship was one of virtual lovers. The details of their correspondence became increasingly erotic and, to his surprise and pleasure, perverse. His aunt revealed a dark sado-masochistic streak to her already fascinating personality. The photographs that arrived as file attachments displayed a gorgeous, mature dominatrix, a dark angel projecting a fundamental sexual power. And as this happened, she felt herself becoming more confident. Aunt Debra's fierce, sensual praise gave Eve the courage to allow her very professional pictures to be posted on a number of TV club websites. She was inundated with messages of praise and desire, many from men, many deeply sexual, many deliciously disgusting; all producing a deep, powerful pleasure.

At work he remained purely Adam, always pleasant, efficient Adam. Under his suits he virtually always wore silky, sexy panties and sheer nylon tights. Adam was now the illusion and Eve was, increasingly, the truth – the true self. He found the work – account management for a number of large investment companies – simple and quickly rewarding. Ultimately, he had no interest in it as a career. It was a means to an end – a well-paid way of servicing the increasingly intricate needs of Eve and, indirectly, his aunt.

Once he was established in his own, independent and fully adult life, the parcels began to arrive, all from America, all from his aunt. Parcels containing clothes, beautiful, expensive and often kinky. Clothes she demanded Eve wear and model via photographic evidence sent over the Internet. Clothes that always fitted; clothes designed to proclaim the absolute femininity of Eve.

In one of these parcels had been the body-shaper, an ingenious tool of transformation that was to bring the final touch of authenticity to the sweet mirage of Eve's physical being. A beautiful basque-like item of underclothing, the body-shaper was designed by an American fetish-wear company to create a totally believable visage of femininity. Made from a satin-lined elastane material, the shaper was essentially an elaborate panty corselette with bra cups carefully filled with a strikingly realistic silicon-based material that provided a highly convincing weight and shape. The shaper was also padded at the hips and between the legs, to provide the lower shape of a fully figured and very sexy young woman. As he had pulled it over his slender, boyish form, a sense of ecstatic conversion had washed over him, a feeling of almost mystical, yet also highly arousing transformation. It was another major turning point orchestrated by Aunt Debra. And once it was positioned, once his silken form was fully and strikingly consumed by its tight, yet teasingly soft contours, he had stared into the full-size, stand-alone mirror that stood next to the elegant dressing table and sighed with a terrible, unyielding pleasure. A sense of deep contentment filled his feminine heart. This was the perfect form, the ideal representation of Eve.

The final touches – a beautiful white silk blouse, a black leather micro-mini, jet-black nylon tights and five-inch-high, black patent-leather stilettos, plus the usual judicious use of make-up and a striking honey-blonde wig – ensured immediate and devastating perfection. He found himself beholding Eve remixed: Eve as the sexiest female he had ever laid eyes upon. And when his aunt had seen the photographs he took a few hours later, her response had been astonishment and excitement. She had called Eve 'her divine and perfect creation', and he had found it difficult to disagree.

And the parcels continued. Aunt Debra seemed determined to provoke and stimulate with every item of attire. As well as leather and rubber wear, there had been uniforms: schoolgirl, nurse, maid. She demanded detailed descriptions of how the costumes made him feel. She had insisted he masturbate while dressed, thinking only of ultra-feminisation, and that he do so to the pictures of Aunt Debra, a command the gorgeous she-male followed without question. Indeed, the control of his sex became a key part of the virtual sado-masochistic ritual of submission and domination, a control he came to desire.

'Your sex is mine,' she wrote to him. 'It has always been mine. I was the first and the last woman to touch it. And when you touch it – even when you piss – you will think only of me, my sexy, sissy slut.'

This was the new tone, and it was one he loved and craved. She was always 'Dear Auntie Debra', no other form of address was permitted. But she was also – in his mind – the Mistress, the Majesty. The Divine High Priestess of Ultra-Feminisation.

And it had been she who had sent him the web link to the Crème de la Crème club. At first, he had been surprised. As soon as he had seen the site, and what it held, he was filled with a terrible and very familiar sense of change. This had been, without doubt, another very significant turning point.

For the Crème de la Crème was precisely that: a club catering for the most convincing and beautiful TVs on the net, a society of striking and expert illusion. Here he discovered all the pictures he had so desperately wished he had been sent by his many TV friends and admirers. Here was a stunning consistency of utterly convincing and gorgeous mirage. Its members referred to themselves as 'The Beautiful Elect'. And to become a member, you clearly had to be both very convincing and beautiful.

The first time he had visited the site, via a weblink sent in one of his aunt's e-mails, he had been astonished and furiously aroused.

'I think you'll like this one, Eve.'

That was all her accompanying message had said. As he looked at the pictures, at the elaborate pink, white and red design motif, at the detailed and carefully written text and the stunning photographs, he knew he was entering a new realm of she-male perfection, a realm in which Eve would be very naturally at home.

Then there had been another message; a few hours later.

'I think you should join. I think this is the moment to consider coming out, my pretty little petal.'

The club was managed by the elegantly and rather melodramatically named 'Priscilla Rouge', a stunning redhead with large emerald eyes, a very tall frame and a carefully presented, highly erotic figure. Her picture, which dominated her own personal page on the website, defined the ethos of the club: ultra-femininity, a striking attention to detail, erotic attire and striking authenticity. The picture showed Priscilla sitting on a high stool, wearing a tight red satin blouse revealing a generous, scrupulously manufactured bosom; indeed, the powerful illusion of femininity she presented was significantly enhanced by the fact that the blouse opened at the chest to reveal two pale rose orbs that looked remarkably lifelike. He wondered if the picture had been doctored. But there had been no doubt about the reality of her legs – long, beautifully shaped, sealed in sheer black nylon and enhanced perfectly by a black-leather micro-mini; legs that travelled down to feet erotically encased in black patent-leather court shoes with fierce heels of at least four inches in length. Yes, she was a splendid spectacle, and he had quickly become hard.

Priscilla gave her age as thirty-three, but she looked younger – nearer Eve's age. She defined herself as the President of the Crème de la Crème club and in her sparkling emerald eyes was a daring confidence. He was immediately and deeply attracted to this gorgeous she-male, the first whose beauty and careful construction truly rivalled Eve's.

Yet there were more TV beauties revealed within the elaborate and expertly structured pages of the website. Indeed, each club member was allowed a single webpage to display a sexy picture and to provide a biography. There must have been at least twenty of these pages, each as stunning and convincing as the next. The quality of illusion was very, very high, and the taste for rather outrageous costumes increasingly apparent. There were blondes, brunettes, redheads; most were white, but Eve noticed a few Asians and one very striking Afro-Caribbean beauty called Cherry. All were posed and photographed in a highly professional and erotic manner, and all had a look of sensual tease in their eyes. It was almost as if they were presenting themselves for sale.

Adam was reduced to furious and desperate masturbation, and over the next few days he returned again and again to the website, making a strange kind of love to these impressive and deeply sexual images, particularly Cherry, to whom he found himself violently attracted. This left him exhausted and elated. Here, indeed, were Eve's glorious, stunning equals; here there was no embarrassment or disappointment. Here was the believable and the joyously confident. Here were she-males experiencing a true freedom in the expression of their instinctive feminine nature. And suddenly he – as she, as Eve – longed to be part of this confidence, this free expression. For the first time he felt a deep, painful need to be with other she-males; to mingle with these beautiful, utterly convincing beauties. To be part of their sensual, elegant society.

Then there had been the clear instruction of her aunt: for the first time in ten years, she was encouraging Adam to extend his – her – true, yet secret self into the real world outside the flat and the Internet; outside their epic, erotic correspondence.

And so he had applied, following the strict, perhaps overly harsh instructions listed on the website, sending a portfolio of photographs and a formal application as file attachments to *Priscilla@cremedelacreme.co.uk*. Within twenty-four hours there had been a reply. There was a formality in the response from Ms Rouge, yet it failed to hide a genuine desire to meet with the gorgeous Eve. Her application had been accepted and she was invited to attend a 'formal interview' at the club *'en femme'*. He read these familiar words and was transported back down the years to the erotic adventure with Aunt Debra, to the twenty four hours that had changed his life forever. *En femme*.

And here *she* is, a week later, about to understand what going *'en femme'* entails. She opens the car door and feels a wave of sudden, powerful panic hit her like an invisible electric wave. Her whole body is shaking as she pulls her legs neatly and modestly out of the car. She feels the cool evening breeze pass through the sheer black nylon and slip beneath the sexy mini-skirt. A truly erotic sensation that almost immediately calms her terrible nerves.

Then, in one quick but careful move, she climbs out of the car and shuts the door. The sound of the automatic locking device seems to echo down the dark, quiet street like an alarm announcing an intruder. A she-male is on the city streets! Call the police!

But then she is on the move, in the manner that has become more natural than the strides she forces Adam to take in order to maintain the illusion of masculinity, the illusion that enables her to function in the real world, in the world she is now entering as Eve for the first time. Yes, she realises that by coming here, by breaking through into the world that has previously been almost exclusively Adam's realm, she is ensuring an important strengthening of Eve and, automatically, a further diminishing of Adam.

The sense of exposure is immediate, terrible and deeply exciting. Bathed in the sodium orange of the street lighting, walking through pools of black shadow, the night breeze gently caressing her nylon-sheathed legs, she feels hyper-real. She feels more alive and physically in the world than at any other time in her life. And with each high-heeled step she takes, this almost ecstatic feeling strengthens. Increased confidence begins to flow through her beautiful feminine form. Eve lives!

Then, in front of her, and approaching at an alarmingly fast pace, are two men. Young men in their late teens. Men dressed for an evening on the town. Men whose cool, appraising eyes fall upon the image of Eve. Her new confidence is blown away by an explosion of terrible, brutal fear. She sees the cruel, suggestive smiles as they draw closer. Surely she will be revealed – surely they will be able to tell that she is in fact a she-male. There will be humiliation and – possibly – violence. Yet even as her heart pounds with panic and she imagines an impending molestation, her sex hardens and her sense of arousal heightens. I am in the world of sex, she thinks; the world of unending physical excitement and possibility. Whatever happens . . .

They confront her and she stifles a cry of ambivalent fear.

'Evening, sexy,' one of them whispers.

'Hello, gorgeous. Going anywhere interesting?'

Their rough, yet good-natured voices indicate one simple, exciting truth: they accept her as a woman without question; there is no doubt.

Suddenly the fear has gone. She smiles, looking them in the eyes, a flirtatious smile. They smile back. There is a shocking instant of pure sexual electricity. Momentarily she fantasises about going with these men, to a club, to a bar, spending the evening with them; then taking them to her flat. Here they discover the truth: here they either beat her senseless or realise – as she is realising – the possibilities of Eve. They walk past her and laugh. She imagines their cocks. Sucking their hard, long cocks. A sudden, violent, furiously sexual image that both horrifies and excites her.

Then they are gone and she finds herself by a door hidden between two store-fronts, one a furniture shop, the other – to her surprise – a fetish-wear boutique. The name on the fetish-wear store-front is Cherry Rose.

The door has no markings, just a simple, slightly battered, wooden door with a row of plastic buttons on a metal panel at the side. Beneath each button is a name. She presses the button marked Crème de la Crème in felt-tipped capitals. As her eyes fall on the simple, amateurish sign, she feels an immediate and worrying sense of disappointment. She had expected more, something elegant, regal; something elaborate and feminine.

When she presses the button there is no sound, no bell or other ring tone. However, immediately above her, fixed to the wall, is a closed-circuit TV camera. She hears a bolt snap back and the door opens inward less than an inch.

She hesitates a few seconds, then pushes the door fully open and minces into the darkness. The door closes behind her and she finds herself in a badly lit corridor that runs on a downward slope towards the back of what appears to be the two stores. She realises that she is actually in a damp, smelly alleyway between two buildings, poorly lit by a series of rather ancient-looking lamps fixed to each cracked wall.

She totters nervously towards the other end of the alleyway. As the sound of her heels striking wet concrete echo around her, she notices a stronger light from a larger lamp directly ahead of her, a lamp positioned over a white door.

At the door, she hesitates and then knocks once. Almost immediately the door opens and she finds herself facing Priscilla Rouge.

'Eve in the flesh. And even more impressive,' the lovely she-male says in a deep, yet not obviously masculine voice.

Confronted by Priscilla, Eve is far more nervous than earlier with the two young men. She smiles weakly and suddenly feels utterly and painfully exposed. This is surely because Priscilla knows the truth: that the judgement in her gorgeous emerald eyes is informed by fact, not assumption. Yet it is also because Priscilla is a stunningly beautiful she-male, the first she has ever seen in the flesh, a creature whose mastery of illusion is even greater than Eve's, and who stands before her armed with a mildly amused and deeply curious smile.

She is dressed in a short, tight black dress that reveals a firm, sensuous figure, with a strikingly realistic and large bosom and long, elegantly tapering legs sheathed in sheer red nylon. Her legs are largely hidden beneath the knees by a pair of stunning black-leather boots, with an intricate wall of lacing and testing five-inch-high stiletto heels. Because she is obviously tall, the addition of the heels gives her the physical presence of a green-eyed goddess. Her beautiful red hair is worn in a single ponytail that stretches down her back like a narrow stream of fire and is secured at the nape of her neck by a large red silk ribbon tied in a fat bow.

'Come inside and meet the other girls.'

Eve smiles nervously and follows Priscilla into the promising darkness.

Her eyes adjust to the red-tinged gloom of a hallway that leads out into a larger, better-lit reception area. Priscilla takes long, confident steps and Eve finds her eyes helplessly drawn to the she-male's exquisite backside. Her dress is so short, it barely covers the curving lower globes of her very shapely bottom and at one point there is the slightest hint of heavily frilled red silk panties.

41

The reception area is a small, circular space with a desk, behind which is a cloakroom. Sitting at the desk is the gorgeous black she-male from the Crème de la Crème website.

'Cherry, meet Eve.'

Eve's eyes betray a helpless, instant physical attraction as Cherry rises from the desk to greet the latest would-be member of the Crème de la Crème club.

Cherry is shorter than Priscilla, even in three-inch-high, white patent-leather stiletto-heeled court shoes. She is dressed in a white mini-skirt, a red satin blouse and white nylon tights. She is also wearing a striking, Monroe-style wig, which, given her flawless chocolate skin, creates a strangely erotic contradiction that Eve finds intensely attractive.

She is ultra-feminine and gorgeous. Her figure appears as real as Priscilla's, and her thick, sensual lips are painted the same shade of red as the blouse. Eve cannot help but be impressed by the expertise of the padding that has produced the utterly convincing bosom straining beneath the blouse.

'It's so good to meet you at last. We've all been desperate to see you in the flesh. And you're certainly not a disappointment.'

Eve smiles and whispers a shy, terribly nervous thank-you, her gaze one of helpless adoration.

'I think she likes you, Cherry.'

Cherry's smile broadens and Eve blushes furiously.

'Well, the feeling is totally mutual,' the black beauty says, her tone suggestive, her eyes filled with a dark, erotic promise.

Priscilla then leads Eve, followed by a smiling Cherry, through a set of red velvet curtains into a very large, open room, which Eve quickly realises is the heart of the club. A number of small, circular tables are positioned in a semicircle around an oval dance floor, beyond which is a large stage draped in more red velvet curtains.

At the tables sit a collection of men and women, most if not all of whom Eve presumes are she-males. However, in the strange red half-light it is very difficult to tell. Priscilla leads Eve through the tables, and is closely followed by Cherry. Eve is fully aware of the eyes fixed on her elegant, erotic form as she minces carefully and apprehensively towards the dance floor.

A long cocktail bar runs across the back of the club and, standing close to it, Eve can dimly make out what appear to be three she-males or women dressed in costumes that resemble bunny-girl outfits.

Then, to her not insignificant surprise and embarrassment, she is pulled on to the dance floor by Priscilla. She is instantly blinded by powerful stage lights that blaze down from a sturdy metal beam attached to the ceiling. She is instantly conscious of an absolute and inescapable exposure and looks out nervously into a sea of sinister shadows.

'Ladies and gentlemen!' Priscilla shouts, her voice now more male than female, yet still oddly feminine. 'Before tonight's show begins, we would like to welcome a new member to our little society. Please put your hands together for Eve!'

Eve is bathed in enthusiastic applause and a few wolf whistles. She blushes an even deeper red and then, in a moment of madness, performs a sweet, dainty curtsey, a gesture that inspires even greater rapture.

Then she is led from the dance floor to a front-row table. Eve's eyes widen with interest as she notices that Cherry is already seated at the table, along with a very attractive man.

'Richard, say hello to Eve.'

Richard, whose eyes possess the same erotic irony as Cherry's, and whose firm, tall form is sheathed in a perfectly fitting black suit, smiles gently and rises from his seat.

'It's very nice to meet you,' he says, his voice quiet yet precise, calm yet also full of a real and distinctly masculine power.

Eve looks into his striking sky-blue eyes and feels the same strange thrill that gripped her when teased by the two men. His power and physical beauty arouse her in a way that is both confusing and very exciting. She looks over at Cherry and then back at Richard, momentarily unsure which one she wants more.

At Priscilla's gentle instruction, she sits between Richard and Cherry and tries to make herself comfortable. She adjusts her skirt and crosses her black nylon-sheathed legs, an action that produces an immediate and very powerful sexual thrill. She looks at Richard and discovers his beautiful eyes consuming her legs with a very obvious sexual interest. She blushes and quickly looks at Priscilla.

'I thought there'd be a test, an interview. Some form of process.'

Priscilla laughs. 'As soon as we saw you, you were in. It was just a matter of confirming you were real, Eve. You're by far the prettiest catch we've made for ages. We've got no intention of letting you go.'

Eve blushes again. Then she gasps with shock as Richard slips a hand under the table and lets it rest gently on Eve's nylon-sheathed knee. She feels her cock stiffen and her heartbeat increase. Yet the shock passes, to be quickly replaced with arousal. She looks up at him, then, emboldened by something she can't quite define, gently pulls the elegant hand from her knee. He smiles ironically and holds her hand for a few delicate seconds. She swallows back a violent, even sickening sense of sexual excitement and feels a terrible heat burn into her cheeks. He releases his grip and then the stage curtains suddenly open.

There is an explosion of loud, electronic music. Eve jumps and Richard laughs. She looks at him angrily, but as soon as their eyes meet, she is filled with a painful sexual arousal.

A deep elaborate set is revealed and Eve's pretty eyes widen in astonishment, for she is looking at a very convincing reconstruction of a torture chamber. Before her are dark, brick walls from which metal shackles and chains hang, as well as terrifying weapons: axes, swords, spears. In the centre of the stage is a burning brazier and a long wooden rack. To the left of the rack is a metal table upon which is a collection of sex toys.

44

The music is loud and hypnotic, its computer-generated beat fractured by strange clashing cries that resemble whip cracks. Then there is most definitely a real whip crack. Eve starts again and Richard's hand is quickly back on her knee, or rather just above it.

'It's only a little entertainment, Eve. No need to worry,' he whispers.

Then his hand slips beneath Eve's short skirt and she makes no attempt to remove it. The hand presses upward towards its intimate goal and Eve releases a helpless moan of pleasure just as a tall, stunningly beautiful woman strides on to the stage. She is dressed in a striking leather basque covered in silvery metal studs. Her incredibly long legs are sheathed in black fishnet tights consumed by thigh-length black leather boots with amazing six-inch stiletto heels. Her black hair is cut in a Louise Brooks-style pageboy. A black velvet choker is wrapped around her slender, pale-rose neck, and fitted at its centre with a blood-red ruby that exactly matches her lips. She wears black, shoulder-length gloves, and a riding crop hangs menacingly from a narrow leather belt.

After coming to terms with the startling spectacle of this image of female power, Eve becomes aware that the woman is tugging angrily on a leash. And it is then that the true nature of this sado-erotic spectacle is made apparent, for on the end of the leash is another woman, or rather a she-male – a beautiful she-male whom Eve immediately recognises from the website. This is Honey, and she is clearly a gifted performer, for she struggles at the end of the leash with great enthusiasm. The leash is attached to a thick, pink leather collar that covers virtually all of her slender neck. Besides the collar, she is wearing a striking pink satin dress. A strange concoction of little girl attire and provocative fetish wear, the dress has a plunging, frilled neckline that reveals a strikingly realistic pair of breasts, presumably the result of carefully constructed padding and make-up. The dress is outrageously short; indeed, its frou-frou petticoating barely reaches the tops of her thighs and leaves a pair of heavily frilled white silk panties on very clear display. A thick, pink leather belt is buckled very tightly, producing a painfully slender waist and stressing still further her more than ample bosom. Her long, perfectly formed legs are sheathed in white nylon tights and her feet are imprisoned in white, silk-lined ankle boots with shocking seven-inch heels that make every tiny step a desperate, panic-stricken totter. Her thick blonde hair is bound in a tight bun with a shimmering silver clasp, and a coat of thick white foundation gives her face the inhuman sheen of a Victorian doll. Her arms have been forced behind her back and tied tightly at the wrists and elbows with thick silk ribbons. Fingerless satin gloves are pulled over her hands and buttoned tightly around the puffed sleeves of the dress. A fat, pink rubber-ball gag fills her mouth and a look of intense and uncontrollable sexual arousal floods her wide, beautiful pale-blue eyes.

Eve looks at this sado-masochistic display and feels a deeply disturbing sexual thrill. As the pitiful, bound and gagged she-male is dragged on to the stage, she remembers the carefully manufactured images of Aunt Debra sent to her over the last ten years, images that have become increasingly perverse and shocking, and thus increasingly arousing. She recalls the more daring images from the Crème de la Crème website, and feels a powerful sense of attraction to these images of she-male submission. To be feminine is, it seems, to be submissive. She now feels the sense of submission at its strongest. And as her cock strains inside the ingenious body-shaper, as her heart pumps desperately, she feels Richard's hand travel further inside her skirt, to the edge of the frilled ridge of the shaper which traverses the outline of her nylon-sheathed sex.

'Do you like it?'

Richard's deep, sensual voice rings in her head like sex bells before some thundering orgasm. She can only nod helplessly.

Honey is a fine actress, squealing and sobbing melo-dramatically, wiggling her shapely backside furiously and shaking her impressive bosom for the amusement of the audience. Momentarily, Eve turns around to study the onlookers. She sees a number of very beautiful transvestites, most of whom she recognises from the website. She also sees women. Despite the beauty of the club members, it is always possible for the trained eye to tell a real girl from a TV. These women sit with the TVs or with men. And there are a surprisingly large number of men, of all ages. Some are with the real girls, but the majority are sitting with the glamorous, elegantly and erotically attired TVs. They sit close. Some are locked in embraces or cuddles. Eve finds herself envying them, as if being the possession of a man is a badge of true authenticity. If a man finds you desirable, then surely you have become truly convincing. She looks at Richard and smiles slightly. He presses his hand against her cock and she moans with pleasure. His gentle smile widens.

Things are also heating up on the stage. The beautiful mistress has bent poor Honey face down over the rack, so that her chest is hanging over the shiny wooden edge, and is working free the thick leather belt. Honey is squealing desperately into her gag and shaking her head, begging for impossible mercy. The belt is pulled off her body and then the dominatrix, in one dramatic, powerful gesture, rips away the lovely satin dress. It quickly becomes clear that the dress has been specially designed to allow this form of explosive removal, but what is revealed as it is discarded on to the stage floor is something even more astonishing: Honey is not wearing a bra, and the large, rosy breasts that are subsequently exposed to the audience (inspiring much cheering and applause) are very clearly real. The dominatrix then takes the unfortunate girl in her firm grasp and holds her upright before the audience so that these splendid orbs are fully displayed. The cheering and clapping increases significantly. Eve is amazed and excited.

'Would you like to be up there?' Richard asks, pressing his hand a little harder.

Eve nods weakly, her cherry lips curved into a bow of desire, and Richard smiles gently. 'Yes, of course you would, my pretty sissy petal.'

Eve again turns to face Richard. He is quite gorgeous in this flickering theatrical half-light. She runs her tongue over her moist, cherry lips and, in a moment of sudden, and unnerving confidence, flashes him a strikingly feminine look of encouragement.

Her eyes, though, are drawn back to the highly erotic spectacle unfolding on the stage. Honey has been returned to the rack. The panties have also been ripped away, leaving the gorgeous she-male dressed only in the gloves, the shimmering white tights and the high-heeled boots. Her own large, long and very hard sex is outlined against the sheer fabric of the tights, a perfect statement of the glorious ambivalence that is the body of Honey.

She is bent back over the rack and the dominatrix takes the riding crop from her belt. There is more desperate squealing and wiggling and then the crop is applied with shocking conviction to the unfortunate she-male's shapely bottom, its petite, feminine contours perfectly displayed by the skin-tight covering of white nylon.

As Honey receives six hard cuts of the crop, her pain is clearly genuine. Yet far from being appalled by this dark turn, Eve finds herself even more aroused. Her arousal, however, holds a simple, nagging confusion: is her pleasure that of the sadist identifying with the dominatrix or the masochist identifying with lovely, helpless and now loudly sobbing Honey? As large and very genuine tears join the sexy satin dress on the stage floor, Eve knows this ambiguity holds a terrible truth about her true self. She shifts slightly in her chair and Richard relaxes the pressure on her tormented sex. Suddenly, Eve feels distinctly sick, or rather overwhelmed by a sensation of intense and not unpleasant giddiness.

'I need to go to the toilet.'

A look of slight confusion passes over Richard's face. Priscilla looks at her with genuine concern. 'Are you OK?'

'I'm fine. I just need the toilet.'

'Use the ladies by the bar.'

Eve pulls herself to her feet, brushes past a wide-eyed Richard and negotiates a path through the tables, her eyes meeting the animated, aroused faces of male, female and she-male. Strangely, once on her high heels and moving forward, she begins to feel better. And by the time she gets to the blood-red-stained wooden door of the toilet, the mysterious sensation has passed. She looks at the emblem for female and smiles. Then she pushes the door open and enters a crystal-white toilet, which is utterly spotless and distinctly feminine.

She finds herself standing before a wide mirror that runs along virtually the entire wall, above a row of sparkling silver wash-basins and taps. In the powerful ice-white light of the toilet, she finds herself revealed, exposed and elated. She considers her reflection and knows that tonight Eve has finally become real, a being in the world. She feels a power of satisfaction and rightness wash over her gorgeous she-male form and with it a new, startling confidence.

'I am beautiful and real,' she whispers, running her hands over the short, tight skirt. 'I can be whatever I want to be.'

She runs her hands over the convincing, but essentially unreal breast shapes built into the body shaper and remembers Honey's proud, stunning tits. Probably the product of hormones and some form of very elaborate plastic surgery. Their quality, however, had been beyond anything Eve had ever seen, heard or read about. Another teasing and exciting mystery of the Crème de la Crème club.

As she turns to leave the toilet, she notices a selection of art works fixed to the opposite wall. Closer inspection reveals them to be pencil drawings by Stanton and Willie, two very famous fetish artists with whom Eve is, thanks to Aunt Debra, familiar. The pictures depict lithe, impossibly beautiful blondes in a variety of torments, their bondage excessively elaborate and ritualistic. She thinks again of Honey, of the sado-erotic fantasy whose function seemed not just to entertain, but to arouse, to inspire overt and powerful sexual desire. Then she thinks of Richard, his wandering teasing hand and the look in his eyes, the look that said he wanted her. A shiver of dark delight passes over her body.

Renewed, she leaves the toilet. By the time she reaches the table, poor Honey has been stretched face down on the rack and is being subjected to graphic anal stimulation by the dominatrix via a large, pink rubber strap-on dildo. Eve doesn't sit down. Instead, she carefully leans over to Priscilla.

'Sorry, I need to go,' she shouts over the loud, ominous techno beat.

Priscilla immediately looks deeply concerned. 'Why? This is just the beginning. Is this too much for you?'

Eve smiles and shakes her head. 'No. It's . . . lovely. I really like it, and this place. Everything. But I'm a bit overwhelmed by it all. This is my first time out as Eve. I need some air.'

Priscilla nods with obvious disappointment and rises from the table. Richard watches them both with a cool gaze. As Honey's punishment for her mysterious crime becomes even more graphic, Priscilla takes Eve's hand and leads her from the main function area back to the red-curtained reception. Eve turns to look at Richard, but now, to her intense disappointment, he is whispering something in Cherry's ear and inspiring a rude, slightly drunken laugh.

In the reception area, where the beat is just a dull background throb, they talk.

'So, we'll see you again?' Priscilla asks.

Eve nods. 'Of course. I want to be part of this.'

Priscilla smiles, clearly relieved. 'I'm so glad.'

Then, to Eve's surprise, Priscilla leans forward and kisses Eve on the cheek. As she does so, her bosom brushes against Eve's arm and the younger she-male is again impressed by the authenticity of her large, soft breasts and swallows hard with an instant, but now useless desire.

'Who is Richard?' she asks, almost without thinking.

Priscilla smiles, amusement in her lovely green eyes. 'A regular. He's an artist, I believe. Quite well known in those sort of circles. He loves TVs. He and Cherry used to have a bit of a thing going, but now he's a free agent. He certainly likes you.'

Eve smiles nervously and nods weakly. 'Well, I'll see you . . . next week?'

Priscilla smiles back. 'I'd rather it was before then.'

There is a moment of powerful sexual tension. Eve feels her sex swell and hears her heart pound. Once again she begins to feel dizzy.

'We're having a dinner party on Saturday night. It'd be great if you could come.'

'We?'

There is a tone of disappointment in Eve's voice, yet also – perhaps – secret relief.

'My wife and I.'

Eve's eyes widen with surprise.

'Yes, I'm married. Very happily married . . . for some time. And yes, *to a woman*.'

They both laugh and Eve relaxes visibly. 'Yes, that'd be really good.'

'And come as Eve. Only Eve. Please.'

Eve nods and laughs again. 'Who else would I come as?'

Priscilla gives Eve her address and they part after another brief kiss. As she leaves the club, she feels a sense of utter peace and tremendous achievement. As she steps back on to the orange glow of the street, she also feels truly real. She takes long, elegant strides forward, knowing she looks great. Her long legs, so sensually sheathed in black nylon, move with an assured purpose. She feels her carefully padded hips sway and her meticulously constructed breasts swing. Barely conscious of the decision, she has turned in the opposite direction to where her car is parked and is now walking towards the city centre. It is as if she has stepped through a hole in the space-time continuum and entered an alternative ultra-reality, a startling world of hyper-colours and sounds, where the physical experience of being is multiplied ten times.

She is suddenly aware of everything around her in a way that is quite astonishing. The sense of joy this new sensitivity brings is astonishing. Once, with a friend at university, she had snorted cocaine. A foolish, expensive adventure, that had brought a few minutes of genuine

51

elation. The amazing impact of the drug, even for the brief period she was 'inside' it, had stuck in her memory. It was a moment of utter happiness and it was, of course, a chemical illusion. Yet now, having truly become aware of the joy of being Eve, and of the full potential of her secret feminine self, she is reliving the same sense of incredible happiness. And this is no chemically induced illusion. This is, she now realises, the Real Me.

Within a few minutes, she is in the heart of the main shopping arcade and then moving into the open city square. Here the young have congregated, preparing for clubs, bars, the carefree pleasure of youth. And she walks among them, hundreds of laughing, flamboyant, life-affirming young people. She feels the eyes of so many men burn into her and secretly experiences a terrible thrill. At last, she is free. After years locked in rooms, she has exploded into the world as it is: a true, shocking, beautiful rebirth.

There are whistles and teasing remarks. The harsh, drink-addled voices of sexed-up young men – all aimed at her. And then there are the eyes of the women, the jealous eyes, the appraising eyes, even the desiring eyes. Yet in this appraisal and desire there is something else, something that cuts through her mood of elation. She senses their knowledge of the illusion through which Eve expresses her true self. They know. By the fact of their physical female being they know.

Eve mingles for maybe an hour, then returns to the car. By the time she gets home, she is utterly exhausted and furiously aroused. A thousand erotic images flood through her mind as she stands before the bedroom mirror, viewing her reflection with new eyes. Beautiful as they were, there hadn't been one member of the Crème de la Crème club who was as convincing and as gorgeous as Eve. She knows this and tries not to admit it in a way that seems arrogant. She could see it clearly in all their pretty TV eyes: a mixture of intense desire and jealousy. And especially in the eyes of Richard. Even the startling, ample Cherry – by far the prettiest of the pretty as far as the club was concerned –

was not as impressive as the lovely Eve. A statement of fact. This recognition, plus the fact that she had felt so relaxed and at ease in their company, had allowed her to feel completely happy about herself for the first time. And this happiness brought a powerful, addictive confidence that had filled her with a near-sickening sense of her own vital being. It had been this shocking truth, this startling confidence, that had driven her out of the club and into the town centre to be among the largest group of others she could find, to undertake the most immediate and realistic test she could set herself in the limited time available.

As she undresses before the mirror, however, there is one thing that she knows she lacks in comparison with the Crème de la Crème beauties: truly convincing boobs. Honey had clearly undergone hormone therapy and cosmetic surgery. The results were spectacular and utterly real. Judging from the busts of Cherry and Priscilla – and of a number of other members – they must have undergone some similar form of treatment. Yet that, surely, was an irreversible act, a final and lifelong declaration of femininity. Indeed, the Crème de la Crème girls seemed to be hovering in some strange, highly erotic grey space between the transvestite and the transsexual. As Eve removes the shimmering, silken blouse and looks at the carefully designed and shaped padding filling the bra cups of the body-shaper, she wonders if she could ever make that sort of commitment.

Yet even as she thinks it, even as she wiggles sexily out of the micro-mini and reveals the full, glorious beauty of her perfect, black nylon-enveloped legs, she knows the answer is yes. A loud and inescapable *yes*. She would give up everything Adam has become to be the new Eve.

She is as hard as she has ever been and finds herself moving away from the mirror, kicking her high heels halfway across the bedroom, pulling the tights and the shaper desperately from her silky smooth, ultra-feminine body and then collapsing naked on to the bed, her cock massive and savagely aroused. She takes it in her hands and begins to masturbate, all the while thinking of the look in Richard's eyes and the feel of his hand pressing against her sex, the buxom invitation of Cherry's amazing sex-bomb body, the terrible trials of the splendid sissy, Honey.

Then she thinks of tomorrow. A miserable Thursday at work. Another pointless working day. But it won't be. She will phone in sick and then head back into the city, in broad, all-seeing daylight, dressed in the sexiest outfit she can find. She will be Eve in a most spectacular and apparent way, for the world to see. She screams her total joy at this adventurous thought as she explodes, as silver stars ignite before her eyes, as wet, creamy come splashes high on to her stomach and chest. A massive, mind-quaking orgasm, that leaves her screaming for more, more and more!

3

Outside the Envelope

The next morning she is up early, before seven a.m. A new sense of purpose grips her; there is a confidence in her elegant, feminine movements: the new Eve is in complete control. Her sex is rock hard and the need to relieve herself of a deep, sexual ache almost unbearable. But she knows today is too special to indulge in idle self-abuse: she must use this ache, this profound hunger for release, turn it into a force that will sustain her determination to take Eve to the next stage of her glorious evolution.

She spends over an hour preparing her body. In the shower, she cleanses her smooth form using a powerfully scented feminine soap. The hot water enlivens her flawless skin and prepares it for the close, careful shaving that follows. She uses an expensive lady shaver purchased from the Internet, working it across every inch of her slender body with an expert attention to detail. She has ensured her skin remains baby smooth ever since moving into her first flat. For twelve years she has taken a deep, eroticised pride in the fastidious cultivation of her body. The first time she pulled sheer nylon hose over freshly shaven legs, she had experienced a truly shocking sexual thrill, a gasp of fierce pleasure exploding from her mouth, and for a brief moment she had felt as if she would pass out from the almost overwhelming impact of this ever fascinating and endlessly erotic material on her smooth, ultra-sensitised skin. And even now, as she checks her bronzed, perfectly shaped legs for even the tiniest speck of hair, she is filled with a teasing anticipation at the thought of their impending envelopment in soft, endlessly caressing hose.

When Eve is finally satisfied that she is acceptably silken, she smothers her body in a powerful vanilla-scented body spray and then slips into a pink silk bathrobe before mincing back into the bedroom. And here, the fun really begins.

By now her heart is pounding with anticipation. It is a beautiful, early winter's morning; from her bedroom window she can see a cobalt-blue sky. The room is warm, thanks to central heating, but outside she can see there has been a frost. The world appears cleansed and fresh, as does Eve. This is a new day and she is the new Eve.

Her erection presses against the soft silk of the elegant, sexy nightgown. She remembers Richard's hand travelling up her hosed thigh and stifles a moan of dark pleasure. She remembers the splendid, hyper-erotic form of Cherry and swallows hard. She can hardly believe what is happening to her.

She flicks on the portable stereo player on a bookcase opposite her bed. A cool, aquatic electronica suddenly fills the room. On the walls there are white-framed pictures of her female idols: the young Elizabeth Taylor in a swimsuit on a beach, her eyes filled with a sensual sadness and provocation; Ann Margaret in a spectacular Las Vegas showgirl's costume; the fetish models Betty Page and Stacey Burke; Marilyn Monroe; a number of famous female impersonators. And more. A gallery of erotic influence.

She moves to the large walk-in wardrobe that traverses one entire side of the bedroom. This is the only major physical change she has made to the house since moving in. It was expensive, but absolutely necessary. For inside the wardrobe is the gorgeous history of her secret self; the story of Eve written in a spectacular collection of feminine attire.

The sliding doors to the wardrobe are painted a light pink, a colour that matches the walls and the silk bed-sheets. She painted the room herself over a weekend, and when the carpet layers fitted the thick, snow-white carpet, she – as Adam – had explained it away as a room for his wife's sister, who would be living with 'them'. A lie, a white lie, one of quite a few she has told over the years – to protect the secret of Eve.

She pulls back the doors to reveal an elaborately ordered display of sensual delights. The wardrobe is much deeper than one might usually expect to find in a new, three-bedroomed, detached house on a housing estate in a large urban sprawl. Its depth provides room for two parallel rows of clothing, both split in the middle by a small gap that enables Eve to enter and move within the rows. As soon as the doors are opened, a soft white light clicks on automatically and the lovely she-male is filled with a sense of absolute contentment. This is me, she thinks – as she always thinks – this is the real me.

The scents of a variety of perfumes and soft, feminine materials tickle her girlish nostrils as she slips into the gap and seeks out the clothing that will create Eve on her first truly public exposure. She is determined to be both formal and sexy, to look businesslike and devastating. There is no point in drawing too much attention to herself; to look like a tart would be to make the classic error of the TV going *en femme*. No: there has to be realism here, realism and a genuine sensuality.

She eventually extracts a short, grey cotton skirt, almost but not quite a mini; a matching silk jacket with white pearl buttons, and a gorgeous white silk blouse/shirt. She carefully places these items on the bed and then returns to the wardrobe. Set into the floor are a series of metal racks, three tiered rows that contain more than a hundred pairs of women's shoes. Every one is heeled: Eve cannot conceive of feminine footwear that is not heeled.

With a sigh of pleasure, she takes out a pair of grey leather court shoes with three-inch stiletto heels. She feels their weight in her hands and admires the elegant and erotic contours of their design. Shoes designed to extend and stress the elegant shape of the female foot, to sensualise form, balance and movement. The first time she had walked in heels slips quietly into her mind, the memory of that nervous totter before her gorgeous, encouraging aunt. How can a day go by when I don't think of her, she ponders. Eventually, she will send Aunt Debra an e-mail, detailing the great adventure that is unfolding. But now she is too involved in the creation of Eve. And this, as always, must be the first priority.

She places the shoes at the foot of the bed, and then, from the end of the front row of the wardrobe racks, extracts the second of her three body-shapers. It is white, made of exactly the same elastane and silk materials as the others, and it remains the core of her physical transformation. The shape of Eve; the perfect form of a beautiful, sexy young woman. A highly erotic exoskeleton of transvestite desire.

She steps into the body-shaper and carefully wiggles it up her scented, shaven form, quietly wallowing in the balletic movements demanded to fit the garment properly, as if the shaper itself was imparting a powerful drug of femininity and beginning a process of profound physical change.

As she adjusts the shaper over her slender body, she feels the perfect weight of the artificial silicon breast packs and again recalls Honey's astonishing bosom. Envy floods her mind and her sex stiffens deep inside the snug embrace of the shaper. And as arousal returns, she remembers the excited gaze of Richard, the teasing words of the men on the street and wonders, for a moment, if there is something else at work here – a latent homosexuality. But even as she ponders this possibility, she knows it is very far from the truth of her being. Although Eve is now in firm control, there has never been a hint of anything other than Adam's helplessly fierce heterosexuality. But then there was Richard and his warm hand caressing her nylon-wrapped thigh . . .

She shakes her mind free of these disturbing thoughts and tries to concentrate on the task before her: the submersion in the sexiest and softest of feminine attire, the true root of all her powerful, irresistible desires.

She begins with the tights. Next to the dressing table is a large white mahogany chest of drawers – five drawers with ornate golden handles that contain Eve's delicate cornucopia of underwear. The top drawer is filled with neatly piled and folded tights and stockings, of every colour and type, most made from sheer nylon, some from expensive, fine silk. She gently sorts through these delightful fetish towers and extracts a pair of 10-denier silver-grey nylon tights. She sits down on the bed and carefully draws the tights up her silken legs. And as the ultra-sheer material presses gently against her skin, she cannot resist a familiar moan of intense physical pleasure. This remains the most startling and arousing part of any dressing, and by the time she stretches the widening film of nylon over her calves and knees, her sex is granite hard. She stands to ease the tights up over her thighs, wiggling her bottom with an instinctive and coquettish femininity. Then she adjusts the thick control top around her waist, painting the lower half of the body-shaper in a mist of grey nylon. She carefully runs her hands over the surface of the tights, expertly smoothing the slightest wrinkle and creating a flawless second skin that accentuates and eroticises the perfect shape of her legs.

With the tights on, she feels Eve's true presence in the strongest possible way. Now she is at her most feminine and thus most real. Her movements become softer, more graceful, more delicately considered. She is a beautiful young woman preparing herself for a day of exquisite adventure.

She returns to the chest of drawers, her steps now smaller, daintier, sexier, her bottom wiggling, her hips swaying. She is becoming, transforming, emerging. From the second drawer she takes a pair of cream silk panties, gorgeous and expensive, with delicately frilled edging running along the legs and waist. She slips into these in one extraordinarily elegant move and pulls them up over her nyloned thighs and waist. She runs her hands over the shimmering, electric surface and coos with girlish delight.

Then she turns to the bed and considers the beautiful, sexy clothing set out so neatly before her. She smiles and minces over to the dressing table, gently lowers herself on to the white leather-backed stool and considers the next part of this wondrous transformation: the creation of the face of Eve.

She finds herself, as on so many other occasions, facing a boyish young woman. Her soft, pale face, with its always feminine and full lips and large, crystal-blue eyes, the face that Aunt Debra had described as 'inescapably female', looks back at her with something approaching erotic fascination. At the heart of Eve is an acknowledged narcissism. She has always been helplessly drawn to her reflection, to its essential ambivalence. She remembers the girls at school and at university, how they would always stare at him with a disturbed ambiguity. 'You're prettier than most of my friends,' one had said, trying to steal a kiss at a party. 'You should be a girl.' Eve, as Adam, a seventeen-year-old Adam, had allowed her to kiss him on the lips and then swooned with a dizzying pleasure. The words had echoed in his head for days afterward and had driven him to helpless, furious masturbation.

Yes, he should have been a girl, and now, finally, *she* will be. Her natural hair is dark and cut very short. She has been careful to look after her hair. The constant wearing of wigs has been a test of its texture and oils, and she has become something of an expert at high-quality mainten-ance. She slips a specially treated and prepared black nylon stocking over her head, gently pulling it into a snug fit, so that the rim of the stocking covers her hair, but does not intrude beyond the natural hairline. There are three wigs resting upon stands on the dressing table – one strawberry blonde, one jet black and one red. The blonde wig is cut in a distinctly fifties, layered style, reminiscent of actresses such as Monroe and the blonde Rita Hayworth in *The Lady from Shanghai* (an enlarged publicity still of the actress in this role hangs within a silver frame, among many other pictures, above Eve's bed). The black wig is styled in a Louise Brooks pageboy cut (her picture sits alongside Rita's). Then there is the red wig, much longer, thicker and detailed, that Eve has modelled after her third idol: Ann Margaret. Her picture rests to the right of Rita's. Yet, deep in her tormented mind, she knows that all of these are subject to the one true divine goddess, whose picture stares up at her from a frame placed on the dressing table: his lovely, all-important and all-pervasive Aunt Debra.

She takes up the blonde wig and, with an artist's crafted precision, pulls it over the tightly positioned stocking. What was once a difficult process of adjustment is now a simple matter, and within seconds she has placed the wig perfectly and is staring confidently at the beautiful reflection of Eve.

The wig is followed by the lightest touches of make-up: a mild tan foundation, a peach-toned and flavoured lipstick, the slightest hint of matching eye shadow. Then, a pair of very simple, clip-on pearl earrings. A minimal intervention to ensure maximum effect: the vision of Eve renewed in new and stronger form. And even this low-level approach to make-up produces immediate and very impressive effects. Years of careful work has enabled her to produce, in a relatively short period of time, a completely believable illusion of femininity. And even though she expects nothing else, she is still impressed by the power of her creation, by its utter authenticity. Aided by a naturally feminine face, by a poise born from ten years of practice, she is able to create a picture of completely convincing femininity within less than thirty minutes.

Once the make-up is complete, she applies a dab of Chanel behind each ear and sets about slipping into the blouse and skirt. And as each piece of this gorgeous jigsaw puzzle of identity is complete, she feels Eve become stronger, surer, more confident. More real. As she sits down on the bed to slip her delicately hosed feet into the deliciously high-heeled court shoes, the bright morning sunlight bringing a fractured sparkle to her nylon-sheathed and perfectly shaped thighs, the sense of ultimate being that she had felt at the peak of the previous evening's adventure returns. A powerful electric surge of supreme confidence flashes across her body, cleansing and vitalising.

Any sense of nervousness or doubt about what she is about to do is blasted away and her feminine heart is filled with joy. At last, she thinks, I am complete.

She stands and adjusts her balance to suit the erotic demands of the beautiful, sexy shoes. She minces up and down the room a few times and then studies herself carefully in the long, full-size mirror positioned just beyond the wardrobe. She sighs with pleasure. I am beautiful. A statement of fact. And she says it. She says out loud, 'I am a beautiful woman', accompanied by the flow of ambient electronica.

She uses a soft brush to adjust her hair slightly, takes the grey jacket from the bed and tosses it over her silk-sheathed left shoulder. Then she goes downstairs to breakfast, fully prepared and furiously aroused.

She eats a bowl of muesli and drinks a glass of orange juice at her dining-room table. She stares out of patio windows at her back garden. Twice a month, a local gardening company tend to this modest patch of green, producing a 'low maintenance visage' that she is rarely aware of. Now she imagines tending to the few flowers in a skimpy summer dress and high-heeled sandals, revealing her secret self to the eyes of her neighbours. A slightly ironic smile skims across her peach-coloured lips.

After breakfast, she slips into the grey jacket and takes her car keys from the living-room coffee table. She walks into the entrance hall and faces the front door. For a few moments, she feels nervous. Last night, under cover of darkness, there had at least been the opportunity to reduce the chances of discovery. Now, in this strong, morning sunlight, she will be seen by all in inescapable detail. This is, she knows, the first and last true test of her authenticity, her believability. But then she recalls the desiring eyes of men, women and she-males from last night and the sense of utter personal victory those looks inspired. I am beautiful. I can do this.

She opens the front door and walks out into the new day.

She drives back into town, on the same roads as the night before, but now in the startling truth of daylight.

Immediately, she is aware that there are more people – on the pavements and in cars. As she moves towards the city centre, she is surrounded by others, hundreds of them. For an instant, they are all looking at her – finally, she has been revealed to the world as a vision of pure and shocking ambiguity. But she is not the centre of attention: these people are indifferent to Eve, as they are indifferent to most of the sights and sounds around them. They are moving in their own worlds, conscious only of their own limited, immediate desires. They are hardly alive. But Eve is conscious of herself in a totally different and truly invigorating way. She is conscious of her intricately feminised physical form and of the soft, elegant clothing that embraces every inch of her scented, silky smooth body. She is conscious of this elegant creature who is Eve, seated in the car, her long, grey nylon-wrapped legs emerging from the teasingly short skirt and down towards the control pedals. She is ultra-conscious of operating these pedals, using the elegant, sensual high heels. Her hosed thighs rub together as she drives and this constant, powerfully sexual stimulation only serves to increase the sense of enhanced consciousness. This is pure sex being, and its absolute, undeniable power fuels her growing confidence and a deep-rooted sense of inner peace.

She parks the car in a multi-storey near the main shopping precinct and, for a few apprehensive moments, sits in stunned, fearful silence. She places her hands on her thighs and feels the heat of her body through sheer nylon. Her heart is pounding, yet she remains strangely calm. There is no going back. This is it. Move!

She opens the driver's door and steps out into the half-light of the car park. She slowly and elegantly swings her legs, held closely together, across the driver's seat and out into the cool air. She places her heels on the tarmac surface and carefully pushes upward. Then she is standing. She takes her leather handbag from the passenger seat, bending forward deep into the car, allowing her skirt to ride up her legs and expose the frilled edges of her pretty white silk panties. An outrageous gesture, a deliberate and perhaps dangerous provocation in which she engages with a startling calmness. She then takes the bag from the car and closes the door.

I must be mad. I *am* mad. Yes, she certainly feels quite odd now. And this is not at all how she had expected to feel: free, elated, eager to reveal all; to challenge the world of others with her authentic feminine beauty.

She locks the car and walks over to the ticket machine. A man, in his mid-forties, is already there, putting in his money, waiting patiently for his ticket. The machine whirls and clicks. He turns at the sound of her heels. The impact is immediate. His eyes widen, a slight, idiot smile crosses his slightly plump face. She returns his gaze with a sudden, surprising contempt. He blushes and looks away, the aftershock of his sexual attraction washing over her splendid form, an attraction which was helpless and real. The attraction of a sad, middle-aged man for a beautiful young woman.

The machine spits out his ticket. He grabs it and dashes from her, turning once to ensure this striking vision was indeed real.

Eve smiles and steps forward. She gets her ticket, returns to the car and then, filled with a strange sense of her own power, strolls elegantly and purposefully out of the garage, the sounds of her sharp, erotically high heels exploding in the silence of the long, dark multi-storey corridors. As she walks, her perfectly formed bottom wiggles with a sensual abandon and her convincing bosom bounces with a cheeky joy.

She descends dark damp stairs without seeing anyone. Then she opens a stained, battered door and walks out into a shockingly busy high street. It is as if she has dived head-first into a freezing ocean. This was not expected. Indeed, her initial response is a moment of truly sickening panic. Then a man, a young, angry looking man, knocks into her. His eyes are filled with hate and violence. His first reaction is to turn and face off this latest contemptible annoyance and unleash casual, spiteful, intense aggression. Then his eyes soften, his mouth opens slightly and desire replaces the brutal fury of his everyday being. Instantly, he is sedated by the beautiful spectacle of Eve, who regards him with a fear-framed curiosity.

'Sorry, love,' he mumbles, his idiot eyes pawing her shapely, hyper-eroticised form.

She smiles slightly and walks on, conscious of his eyes still pinned to her long, grey legs, of the hardness that is spreading helplessly and angrily over his inescapable sex meat. If he fucks or wanks tonight, he will think of her, of this charged collision. And he will wish he had said something; but, as usual, there was nothing in him, no subtle language, no intelligent translation of animal desire into erotic action. As he thinks of this failure to speak, he will be truly defeated, humiliated in a way far more profound than any Saturday-night beating. For this is her power, this is the power that floods through her body. A smile of absolute triumph illuminates her beautiful mouth and she walks deep into this seething sea of otherness.

After a few minutes, she is almost totally relaxed. She has established a careful, but teasing walk built around a gentle, sexual rhythm that attracts helpless glances from so many men and women. In the men's eyes she sees the familiar desire, the animal hunger. At first, she is shocked by the brutal honesty of their gazes, even when they are furtive, snatched in a quick look at this spectacular feminine object. Gazes that express in a cold, even angry way, the male biological imperative. Yet she realises this is what all beautiful women face every day; this animality is normal. And so are most of the gazes she receives from women: also vaguely angry, and most far from desiring. In their eyes she sees envy, some admiration and more than a little aggression (especially from those who are with men).

To be looked at in this way is to experience the truth of physical human being. To be consumed by the desiring and jealous eyes of others is to know that fundamental reality of our waking lives. This is just another jungle, and these are just another collection of hungry beasts.

Her pleasure in her object-ness is intense and, most probably, masochistic. She is being ravished by a thousand eyes and enjoying every second of it.

Over the next hour, she is a beautiful young woman spending a morning shopping. She goes first to a coffee shop. Over a large creamy latte, she idly reads a women's fashion magazine. She has positioned herself in the centre of the café, her back straight, her long legs tightly crossed, her toes pointed slightly downward. As she adjusts her posture, she feels her delicately hosed thighs rub together and has to fight to withhold a moan of pleasure.

Here, the eyes are as focused and hungry as anywhere else, and her response is the same: careful indifference that hides furious arousal.

She pays a handsome young Italian man for the coffee. He thanks her with a blinding, sensual smile and she blushes helplessly, a feeling of genuine feminine shyness that fills her with joy. There is passion burning in his dark brown eyes, and she resists a dizzying swoon.

Then it is time for the moment she has so deliberately withheld, teasing herself with a dreadfully sexual expectation in this theatre of elegant exposure. Now, finally, she will visit the clothing stores. Here she will take the ultimate test.

She begins with a large department store, walking through its glass doors with a sense of focus and determination. There can be no doubt now: she is beautiful, elegant, sexy Eve.

The women's section is virtually the whole of the ground floor, a cornucopia of stylish femininity, a paradise of Eve's most secret and desperate desires. The racks are formed in carefully organised circles, islands of dresses, blouses and skirts around which female shoppers walk, stopping to assess, sometimes to remove an item and take it to the changing rooms. Eve's eyes glide across the racks and she feels a very familiar and powerful sense of beauty. For as long as she can remember, the sight of female clothing has not only aroused her, but also inspired a sense of aesthetic interest. It is as if she is in an art gallery, appraising not just function, but the principles of design and form. Here the exhibit is an erotic creation, in silk, in nylon, in satin and cotton, fabrics whose essence are used to express identity and desire.

She moves closer to a rack neatly loaded with a variety of silk blouses, all expensive, all rather beautiful. She runs her hands across the fine, electric material and feels a shiver of sexual delight. Silk and skin: a perfectly eternal combination. She takes a blouse from the rack and holds it against her own, carefully manufactured form. It is dark red and terribly sexy. She feels her sex stiffen as she imagines wearing this gorgeous item. She replaces it on the rack with a stunned smile. She is lost in a scented fog of sheer bliss.

She has more than £100 in cash in her handbag, but if she were to buy the blouse she would have less than £20 left. She decides to look for something a little cheaper.

As she turns to view the rack opposite, she collides with another shopper, a tall man. He appears shocked and almost immediately apologises. Eve is briefly stunned and then also apologetic. She mumbles a rather deep and clearly masculine sorry and then freezes in horror. For she finds herself facing Richard, the handsome man from the club, the man whose hand had teased and tormented her so effectively.

At first, Eve considers running from the shop, so great is her sense of panic. Yet a calmer voice is telling her to remain, to continue as if this was just a random encounter with a stranger, that this is perhaps the greatest test for Eve.

Then she is looking directly into his large sky-blue eyes and she feels her nylon-sheathed knees turn to jelly.

'Eve! I thought it was you! Sorry about the clumsy introduction.'

He has a light, easy and cultured voice. There is a calmness in his tone and in his posture. He is relaxed and confident. Yet, at the same time, she can see his passion . . . for her.

Eve averts her gaze, blushing furiously, unsure what to say or do. She smiles weakly.

'Sorry . . . is this a bad time?'

She shakes her head and whispers a very nervous 'No, it's fine . . . it's just I wasn't expecting . . .'

He smiles warmly and nods vigorously. 'Yes, of course. Now I can see.'

He hesitates. She looks up at him. Even in her heels she is shorter. He must be at least six feet three. His hair is thick, dark blond. He has a long, gentle face, very broad shoulders, an athletic frame. He is, with a doubt, a classic example of masculine beauty.

'Look, I'm sorry. I thought you'd be OK about this, but I've obviously imposed.'

He turns to leave, but then she grabs his arm, a sudden, almost desperate gesture.

'No, don't go,' she whispers. 'It's just that I don't, I haven't done this . . .'

There is a moment of terrible awkwardness. She is painfully aware of her voice, of Adam's voice, shattering this elegant, careful visage with its helplessly male tonality. Then Richard smiles gently. There is care and concern in his eyes.

'It's your first time out on your own?'

She nods, begging for a bottomless hole to swallow her up.

'You don't need to worry, Eve. You're absolutely gorgeous. Nobody would ever know.'

She looks up at him then, sees the confident power of his desire and feels a violent, dizzying sexual thrill.

'Look,' he says, taking her hand, 'why don't I buy you a cup of coffee? Somewhere quiet. Where we can talk.'

All she can do is nod helplessly. Then he takes the blouse from her shaking hands.

'And let me buy you this. It'll look fantastic on you.'

Her eyes widen with surprise. She begins to shake her head, aware of the cost and also the power she is in some way giving him if she agrees. But then he gently extracts the blouse from her already faltering grasp and whispers 'please'. All resistance melts and she nods weakly.

He pays for the blouse with a Gold American Express card. The girl at the counter, a pretty teenage blonde, stares at Eve with genuine envy, the look that one woman would reserve for another, a look that fills Eve with a tremendous sense of success and also a very deep arousal.

Then she is carrying the bag with the blouse and being led from the store by Richard, stunned, astonished, elated.

Richard is wearing a tight pair of Levi jeans, brown suede shoes, a pale-blue denim, open-necked shirt and a tan-coloured jacket. He looks casual, yet particularly well groomed. Eve notices other women looking at him with obvious sexual interest, and then at her – with envy.

It is only as they enter the small, quiet café on a side road off the main shopping precinct that Eve begins to feel just a little uncomfortable. This is not what she had planned for today, this is also not what she had ever considered when she applied to the Crème de la Crème. A man! A man who obviously admires and maybe even desires her! Yet, despite her concerns, despite a desperate confirmation of her fundamentally male sexuality, she follows him. Somehow this is the absolute final affirmation of her femininity. And to have this happen – to have a man desire her as a woman – is to experience a violent sexual thrill.

They sit in a quiet booth in a corner of the café and are almost immediately served by a pretty, plump brunette in the skimpiest of mini-skirts. Eve notices her long, beautiful legs sheathed in opaque black nylon and feels a twinge of desire. Then a smile crosses her beautiful face. I look at her and feel sexual attraction; I look at him and feel . . .

Richard orders two lattes. Eve places the bags on the floor and then crosses her legs tightly. The mini-skirt rides up her legs to reveal a little more of her grey nylon-sheathed thighs and she is instantly aware of his eyes appraising her ultra-feminine form, an appraisal that causes her to blush with a terrible, aching and deeply disturbing pleasure.

'How long have you been dressing?' he asks, his question neutral, but his eyes filled with a dark, erotic interest.

'Since I was sixteen. About twelve years.'

'And you've only just come out?'

'Yes. The visit to the club last night was my first time.'

His smile widens and he shakes his head. 'I find that very hard to believe.'

69

'Really? Why?'

There is a false modesty to her question that they both recognise. 'Because you're so very beautiful. And you know it.'

She squirms with pleasure and averts his clear, frank gaze.

There is a slightly unpleasant silence then, as his eyes continue to roam over her body. The intensity of his examination, without conversation, is almost too much to endure.

'How long have you been going to the club?' she asks, desperate to relieve the pain of this silence.

'Me? About a year. Ever since they asked me to work for them.'

'Work?'

'Yes, I'm a photographer and film maker. I help them with their publicity and do some video work.'

She nods carefully, aware of his hand moving from the table to his side, falling loosely between them and brushing ever so gently against her skirt.

'I'm sorry about last night,' he says suddenly, guilt-edged concern briefly replacing the desire in his beautiful eyes.

'Sorry? Why?'

'For the way I acted . . . the way I touched you. It was terribly crass of me. Given I hardly knew you. I was drunk, and you were . . .'

'I was what?'

He smiles slightly and raises his eyes up towards the café's long bar, as if searching for the right word.

'You were perfect, Eve.'

She blushes and shakes her head.

'No . . . seriously. I mean it. I've seen all of them . . . all the Crème de la Crème girls. And none of them come anywhere close to you. Not even Cherry. And Cherry is fucking gorgeous.'

His passion is sudden and shocking. He leans forward and places his hand directly on her warm, nylon-sheathed knee.

'But my voice,' she says, aware of the one thing that destroys this image of feminine perfection.

He nods in that strangely sage way and his smile fades. 'Your perfection isn't about being a totally convincing female. It's about something else. It's about the illusion of femininity.'

A mild anger suddenly fills Eve's eyes. 'It's not an illusion . . . I'm not an illusion.'

Richard smiles slightly, clearly confused by this testy answer.

'Then what is this?' he asks, pointing directly at Eve. 'The smart suit, the sexy, city girl look? The tights and heels. The careful make-up? The wig?'

'It's the real me.'

Eve knows this sounds wrong and then attempts to elaborate. 'It's the way I express the real me.'

Richard nods again, thoughtful, considerate. 'OK. That makes sense. But it can only help you go so far. And anyway, what's the true you? What's your name?'

'Eve. I am Eve.'

'And I'm Richard. And I'm really pleased to meet you, Eve.'

Eve smiles without conviction. 'Why?'

Richard smiles again, still slightly confused. 'Why what?'

'Why are you pleased to meet me?'

His smile widens, he relaxes. He leans further forward, his handsome face a few inches from Eve's.

'Because I love TVs.'

She feels his hot, coffee breath against her face and her cock strain inside the shaper. Her heart speeds up. She swallows hard.

'I can't help it,' he continues. 'I've had this thing about transvestites since I was a kid. At first, I thought I was a transvestite. But I've never wanted to dress up. It's . . . well, it's pretty fucking weird I suppose. Let's just say I'm an admirer of beautiful cross-dressers. That there is something in the ambiguity they represent that I find . . . arousing.'

'Am I ambiguous?'

71

Richard laughs, but his eyes betray the slightest irritation with Eve's monotone interrogation. 'Of course. And I find the ambiguity exciting. This strange middle-ground between male and female. This, I don't know ... this subversive middle-ground. People like you question us all. The simple definitions of sex and gender begin to fall apart. I like that. The way you fuck up the desperate truths of morality.'

Eve listens politely to the subversion argument. She has heard it a hundred times and never been impressed.

'Do you like girls?'

There is no hesitation. 'Yes. But not all the time. I suppose I'm bisexual.'

'Have you had sex with a transvestite?'

She is surprised by this hard, frank retort.

He nods and then moves his hand on to her thigh. 'Yes. Yes, I have.'

Eve feels the room begin to move beneath her. A terrible, desire-framed giddiness similar to the one she had felt at the club the night before. Richard's hand slips beneath the skirt and presses against the crotch of the body-shaper through the silk panties. She feels an almost unbearable hardness deep in her sex, a hardness she has never felt before; a hardness that threatens to explode into terminal stars.

Richard, noticing her strange reaction, withdraws his hand.

'Are you OK?'

The room slows. The sickness passes. 'Yes,' she says. Then she leans forward and kisses him on the cheek. 'Take me shopping. Then let's go back to my place.'

4

A New Love

The next few hours are some of the happiest Eve has
experienced. In the company of Richard she feels as
relaxed and at ease as she has felt with anyone. As they
move from shop to shop, as he spends hundreds of pounds
on her with utter indifference, she is truly at one with
herself; yet she is also aware of her limits. In the shops,
their conversations are muted; even when Richard teases
the gorgeous she-male, they are both careful not to draw
too much attention to Eve's voice. Yet despite the caution
at the heart of their communication, the tone is heavily
eroticised, and it is this that draws Eve closer and closer to
Richard. He frequently comments on how a certain dress
or skirt or blouse will look on Eve, complementing her
figure, her legs, her grace; making it all sound so very
natural and proper. And poor Eve is lost in a near ecstasy
of contentment, her deepest fantasy of acceptance brought
to stunning, erotic life. She knows she will take him back
to her house and that something will happen. Something
she had never imagined possible.

By the early afternoon, both are loaded down with
purchases and, after lunch at a small café, Richard suggests
they go to the cinema before returning to her house. There
is a film he wants her to see. Eve is excited by the
suggestion and agrees without a second's hesitation.

'We can put the bags in your car,' he says. 'I can come
and pick mine up in the morning.'

He looks at her with expectation and desire. She nods,
knowing what she is agreeing to. She is so terribly aroused.

'I'll make you a pasta dinner,' she says, and his smile becomes a beam of beautiful joy.

To Eve's surprise, they end up in a small art-house cinema that is showing a trio of French films called the *Three Colours Trilogy*, one after the other for two weeks. They pay for the showing of the first film, *Three Colours: Blue*, and are soon sitting in a virtually empty cinema which smells of exotic coffee.

Eve knows very little about foreign cinema, but it is clear that Richard is a well-informed cinephile. He speaks highly of the film's star, the French actress Juliette Binoche. Eve has heard of Miss Binoche and has actually seen her perform in one or two rather overblown Hollywood movies. She remembers a cool, dark-haired beauty, but what she experiences once the film begins is a pure revelation. In this intimate and secret darkness, a space that is both painfully private and so very clearly public, she is exposed to the narrative precision of true art cinema and the elegance and intelligence of one of the world's greatest actresses. Photographed in shades of crystal-blue and telling the story of a tragedy and, perhaps, a deception, the film's style and highly developed narrative are part of a European cultural tradition to which Eve, despite her love of the glamour and flamboyance of American cinema, has never truly been exposed. Then, there is the revelatory beauty of the actress and of her performance. Eve is overwhelmed with admiration and desire. This sophisticated representation of a woman and her life holds a new insight into the possibilities of femininity. Eve finds herself watching movement and dress with a fetishist's rapt interest and seeing another model for her own being, another icon to frame and hang on her bedroom wall.

Her attention is diverted periodically by the gentle caresses of Richard. Although he appears as smitten by the film as Eve, it is clear he also welcomes the cover provided by the cinematic darkness, for, within seconds of the light dimming, Eve feels a warm hand slipping once again beneath her skirt and seeking out the edge of the body-shaper. Enthralled by the film, aroused by the caress, Eve is almost overwhelmed by sensory stimulation. Richard moves closer, presses his body tightly against her.

'Are you enjoying it?' he whispers.

Eve nods and fights a gasp of surprised pleasure as Richard manages to slip his hand directly between her legs. Yes: she is enjoying the film and these illicit, ultra-erotic caresses, and she responds by nervously placing her own hand over Richard's crotch. The denim-covered hardness she discovers sends a shock of pleasure and fear through her body. In the darkness, it is perhaps too easy to make this bold and – in terms of wherever today is going – potentially profound move. Richard turns towards her and moans. She then feels his lips brush against her neck.

In the film, a dead composer's wife is – perhaps – gradually revealed as the true creator of many of the works that have been presented under his name. Behind the façade of the male, the truth of the female. Eve is amused and disturbed by this, aware that Eve is the truth behind Adam. Yet a fractured truth, or rather a form of refraction. For today she has learnt, in the pure moment of her most daring exposure, that the deeper physiological truth of her maleness is inescapable. And this inescapability has widened Eve's understanding of her being: neither male nor female, but she-male.

After the film, they walk to the multi-storey car park. It is after five p.m., and the winter darkness has already set in. As they walk up the dank stairwell of the car park, Richard asks, 'Would you like to be with a man? Sexually?'

It is a frank and shocking question that takes Eve completely off guard. Yet her answer surprises even Eve.

'Maybe.'

Richard laughs and then suddenly and violently grabs her. Eve's first response is to resist, but this fades as he presses himself tightly against her body, as his hands fall upon her backside, as he nearly pulls her up off the ground. His hard cock presses against the front of her skirt. She cries out with a terrible, confused pleasure.

'Please,' she whispers, her voice so weak, so exactly feminine. 'Not here.'

The dark, animal light fades. A look of horror washes over his handsome face.

'God,' he mumbles, releasing her as suddenly as he had grabbed her. 'I'm so sorry.'

She straightens her skirt and smiles shyly. 'You're very . . . strong.'

'I really am . . .'

'Don't apologise,' she says, her smile deepening, her eyes filling with a slightly teasing irony. 'I don't mind. I . . .'

Then she has to face the simple truth: as he had held her so very tightly, as he had attempted to ravish her, she had felt a huge charge of masochistic sexual pleasure.

'I liked it.'

His look of self-loathing fades. 'Really?'

'Yes. Really. And if you want me to play with you, then I will. But not here.'

He nods then, eager, understanding, his hot breath forming clouds of hungry need – a sex mist.

She leads him to her car. She unlocks the doors. Then they are inside. And as she slams her door shut, they are trapped – momentarily – in a strange, unnerving, erotic silence.

She starts the car. Then she turns to him, suddenly so much more confident and ready to face the truth of that violent embrace.

'We can go back to my house and you can do what you like. But not here.'

Her words are precise: she is giving the orders. Yet she knows this is not what she wants. She wants him to give the orders. Him to control her. But only on her terms.

Evening traffic makes the journey back to Eve's house frustrating. Richard tries his hardest to talk through the silence of intense sexual anticipation.

'Did you enjoy the film?' he asks, his voice broken by nervous need.

'Yes. Very much.'

'We should see the other two. You'd like them.'

Eve nods, fighting to maintain her concentration.

'We should dress you up like Juliette Binoche,' he continues, recovering his teasing humour. 'She had some

76

really great outfits. Short, dark dresses, black tights, heels. Get a black wig. You'd look great.'

There is an element of instruction in Richard's voice now, a forceful tone. Eve nods and smiles. She likes the way he is talking to her. She wants more of it.

Eve looks at Richard then, for a brief moment, at his newly confident, commanding stare, and nods again. 'Yes, I'd like that.'

Eve returns her pretty, girlish eyes to the road and ponders the rapidity of things. She is elated, yet also disturbed. She has allowed herself to fall head-first into it without hardly a moment's hesitation. Yet now, alone with Richard, she finds herself reflecting on the coincidence of their meeting. Suddenly, Eve wants to ask him if his arrival in the shop was just a coincidence; if, in fact, there was some connection in between her arrival and the events of the night before. This now seems the only logical explanation. Yet it is an explanation Eve chooses not to pursue. Because Richard is opening up a whole new possibility of Eve, a possibility both deeply disturbing and tremendously exciting, a possibility she is choosing to pursue with an almost reckless abandon.

It is nearly six p.m. by the time they arrive at Eve's house. They carry the many bags from the car, surrounded by a thick air of expectation. In the darkness of the teatime streets, there is little possibility that anyone will see them and, if they did, they wouldn't see anything other than a man and a woman heavily laden with the booty of an extravagant shopping trip.

Richard is obviously surprised by the house and its quiet, middle-class location.

'I didn't think you'd be the sort for suburbia,' he teases, as Eve flicks on a hallway light and lets her new friend into the house.

They enter the living room and dump the bags on the floor. Richard looks around him, examining everything with a surprisingly cool eye, seemingly seeking out some indication of Eve's true character and motives. And while he does this, Eve finds herself examining with an equally careful eye this attractive, mysterious man who has exploded into her life.

'Show me around,' Richard says, turning to her, his gaze stricken by desire, his voice filled with demand. 'Show me all your secrets.'

And so Eve shows him the house, the neat, carefully decorated house. Overall, she knows the tone is minimalist, even Spartan. Except for the bedroom, the elegant lady's room that, while not exactly overwhelming in terms of design or decoration, possesses a certain identity lacking in the rest of the house: the identity of Eve.

They place the large pile of bags by the bed and Eve shows him her most intimate abode. Richard is particularly interested in the bedroom and insists on being shown every detail, of seeing inside the elaborate multi-layered closet, inspecting the drawers, the dressing table. He ponders the books on the bookshelf and the pictures of Eve's icons. His tone and manner are increasingly authoritative, his shimmering eyes filled with a powerful sexual light that will stand no resistance.

'You've got a lovely house, Eve. Particularly this room. I bet you spend a lot of time up here.'

She smiles weakly and nods, the sound in her head of her heart beating a terrible indication of her almost uncontrollable sexual excitement.

Then Richard sits down on the bed.

'Now you can strip.'

Eve feels her knees weaken and her heart skip a beat. This is the point at which trust and paranoia collide with the most powerful and brutal of sexual desires.

'Put some jazz on and entertain me.'

Dizzy with need and a dark apprehension, Eve totters over to the portable stereo and, her hands shaking, inserts a Miles Davis CD into the machine. The slow, bluesy jazz that fills the room is soaked in a thick eroticism – a perfect ambience for the striptease that Eve is now to perform.

The gorgeous she-male turns to face Richard. She feels her granite sex and her beating heart, and then the wall of fear and nerves begin to fade, just as they had faded as she climbed from her car the night before. At the same time she begins, instinctively, to move her hips to the lazy, elegant, very beautiful music. *A Kind of Blue*. The most famous and popular of Davis's albums, with its carefully placed and utterly unique trumpet phrases and the sensual, effortless piano playing of Bill Evans. Yes, it is the piano more than anything, the piano and the subtle elegance of the overall tonality that Eve finds so attractive, so stimulating. And as she lets the music wash over her, she feels inhibition and suspicion subside. She feels her body begin to move with a deliberately erotic provocation. She meets Richard's hungry gaze and runs a dark, wet tongue slowly over her moist lips. Then she begins to unbutton the grey jacket, each button released with erotic intent, her eyes never leaving Richard's. She edges the expensive silk jacket off her shoulders and lets it fall to the floor. She considers kicking off her shoes, but then realises the importance of the sexy high heels and how they must remain to accentuate her long, almost perfectly feminine legs for as long as possible. So next she wriggles languidly out of the pearl-grey mini-skirt, turning as she does so to expose Richard's increasingly aroused gaze to her tight, petite bottom. She wiggles the skirt down to her thighs and then lets it join the jacket on the floor. Stepping away from the skirt, she turns back to face Richard, who is now smiling weakly, a look of intense pleasure lighting up his face.

She then begins very slowly to release the buttons on the blouse and edge it over her shoulders. She lets it roll like a silver-grey cloud down her tanned, muscular yet still slender and feminine arms to reveal the top half of the body-shaper. Richard's eyes widen, more with an instrumental curiosity than arousal: briefly he seems to be studying the body-shaper with an almost technical interest.

Eve slowly and very sexily wiggles out of the pretty frilled panties, leaving only the sheer grey tights, the fine nylon fabric, shimmering in the soft electric light of the room, covering the lower half of the elegant, intricate body-shaper. It is then that Richard stands up and walks over to her. Never taking his eyes away from Eve's, he slips his hands over the slightly thick waistband of the tights and begins to ease them down over the body-shaper towards the gorgeous she-male's thighs. Eve gasps with pleasure as Richard presses closer to her tightly restrained stomach. He pulls the tights down to Eve's lower thighs and then slips his hands between her legs, directly beneath the body-shaper. Thanks to the way Richard has left the tights, Eve finds herself immobilised and unable to resist Richard's exploratory ministrations.

'Where's the catch? How do I open this fucking thing?'

Richard's voice is rough with sex now, riddled with the animal urgency of desire.

'It's at the front, not underneath,' Eve whispers, over-come, charged with sex electricity.

Richard's hands slip from between Eve's hot thighs and quickly find the Velcro fastener that allows the front flap to be opened. He rips it back and allows Eve's rock-hard sex to pop up almost immediately, finally free and gasping for sexual satisfaction.

'Jackpot!' Richard laughs, taking the red, painfully hard cock in his hands.

Eve releases a squeal of intense pleasure. This is the first time anyone – man or woman (other than Aunt Debra) – has touched her sex. This is the first moment of true sexual intimacy. Richard, with an expertise that betrays signifi-cant previous experience, runs his nails over its hard, still vaguely rubbery surface, pressing just a little too hard and adding a sado-erotic pain to Eve's all too apparent pleasure.

'Time to get this kinky little device off, I think,' Richard gasps, suddenly releasing Eve's hard, boiling cock and gripping the slender silken shoulder straps.

Eve smiles nervously, momentarily fearful that Richard's enthusiasm will lead to a broken body-shaper. She gently pulls Richard's hands away from the straps and slips them over her shoulders. She then carefully stretches her hands behind the body-shaper and unclips the three top hooks that secure it tightly in place. This allows her to inch it free of her chest. Then, after a few more erotic wiggles it falls down to her thighs, where it is held fast by the tangled tights. Richard helps Eve remove the tights and step out of the body-shaper. Then he faces perhaps the true Eve: the silken-skinned, helplessly feminine visage of a beautiful young man, with a large and angrily erect cock.

'You're beautiful,' Richard whispers. 'So beautiful.'

Eve smiles and allows the gorgeous, strange man to return to caressing her sex.

'Put the tights back on. Just the tights and the shoes,' he says, his tone hard, firm – another order.

Eve's hands are shaking with a fear-edged desire as she picks the slightly damp tights from the floor and then slips back into them with a series of elegant, teasingly feminine movements. She pulls them tightly up over her sex, which remains hard and exposed, leaning forward and pressing angrily against the sheer, teasing fabric of the nylon hose.

A thick sweat of arousal now covers Eve's face and her heart pounds against her own perfectly flat chest.

'Put the shoes on and stand with your hands behind your back.'

Eve obeys and stands before Richard, her breathing rapid with confused but very powerful desire.

'Good girl,' Richard whispers. 'Now come here. And keep your hands behind your back.'

Eve complies without a moment's hesitation, tottering forward carefully, hands clasped tightly behind her back. Then she is standing just a few inches from his handsome form.

'You're very beautiful Eve, but also very, very naughty. I think you most definitely need taking in hand. Am I right?'

Eve looks down at him and nods weakly. 'Yes,' she whispers. 'Yes – I'm very naughty.'

Richard smiles darkly and places his hands on her nylon-wrapped hips.

'And naughty girls get spanked ... don't they?'

She nods again, lost in his cruel, amused, deeply aroused gaze.

Very quickly he turns her around and pulls her down on to his lap. Almost immediately, she feels his hard, long sex press into her backside. Then she is being pulled over his knees, positioned for an apparently much-deserved spanking.

The first slap is somewhat casual, even tentative. She squeaks with surprise rather than pain. The second slap, however, is much firmer and, as his hand vibrates off her helplessly wobbling buttocks, a streak of genuine pain shoots across her delicately feminine body.

He then proceeds to administer ten sharp, committed blows that leave her sobbing for mercy. She stares down at the carpet through heavily tear-stained eyes and feels his cock press angrily against her own. After completing his kinky task, he pulls her up on to his knees and looks down at her straining, desperate sex. She wipes thick, hot tears from her eyes and beholds his desiring and deeply masculine gaze.

'Thank you, master,' she whispers through quivering, cherry-painted lips.

His smile widens, his eyes fill with a very obvious elation. He leans forward and kisses her gently on the lips. She feels her heart skip an aroused beat and falls inside this soft but passionate kiss. He takes her head in his hands and she is totally overwhelmed. She is being taken by a man, ravished, possessed in the most potent manner imaginable.

He releases her and holds her terribly excited gaze, his eyes streaked with desire.

'Now you can suck me off.'

She looks at him with dazed eyes. Her shock at these words is immediate and terrible, yet she is also helplessly turned on. She knows this is a test, a simple, brutal test designed to demonstrate her absolute acceptance of what is happening between them. She also knows that she will pass the test with flying colours.

She is gripped again by the confidence that seems to emerge with each new challenge presented by the development of Eve. She smiles at him with a calm passion, and he is clearly impressed when she nods and slips off his lap.

Her feminine grace is apparent in every gesture and movement. His arousal is total.

She kneels before him.

'Open your legs,' she orders – now she is in control.

He does so without a second's hesitation. She then shuffles between his legs on nylon-sheathed knees and begins, with careful, gentle moves, to unzip the fly of his jeans, the zipper tracing the significant length of his rock-hard cock as it is lowered.

There is a moment of hesitation. Eve is unsure whether she is nervous or just teasing him. He is wearing white underpants and he gasps with a furious pleasure as she rather tentatively inserts her right hand to pull down the pants and carefully extract the dark pink, hard rubber meat of his highly agitated sex.

'Jesus,' he mumbles, as she takes the boiling tool in a firm grasp and then eases it out past the zipper. 'Oh fuck!'

She has felt her own sex many times and his is, in a way, little different (although rather bigger). Yet, within this very basic familiarity, there is also a terrible and highly arousing strangeness. As she runs her hand along its considerable, heated length, she is surprised at how aroused she is by the thought of putting it into her mouth. There is little thought of homosexuality now: her powerful attraction to Richard seems linked fundamentally to the development of Eve, to the mental context of Eve. She remains locked tightly into a somewhat confused but nevertheless real heterosexuality, but is – at the same time – highly aroused by the act of feminine surrender at the heart of her new relationship with Richard. By doing this, she is affirming Eve in the most extreme and transparent way, and it is this as much (if not more) than her attraction to Richard which is so exciting her.

It is then that she leans forward and runs her long, pink tongue along the length of the hard, tormented shaft. He cries out again and begs for mercy and release. She feels the hot, hard vein traversing the length of his cock throb against her tongue and again experiences a fierce sense of power. This strange, shifting dialectic of she-male desire, she thinks, holding the cock in her hands and staring at its cold single eye with a sense of grim amusement. She then slips it into her mouth, a free and relaxed gesture free of question and guilt.

He shouts out his pleasure and she gasps as the full extent of his masculinity fills her mouth. There is a taste of salty rubber and metal. A strange, unexpected taste; not pleasant, yet not disgusting. A taste of the most intimate human flesh.

There is something strangely instinctive in the way she adapts to the presence of this hot, angry length inside her mouth. The bulbous, throbbing head presses her tongue down, but her saliva lubricates easily and reduces the sense of gagging that accompanied her first sensations.

Then she begins to move her head, to establish a careful but relaxed rhythm and tease him towards orgasm. His moans quickly become louder and deeper and her sense of control over the process of stimulating him to ejaculation is complete. As she intensifies the rhythm, she uses her tongue to caress the base of his hot, trapped cock. There is a strangely sadistic urge to nibble, to bite, to inflict a sudden, stunning pain at the point of absolute and uncontrollable pleasure. It is an urge she only just manages to resist before he explodes with volcanic intensity.

'Fuuuuuucckk!'

His scream of fundamental animal pleasure bounces off the walls like a loud, brutal slap. She grips his broad, muscular thighs, almost as if trying to prevent herself being washed away on a wave of thick, creamy cum. The hot liquid crashes against the back of her mouth. She tastes salty steel and finds herself with no other option but to swallow it down into the heart of her. It is like speed-drinking a pint of beer, and for a few moments she begins to choke. But then he has finished the jerking, gasping coming and she manages to extract herself with a cry of alarm. She falls back on to the carpet. He falls back on to the bed. Cum trickles from her mouth, over her chin and down her neck. Her cock presses violently into the front of the grey tights.

The taste of him seems to consume her body, as if she has been ecstatically poisoned. His pungent male flavour combines with the raw masculine scents of his body to form a lingering and terribly powerful impression of Richard, the powerful, dominant yet vulnerable man who is now, surely, her lover. Her lover! She can hardly believe it.

He is lying on his back, on the bed, his arms spread out in an image of sex crucifixion. His eyes are closed; his mouth is open. His chest is rising and falling like some spastic bellows. Then his eyes open and he looks up at her, a smile of helpless satisfaction spreading across his handsome face.

'That was amazing,' he whispers. 'Utterly amazing.'

She smiles at him, weak, dazed, her cock still granite rock-hard. 'I need to clean myself up.'

His smile widens. 'So do I.'

The shower is almost as exciting as the blow job. Beneath a wall of hot, steaming water, Richard insists on using one of Eve's large, circular sponges to cover the she-male's silken body in a thick layer of scented soap. Within seconds, her cock is even harder and she is moaning with heart-wrenching pleasure. Richard pays particular attention to the she-male's impressive sex and whispers words of teasing encouragement as it stirs restlessly in his warm, wet hands.

'There, there,' he whispers. 'Time for you to come back out of the box.'

Then, to Eve's further surprise and intense pleasure, Richard slips a hand between her legs and gently slides his index finger between the she-male's tight, girlish bottom. The finger quickly seeks out her anus and begins to work its way inside.

Eve lets out a squeal of shock and delight and relaxes slightly to allow Richard to probe deeper.

'Feel good?' he asks, pressing his beautifully muscular and water-slicked body closer to hers.

Eve nods helplessly and moans louder. Richard laughs and presses a little harder.

'It'll be a little while before we can get my cock in here. But we can work on it, in the coming weeks.'

Her cock rises up and she is seconds away from exploding. These teasing words drive her towards the very edge of sex madness and uncontrollable orgasm. But Richard is clearly experienced in the matter of cock control and, seconds before the point of no return, he removes his soapy finger and sends the sexy she-male plunging into a vat of terrible frustration.

After the shower, they spend another erotic twenty minutes drying each other's bodies. Eve studies Richard's impressive form with wide, sex-maddened eyes and he teases the she-male relentlessly.

'You look really gorgeous, Eve. Even like this you are so perfectly feminine.'

Eve smiles nervously and blushes furiously, her hard cock a simple and inescapable confession of how much she is enjoying being with Richard.

Then they dress. Richard slowly dons his simple male attire and asks Eve to dress for him – the exact opposite of the striptease.

'Impress me, my sexy little she-he,' he teases.

Eve, still naked, smiles. Yes, this will be a simple matter: dressing for this strange and beautiful man, creating a new Eve for his entertainment and arousal.

From beneath the dressing table, she takes a pair of pink patent-leather, stiletto-heeled court shoes. She slips her feet into them and is immediately elevated by four inches. Then, otherwise naked, she wiggle minces across the room in front of Richard and enters the wardrobe, her perfectly formed and very feminine backside performing an erotic and deliberately teasing dance of desire.

From inside the wardrobe, she extracts a white satin-panelled body-shaper, a white nylon sweater and a pink leather mini-skirt. She returns to the bedroom and places the clothes down on the bed, where Richard is once again sitting, her stiff, considerable sex swaying before her like a totem pole dedicated to she-male beauty. As she turns, she smiles briefly and promisingly at her new lover.

From the chest of drawers she extracts a pair of white silk panties and a pair of white nylon tights. She carefully lowers herself on to the dressing table stool and places the tights on the floor. She draws the panties up her long, silken legs, which she stretches out before her to accentuate their intensely erotic contours. When the panties are in position, she returns to the bed and takes up the virginal body-shaper. Then, standing close to Richard, she draws the ingenious, transformative device up her legs and over her body. Once the shaper is tightly positioned against her slender form, she returns to the dressing table stool and proceeds to draw up the soft, very sheer tights, again stretching her legs out before a fascinated and obviously aroused Richard. The tights accentuate the already sensual shape of each leg and reveal the true depth of Eve's feminine soul. Richard's eyes betray a helpless attraction to the erotic ambiguity at the heart of this revelation and they smile at each other with a deep, desperate longing.

Once the tights are snugly positioned, Eve rises from the stool and minces back to the bed. She takes up the skirt and gently wriggles into it. As she does so, Richard places a warm hand on her nylon thigh and strokes it lovingly. Eve smiles and steps back, removing the hand and then picking up the sweater. She gracefully lowers this confection of soft white wool over the substantial bosom provided by the shaper and tucks it into the skirt. She returns to the stool and steps back into the pink patent-leather court shoes. She takes the sumptuously curved blonde wig – the wig that has been her erotic companion all day – from the stand, and carefully places it on her still damp head.

Then a few dabs of make-up: a hint of pink eye shadow and matching lipstick and a touch of foundation. Subtle and modest. She runs a teasing brush through her renewed blonde locks and turns to face a smiling, clearly *very impressed* Richard.

'Incredible,' he whispers. 'Absolutely incredible.'

Eve performs a mock curtsey and Richard's smile broadens.

The rest of the night is lost in a whirl of erotic romance and role-playing, fuelled by good food prepared by Eve's expert hand, plus strong wine. Richard takes every opportunity to order Eve around the house in a masterful manner and also to caress and sexually tease the lovely TV. Eve is lost in a maelstrom of arousal, feeling her powerful sense of feminine being collide head-on with a helplessly masculine desire that is tormented and blurred by her attraction to Richard. This is the inescapable reality of the middle ground. Yet as she enjoys this intensely erotic silver-grey space between the feminine and the masculine, she is also becoming aware of something else – the pleasure of submission.

As the evening progresses, Richard makes his dominant presence felt through the power of his calm, easy-going yet forceful and controlling personality, and a series of more precise and definite orders. Eve is ordered to serve the food and drink as a maid, and to curtsey meekly before her master. At first it is an amusing game. But as they both fall under the influence of alcohol, all inhibitions are removed. Richard becomes even more forceful and Eve, instinctively, even more submissive. This increase in the polar power relations reaches its peak when Eve accidentally spills a drop of wine on Richard's jeans and receives a harsh rebuke. To her secret delight, Richard grabs the gorgeous she-male by her wrists and hauls her once again over his lap. Then he administers an even harder, painful and furiously erotic spanking. At first Eve struggles angrily, but as the blows become more focused – an alternating slap to each buttock – she begins to feel a terrible, profound and all-pervasive pleasure. Her moans of pain edge into ambivalent squeals of a dark she-male pleasure and her stiff sex presses desperately through the body-shaper against Richard's own revived weapon.

Then Richard pushes Eve from his knees.

'Right, let's get back upstairs. I need another really good sucking to help me sleep.'

The lovely Eve obliges. But this time it is beneath the sheets and they are naked. And Eve services Richard's every need for over an hour.

That night – and it is well after midnight by the time they sleep – Eve shares her bed for the first time in her life; the end of a bizarre and beautiful day that has brought so many of her most secret dreams to life. Yet she is too exhausted to comprehend fully the adventures of the last twelve hours. However, even as she quickly slips into a deep and dreamless sleep, she finds herself – however briefly – pondering, once again, Richard's true intentions, and whether there is some sinister link between their encounter in the shop and the Crème de la Crème club.

5

A Cruel Desire

When she wakes, it is after eight a.m. and Richard has left.
There is a note on the dressing table.

My love
Last night was fantastic. I'll be in contact.
R

Eve reads the words and feels the familiar collision of fear
and desire that has framed the last two days. Confused and
excited, she quickly showers, then slips into a pair of white
silk panties and very sheer black nylon tights. Then, as an
added extra, she wriggles into a sexy white silk teddy
covered in a fine pattern of elegant roses. Over this
delightfully feminine confection, she places her male
clothes: a fresh, white cotton suit, a simple red silk tie,
dark-grey trousers and an exactly matching jacket.

On the face of it she is once more he: Adam, the senior
manager; the typical male. She wears male body spray,
black leather shoes and a dark-blue raincoat. When she
walks out to the car, nearly twenty minutes late, she
feels stranger than ever. This is my true disguise, she
thinks, climbing into the car, remembering her previous
journey to the Crème de la Crème club, remembering
driving Richard home the night before in a state of
utter sexual delirium. And as she drives now, entering
the chaotic morning rush-hour traffic, she recalls
Richard's body and his strange, disturbingly elliptic

personality. She also recalls one of the most amazing nights of her life.

Despite the feminine frillies teasing her silken body, she finds Eve now has less power and control. In the suit, in the car, stuck in traffic, worrying about the day ahead, the weight of her male life begins to press upon her mind. Adam is now a day behind, and she knows that as soon as she sits down at the desk in his office, this weight will increase, that the problems will begin to mount up. A year ago, she had found all this a challenge, but now – especially today – it all seems a dreadful waste of time. A strange sense of dread washes over her. This is not what I want to do, she thinks. This is not the truth of my life.

By the time she leaves his car in the underground car park beneath the large office building that houses the regional headquarters, she is enveloped in a sense of numbing gloom. This gloom descends deeper and darker as she takes the lift up to Adam's floor and the open-plan office he manages. As she walks through the jungle of desks, as the entirely female staff wish her good morning, she imagines that everyone knows 'he' is actually a she. She imagines that these many female eyes can, in some strange and miraculous way, see through the suit and into the truth of her feminine undies. This thought relieves the gloom a little, and, by the time she reaches his office, she manages a smile for Angela, Adam's handsome, ultra-efficient secretary, a woman in her late forties whose calm, unflappable personality he has come to rely on during his time as section manager.

She talks about messages, demands, paperwork and Eve fights to listen. As she slinks into Adam's office chair she feels a little less horrified. Angela's calm description of the work ahead is strangely relaxing. She knows that work in itself rather than contemplation of it is the key to surviving the day and the days that are to follow.

Eventually, she is lost in Adam's work, lost inside the problems and challenges that have always been so simple for her to address. Every now and again, she pauses to reflect on the night before, to think about Richard, about the Crème de la Crème, the amazing adventure of her new life. At these points the office seems to fade out and the tacky dance floor of the club is before her. She is dressed in a beautiful ball-gown, a fifties-style confection of white satin. She is dancing with Richard. Then she is dancing with Cherry. Her eyes widen as she remembers the gorgeous, dark-skinned TV. She imagines being with Richard and Cherry, a spectacular sexual adventure whose possibilities seem endless.

Suddenly, her body is tormented by the sensual fabrics beneath the suit and she is desperate to be Eve again, to be wholly transformed and to be with the gorgeous Cherry and the handsome, gently cruel Richard.

By four-thirty p.m., her cock is threatening to explode independently of any external stimulation. She makes Adam's excuses and leaves an hour early.

She drives home through Friday evening traffic in a total trance, managing to avoid a road accident by instinct rather than intention. And once she is inside the house, she rips off the male clothing and spends twenty minutes soaking beneath a hot, steaming shower. The urge to masturbate is appalling and ever present, but she knows that to relieve herself of the deep, dark ache now would be to undermine the dynamic of the evening ahead. She needs to be fully aroused, totally sensitised and completely at the mercy of Richard.

After the shower and a long, teasing drying, she begins the process of transformation once again, a willing disappearance into the freedom of the secret self.

She has known all day how she will dress: tonight the model will be Juliette Binoche; cool black and blue.

She selects a short black dress with long sleeves, the red body-shaper, a very expensive pair of Italian-made black tights, woven from silk-impregnated nylon, a pair of black silk panties, a pair of black velvet-lined leather pumps by Gucci, with relatively modest three-inch heels, and a black cashmere jacket. Before dressing, she applies a hint of Chanel and a very dark red lipstick. The slightest touch of powder foundation and a light-blue eye-shadow complete the make-up.

Once she is dressed, her body alive with the sensual pleasures of the various soft, elegant and deeply erotic fabrics, she returns to the wardrobe, to a large wooden box placed by the shoe-racks. She kneels down, causing the short skirt of the lovely dress to ride up her legs to reveal her black-nyloned, perfectly shaped thighs and send electrical waves of narcissistic pleasure coursing across her she-male body.

From the box she takes a new wig, one of four balancing on polystyrene 'phantom heads'. This is black, medium-length and straight, a slightly longer and thicker version of the classic Louise Brooks wig. She totters back to the dressing table and carefully slips the wig over her own short hair. The effect is immediate and stunning: the final touch which opens the doorway leading to the she-male beauty Eve. She sits at the dressing table, her hands rest on her warm, finely hosed knees; then they slip beneath the skirt of the dress. She moans with pleasure as she remembers the previous evening and the adventures that await her this evening. She remembers Richard's hand inside her, his helpless cries of pleasure as he came in her mouth, the taste of his cum, the strangeness of being totally naked in his powerful arms and still feeling so totally Eve, and thus so totally feminine. Then she remembers the spanking and the terrible, fundamental physical excitement it produced in her, an excitement that is now renewed in her memory and leaves her gasping with a helpless, fierce pleasure.

She is shocked from her erotic ponderings by the clear, hard ring of the doorbell. She knows it is Richard. All day she has known he will come to her tonight and that she will give herself to him in any way he wishes.

Her heart pounding with a terrible anticipation, she tries to move as quickly as possible without undermining her naturally feminine and graceful stride. She knows she looks beautiful and convincing, she knows he will be impressed and aroused. The thought of this new revealing, however, is laced with a strange nervousness. Tonight will be far more profound in its consequences. Tonight is the next stage in the true revelation of Eve.

She opens the door with a beating heart and a rock-hard cock. Then she is before him, elegant, beautiful, so very carefully revealed.

He is dressed in a black sweater, a black leather jacket and black jeans. His eyes are filled with the dark passion she finds so terribly exciting.

He smiles warmly at the beautiful sight of her.

'My God,' he whispers.

He steps into the hallway. She notices he is carrying a black leather sports bag.

'You look gorgeous,' he says, putting down the bag and taking her in his arms. She feels herself momentarily lifted off her feet and then his mouth is pressed against hers. She parts her lips and the kiss they share is long and hard. His hot, minty breath washes over her face and she feels a quiver of feminine surrender pass across her body.

He releases her and she sighs with pleasure.

Then he takes her by the arm and leads her into the front room. She totters alongside him, feeling utterly feminine, in a way that is now more complete and intense than in any other point in her life.

He leads her to the middle of the room and makes her stand with her hands behind her back as he carefully inspects every inch of her slender, elegant and very beautiful form.

'Perfect,' he whispers. 'Utterly perfect.'

She blushes and thanks him.

'Stay there,' he whispers, and then rushes from the room, returning in a few seconds with the bag.

'What's in it?' she asks.

'Toys,' he says, the fire in his black eyes burning bright.

She swallows hard and looks down at the bag.

'And wine.'

He opens the bag and takes out an expensive bottle of red wine.

'What's for dinner?'

She looks at the clock. It is already six-thirty p.m.

'Chicken. A sauce. Nothing too elaborate.'

While she cooks, he prowls around the kitchen. Now and again he moves closer to her, running his hands over

94

her body, especially her legs. She moans with pleasure and fights to concentrate on the cooking.

'You smell fantastic,' he whispers, moving closer, kissing her neck, his hands running up her hosed thighs.

She moans and pushes her shapely, tightly pantied bottom into his eager palm. A finger slips between her legs and she squeals with girlish delight.

'I saw Cherry today,' he says, his voice thick with sex. 'All she wanted to do was talk about you. She likes you very much, Eve. Very much.'

Poor Eve can barely respond. A vision of the gorgeous Cherry floods her teased and tormented mind.

'We should get together sometime. All three of us,' he adds, pressing his finger hard against her silk-sealed arsehole.

'Yes,' Eve gasps. 'I'd really like that.'

He removes his hand and strokes her neck. She lets out a meow of kittenish pleasure.

She serves dinner wearing a heavily frilled pinafore, a fifties housewife serving her man.

'I like the pinny, Eve. Very sexy. I'd love to see you in a full maid's uniform.'

She totters before him in the sexy heels, her long, dark legs tightly together, her thighs rubbing through the sex-film of sheer nylon, carrying plates, bottles, glasses. Her bottom wiggling in the tight skirt, her beautiful eyes wide and flashing with a bright, confident arousal. As the evening progresses, she is becoming more and more confident, yet in a slightly paradoxical and deeply delicious way. For the more confident she becomes in her femininity, the more she desires absolute submission. Once again she recalls the spanking; then she remembers the erotic sufferings of the lovely and unfortunate Honey. Her cock stretches and she sighs. The pleasure she feels is beyond words.

They eat the meal with surprisingly little conversation. She is very aware of him watching her, marvelling at her perfect feminine gestures, at her striking authenticity.

'I have one upstairs,' she says, suddenly, between small, careful mouthfuls of tender, moist and savoury chicken.

Momentarily, Richard is confused.

'Sorry?'

'A maid's uniform. You've seen it. I'll put it on for you.'

His confusion passes. He smiles. Erotic cruelty returns to his gaze.

'Yes. But not tonight. I've got other plans for tonight.'

Now she is confused. He laughs. 'Just a little test for my pretty petal.'

She swallows with nervous desire and avoids his eyes. She knows she will do anything he wants. And the thought fills her with a dizzying sexual thrill.

After dinner and two glasses of wine each, they return to the living room. He sits down on the sofa and she stands before him, hands held behind her back, a posture of gentle but absolute submission.

'Sit on my lap,' he orders.

She smiles and carefully lowers herself on to his knees. As she does so, she is aware of the skirt riding up her thighs and of his eyes pinned to her increasingly apparent and shockingly sexy black nylon-sheathed flesh.

'What's the test?' she asks teasingly, settling her bottom over his hard, large sex.

'I need to know how much you trust me. So let's call it a test of trust.'

She smiles, but there is an obvious concern in her eyes, a crack in the façade of she-male self-assurance.

'I trust you . . . I think.'

They both laugh at her coquettish reply.

'I want to tie you up.'

Her eyes widen. Her body stiffens. His smile turns into a cool grin of sadistic appraisal.

'Tie me up?'

Her voice is filled with a fear-edged desire.

'I want to play a game. To test you and to amuse me. I like playing games.'

Her silence expresses a real and disturbing doubt.

'I don't know,' she says, stumbling into a new realm of real concern.

Maybe she has made a terrible mistake. Maybe Richard

is quite mad. Maybe she is in the hands of some weird sex criminal.

His smile widens. 'You're frightened. I like that. I want you to be frightened. Yet your fear can be overcome by desire, Eve. By your desire for the ultimate feminine submission.'

Her eyes widen, her mouth slips open slightly. She shakes her head slightly.

'Get up,' he orders, his smile fading, a look of grim, very dark determination washing over his handsome, lean face.

She obeys and stands before him with frightened eyes, arms at her side, her heart beginning to beat faster, with fear and very genuine trepidation.

He rises from the sofa and goes over to the bag. From inside, he takes a coil of white nylon rope. She looks at this and shakes her head. 'No . . . please,' she whispers.

'Put your hands behind your back.'

She stands still, doesn't move an inch. He then quickly steps forward and grabs one of her wrists. She shouts 'No!', a firm refusal in the voice of Adam. But Richard is strong; in fact, he is much stronger than Adam ever was. They struggle now, but it is a relatively simple task for Richard to pin Eve's wrists behind her back and then tie them tightly together with the rope.

'Please,' Eve pleads. 'Don't . . . you're frightening me.'

He laughs and returns to the bag. In the heels, with her hands bound, she is unable to move quickly enough even to contemplate escape. Then to her horror, he produces a thick roll of wide, silver-coloured duct tape and what appears to be a pair of white silk panties.

'And you're talking too much.'

He grabs her by the neck and she screams. He then shoves the heavily scented panties deep into her mouth. She gags and tries to spit them out. He clamps a hand over her mouth and pushes her back on to the sofa. Her legs kick out desperately, causing her skirt to ride back up her thighs and reveal her sexy panties. To her amazement, she suddenly realises her erection is stronger and harder than ever.

He holds her down with his body and tears a long strip of tape from the roll. The thick, harsh tearing sound fills the room and her eyes plead for mercy. Then he spreads the tape over her mouth, pressing it hard against her lips and bulging cheeks. She squeals angrily and he bursts out laughing.

'What a lovely damsel in distress you make, Eve.'

His terrible, deeply physical masculine power is now apparent in every gesture, every rough manipulation. She is bound and gagged, totally at his mercy. He can do anything he wishes to her. She is terrified and, to her astonishment, furiously aroused.

He releases her and sets to work on her long, black nylon-sheathed legs, binding her ankles and her knees very tightly together with more lengths of the nylon rope. She moans her fear and tries to struggle free, but he is a true rope expert, and she is painfully secure and thus utterly helpless.

When he has finished with her legs, he makes her sit up and then uses another length of rope to bind her elbows painfully together. She gives a furious, outraged look as he completes this particularly sadistic part of her encasement in dark bondage.

Then he sits back and observes his perverse handiwork.

'Superb. Absolutely superb.'

Tears of terror trickle from her eyes and this just seems to make him all the more aroused. She looks down at his jeans and sees the hard, long length of his sex press against the front. There is truly no escape.

He returns to the bag as she struggles pointlessly in her bondage, wiggling and squealing, her skirt now pulled fully up around her waist. Yet it is as she struggles, as her large, artificial chest wobbles desperately before her, that she begins to feel something new, yet also quite old: a deep sense of femininity. As she wriggles and moans, she finds herself exaggerating the movements, stylising them. She has seen many films where beautiful women are bound and gagged; and she would be lying to herself if she didn't admit a sense of arousal, a sense of very dark but also, she feels, quite natural, sexual excitement. The idea of the damsel in distress is universal; the collision of beauty and peril seems unavoidable. And as she struggles, she begins to realise she is expressing her inner femininity in a particularly powerful and erotic manner.

His hands are on her again. His large, controlling, confident and beautiful hands.

And it is then that he holds the vibrator before her. A thin, quite small vibrator made from pink plastic.

'It is time to begin your training, my love.'

He quickly turns her on to her stomach, so that her face is pressed down into the sofa and her bottom is left jutting provocatively upward. She is aware of him kneeling directly by her backside. Then his hands are carefully pulling her panties down around her knees and working the tights down after them. She squeals angrily into the gag and he slaps her left buttock very hard, inducing a high-pitched squeal of pain.

Then his hands are working between her legs on the gusset section of the body-shaper. This shaper has a gusset-based lock and he slowly removes the clips that hold it tightly in place between her pert, perfectly formed and very pink buttocks.

Then the gusset is free and he is pulling the body-shaper up her bottom and hauling her skirt with it, so that both end up wrapped around her lower waist. Then his hands are again between her legs, but this time they dig deeper, reaching over her bulging, aching balls and grasping the base of her rigid, straining sex.

She squeals and wriggles and his harsh laughter fills the room.

'Hard as a rock,' he snaps, a voice full of sadistic amusement.

Then he releases his tight grip and her sex is left to press desperately into the side of the sofa.

Richard administers four more hard slaps to her exposed backside before beginning the next phase of this ultra-kinky sex torture. Each slap is greeted with a well-gagged cry of anger, yet this is an anger laced with desire, with arousal, with the secret confession of masochistic enjoyment.

His fingers are working at her buttocks once again, now carefully parting them, creating an access way to her totally exposed anus. Her squeals are high and desperate and her erection on the very edge of a violent orgasm.

'If you come, I'll put you in a hog-tie and lock you in the broom closet for the night,' he snaps as the low, deep, terrifying buzz of the vibrator begins to fill the room.

Her squealing lessens, as a terrible anticipation grips her consciousness. The tip of the cool plastic touches the red-fleshed edge of her arse. Her squeal becomes a helpless, sissy meow and then the buzzing of vibrator, combined with the sensual heat that is spreading from her well-spanked buttocks, between her legs and into her rigid sex, ensures a complete and utter surrender. All fear fades as the vibrator is pushed with great care and gentleness into her slowly parting anus. This slender, tiny device has only one purpose: anal stimulation, and as Eve begins to understand the true sensitivity of the back passage and thus its ability to give pleasure, she becomes Richard's gorgeous sissy pet. She knows now there is nothing to fear, that this tight bondage is a test of the true depths and nature of Eve. She bites down on the panty gag and tastes an expensive French perfume. She closes her eyes and sees sex stars exploding across a universe of endless desire. Richard pushes a little harder and she feels as if she will split in two.

'There, there,' he whispers gently as she grunts with discomfort. 'Just a little further, my love.'

As the vibrator moves deeper into her, the vibrations spread across her anal walls and then deep into her balls. The growing sexual stimulation is astonishingly powerful. She fights desperately not to come, her squeals now filled with furious, irresistible sexual hunger. The muffled cries are cries of unbearable pleasure, cries of sweet, intoxicating and eternal surrender.

Then there is a slight pop. The vibrator moves deep within her and slides to a halt. She feels her buttock cheeks lock around it, ensuring a weird, highly exciting self-sealing.

'That was surprisingly straightforward,' he says, pulling the body-shaper back into position and carefully clipping it into place. The shaper is followed by the gentle repositioning of the tights and panties. He then pulls the skirt back into place and softy pats her helplessly twitching bottom.

'You'll be ready for me in two to three weeks, I'd say. I think we'll need an hour every night until then.'

Her eyes widen in surprise and eroticised horror at the thought of being plugged like this every night for the next fourteen to twenty-one days!

His arms wrap around her waist and carefully pull her up before gently lowering her face down on to the floor. She squeals with increasing pleasure as her face touches the edge of the carpet.

She watches his feet move around the room. Then she can feel him attaching another length of rope to the one binding her ankles so tightly and inescapably together.

There is a sudden, rather violent tug on the end of this rope and her ankles are being pulled across her body towards her wrists. Fear and pain return as the cruel hog-tie is secured, leaving her bound helplessly, face down on the carpet, the vibrator buzzing wickedly deep inside her arse.

'There,' he gasps. 'All done. I need to get us some more wine for later and make a phone call. I'll see you in a hour or so.'

She squeals furiously into the gag as he leaves the room. But then the front door slams and she knows she is alone in the house. Alone and utterly helpless. She moans and squirms with a terrible pleasure as the vibrator seems to drill even deeper into her tightly tethered form. The bondage is absolute and inescapable. She is pinned helplessly into position, a sexy she-male package ready for the pleasure of her kinky, cruel master. The feeling of helplessness is a truly startling aphrodisiac, and as she stretches against the unyielding ropes, she experiences an increasing level of submissive femininity. She recalls his firm, power-ful, yet always caressing hands applying the rope to her body and she is lost in a bright, soul-enveloping bliss. This, she realises, is the burning light of masochistic desire that resides at the very heart of Eve.

For the next hour or so, she is lost in a strange contemplation of the adventures of the last twenty hours. Eve is free. Even tightly bound and gagged, she experiences a freedom beyond her imagination a week ago. Yet the rapid pace of events is dizzying. She has moved from a carefully closeted cross-dresser to a member of the most renowned transvestite club in the country. Now, she even has a boyfriend. A boyfriend who spanks her and places her in tight, perverse bondage.

As the vibrator sends waves of pleasure crashing across her tethered, so carefully feminine form, her hard, angry sex presses through silk and nylon against the carpeted floor of the living room. She unleashes a slightly melo-dramatic squeal of frustration. Images of a dark eroticism flood through her sex-addled mind. Her thighs, so com-pletely sealed in the sheerest, most expensive nylon, rub helplessly together and create a hyper-erotic sex static. I am filled with sex electricity, she thinks. This is truly the Body Electric, a beautiful she-male machine powered by a dark and perverse desire.

An image of Cherry returns to her now, along with Richard's teasing words. She imagines the three of them together. Then she imagines she and Cherry, alone, gorg-eous she-male lovers. Yes, this is the image that sticks. With Richard, there is a strange extension of the narcissism at the heart of the transvestite sexual experience. She finds him attractive only so far as he heightens her awareness and realisation of Eve. Yes, even when she was sucking him to that volcanic eruption of hot, salty cum – an act she found far from unpleasant – the core of her own pleasure was the simple fact that to give Richard this pleasure made her feel all the more feminine, all the more submissive. All the more Eve. Yet with Cherry, with the looks they had exchanged in the club, there was a desire that moved beyond herself, a desire that was directed towards an object that was not Eve. She imagines running her hands over Cherry's firm, nylon-sheathed thighs; she imagines holding Cherry's buxom form in her arms and pressing her lips against the black beauty's full, blood-red mouth. She imagines them tied together like this, bound and gagged by Master Richard. And this thought is flooding her mind like blinding golden water or a loud blast of some perfect sex chord when the front door, which has been left teasingly on the latch, is pushed open and, a few seconds later, Richard enters the room.

He stands over her in silence for a long time. She moans into the gag and awaits her no doubt erotic fate.

Then, suddenly, he is kneeling before her.

'Did my pretty petal enjoy her bondage?'

Poor Eve can only nod, a simple confession of the truth. Yes – she has enjoyed every tightly restricted minute.

'Well, you can look forward to lots more from now on.'

She looks up at him with beautifully apprehensive, doe eyes and moans with a helpless delight. His smile softens.

'God, you're so beautiful,' he whispers.

Then there is a silence, a strange, important silence in which a new level of feeling becomes apparent, a silence broken only by the steady, tiny sound of the vibrator deep inside her.

Then, slowly, gently, with an intense love, he begins to untie her, his hands travelling her body between the removal of each coil of restricting white-nylon rope.

Eventually, she is free of everything except the gag and the vibrator.

'You look so good gagged, Eve. It really brings out the sensual beauty of your eyes. Let's keep you gagged for the rest of the evening.'

She nods and he helps her to her high-heeled feet. Then he helps adjust her clothing and gives her a few minutes to straighten her hair.

As she looks at her reflection in a compact mirror, she quivers with a terribly masochistic pleasure. The tape gag covers her lips in an exact rectangle, transferring all possibility to her beautiful, dark-brown eyes. She moans her helpless arousal and turns back to Richard. They exchange a look of intense desire.

They sit together on the sofa. He drinks wine, but she must go without. He caresses her thighs and teases her with words of love and control. She can only moan and squeal and lose herself in a whirlpool of endless submission.

He presses the palm of his hand against the gusset of the body-shaper. Her eyes close and she gasps into the fat, scented gag.

'I think it's time I gave you a little relief.'

Minutes later they are back in the bedroom. They sit on the bed. He helps her out of the skirt and panties. Her eyes are wide with a dreadful, aching anticipation.

'It seems such a shame to takes these tights off. I'm really quite mad about them, you know – my big fetish. The softness of them; the way they shape the legs – the way they eroticise them.'

She nods, agreeing completely, but also so terribly eager for the relief he has promised.

Reluctantly he lowers the tights to her knees and then works free the gusset of the body-shaper. Now, more than ever, she is his object, his possession. Once again, she quivers with submissive delight. He gently rolls back the shaper and her long, hard, crimson cock pops up, its need all too obvious.

His smile widens.

'Lie back my love,' he whispers. 'Lie back and relax.'

She does so and her cock rises up before her like a beautifully erotic craven idol.

She turns her head and watches as he pulls a black nylon stocking from a pocket in his jeans. He smiles down at her and then carefully rolls the stocking up into a ball. Her eyes widen with desperate arousal and pleading as he holds the bunched-up stocking directly over the dark-purple, straining head of Eve's cock.

Then, to her deep excitement, he begins very slowly to ease the stocking over her enraged sex. She squeals furiously as the soft nylon kisses the edges of her boiling

104

sex meat. She wiggles and bucks and he rests a firm, strong hand on her tummy.

'There, there, my pretty. You'll soon get a little release.'

He pulls the scented stocking down around her balls and ensures it is pulled tightly and snugly into position. Then he begins very gently to massage the nyloned cock, a dreadfully arousing and expert tease that brings Eve to the edge of orgasm.

Tears of angry, agonising frustration spill from her eyes: his touch is expert and thus deliberate; he is holding her back from the explosive brink quite deliberately.

'I spoke to Cherry when I was out,' he says. 'I told her that you were all tied up on the floor, all helpless. I told her how beautiful you looked tightly bound and gagged. She sounded terribly turned on. She says she is so looking forward to meeting you again tomorrow night.'

A look of surprise suddenly fills Eve's girlish eyes.

'Oh yes, I know you'll be visiting Pris and her wife. I'm sure that'll be fun. Cherry will be there as well, plus some others. I would go, but there's a little business I need to sort, I'm afraid. A job for Crème de la Crème, actually.'

He begins to press harder and to increase the rhythm of his dark massage. She cries into the gag and imagines Cherry here now, watching, waiting her turn. She imagines being in Cherry's arms. She . . .

The explosion is massive. An atomic coming that leaves her bucking like a wild bronco and screaming love and lust and sex madness into the black hole of her endless she-male desire. She wants to scream *fuck fuck fuck*! into an oblivion of eternal orgasm.

The stocking fills with her thick, creamy cum and soaks through the sheer material to leave a steel-white liquid head on top of her black nylon-enveloped sex. Her heart pounds against the wall of her chest. She feels a sudden, ecstatic physical relief wash over her. She collapses into a soft white pit of serene and total bliss.

And when she wakes up, she is naked and under the silk sheets, tucked in snug as a bug. She is still gagged, but also still free from any other form of bondage. Her clothes are neatly folded on a bedside chair. And on the chair is a note.

> *My pretty angel, ring me Sunday morning. Leave the gag until morning – for me.*
> *All my love*
> *R*

She slips the note beneath the sheets and holds it close to her heart. Then, within seconds, she is asleep again.

6

At Helen's House

She rises at dawn and carefully removes the gag, her mouth
filled with the taste of expensive French perfume. After a
long, deeply relaxing shower, she dresses in simple house
clothes: a navy-blue sweater, a short, pleated black skirt,
black cotton panties and opaque black tights. There is no
body-shaper, no make-up, no wig. She stares at herself in
the wardrobe mirror and is shocked and deeply pleased at
how feminine she remains without the intricate tools of
feminine illusion that are her make-up and the body-
shaper. This is Eve. Simple and true. The real me. The
person resting in the grey space between male and female.

She has a light breakfast and then logs on to the
computer. It is four days since she accessed her e-mail
account and there are three new e-mails from Aunt Debra.
At first, Eve is horrified. For the first time in over twelve
years, she has failed to respond to her aunt's contact. Yet
the tone of Debra's e-mails is far from outraged or hurt.
Indeed, she appears amused that Eve is not responding,
saying that she must be having lots of fun with her new
friends, that she should write as soon as possible and let
her know all her she-male niece's kinky adventures. And
then, with the third e-mail, there is a picture, a picture with
this simple heading: 'Just to remind you what you're
missing'. Eve gasps as she beholds this latest startling
display of her aunt's considerable charms. For the picture
that is attached to the e-mail shows Debra dressed in a
striking black leather and red satin basque, with very sheer,

seamed tights and five-inch heeled, black leather pumps. An astonishing and violently erotic image. She is sitting on a stool, her long, curvaceous legs tightly crossed, her large, pale bosom straining tightly against the bra-section of the basque. Her thick, still almost perfectly black hair is bound in a tight bun, and her lips are painted a bloody red. In her brown eyes there is the flame of a highly imaginative and intense passion, in her slight smile there is a very obvious and terribly teasing promise.

Instantly overwhelmed, poor Eve masturbates to a stunning, screaming orgasm, staining her panties and tights with an indifference that only becomes apparent once she is spent.

As she cleans herself up, she is already hard again, thinking of the picture and of the long erotic history that binds Aunt Debra and Eve so tightly together.

A few minutes later, in fresh panties and tights, Eve is back on the computer, sending her beloved and desired aunt a long and detailed e-mail. Telling her everything with a terrible, desperate abandon. Detailing the Crème de la Crème, the shock and delight of her first exposure in the outside world, and always the surprise at how easy it was for her 'to pass'. Then there is Priscilla and the hungry gaze of so many men. And then, most importantly, there is Richard. And finally, as a helplessly erotic coda, she thanks her aunt for the picture and confesses the immediate impact it has had upon her, confessing in a detail she knows will excite and amuse her.

She finishes her long, detailed reply just before lunch. The message is so long she has to transfer the text into a Word file and send it as a file attachment. Then she stares at the picture of Aunt Debra once again. She is in her late forties now, but still utterly stunning. And Eve's love and desire for her, despite the events of the last few days, is as strong as ever.

Despite Richard and whatever follows, she knows that this startling woman, her glorious Aunt Debra, is the one and only true mistress of her heart.

In the afternoon, dressed in a white sweater, a sedate grey check skirt, black tights, modest heels and the black cashmere jacket, Eve ventures out. Her form made buxom and sexual once more by the body-shaper, she drives into town and spends some time quietly walking among the busy Saturday afternoon crowds. She walks through the main arcade and window-shops. She does this for maybe an hour. And the purpose of this brief excursion is simple: to reinforce her confidence before the visit to Priscilla Rouge. To strengthen her she-male soul and prepare her for a new and no doubt exciting challenge.

She arrives home just after five on a dark winter afternoon and spends the next two hours carefully preparing herself for the dinner party. After another long, scented shower, she selects a suitably striking, but also relatively modest costume: a knee-length, black silk dress, with long, semi-transparent arms, a pair of expensive black nylon Italian tights, a pair of three-inch-heeled, black patent leather pumps and a black leather jacket with elegant silver buttons. She decides on the same blonde wig she wore for her visit to the Crème de la Crème club and the same minimal make-up, plus a subtle, but highly noticeable perfume. Beneath the dress she wears the black silk body-shaper and a pair of black silk panties.

As she studies herself in the wardrobe mirror, she feels a sense of supreme confidence return, the sense that has driven her directly into the adventures of the last three days and which seems to be leading her to a new understanding of the potential of her self and the highly erotic world within which she now moves.

She decides to take a taxi to Priscilla's house and cannot help noticing the admiring gaze of the taxi driver as he helps her into the rear seat. In the darkness of the car, the driver attempts to make conversation and Eve is immediately on her guard. She whispers simple yes and no answers in a lighter, more high-pitched voice, but is very wary of indulging in any form of significant discourse. And all the while she can see his eyes in the rear-view mirror, lit in fragmented flashes by the passing street lights, eyes filled with the familiar male hunger that is both so arousing and so very disturbing; the hunger that so powerfully reminds her of Richard.

As they drive into the street where Priscilla lives, Eve immediately becomes aware of a simple fact: either Priscilla or her wife is very wealthy. This is because the relatively new, small estate of exclusive five-bedroom houses betrays an affluence far beyond most people Eve knows, a fact that is made doubly apparent by the cars parked in the huge driveway: a large silver BMW and a Mercedes estate, both less than a year old.

The driver takes Eve's money with a quizzical smile and wishes her a good evening. She stands in the cool night air staring at the large house and wonders whether she should go in. Then, realising she has come so far in the last few days, and that a visit to Priscilla's home is, by comparison, a minor challenge, she walks up the drive, her heels echoing across the driveway and down the street. At the large black door, she uses an elegant brass handle to announce her presence and feels her confidence return. But when the door opens, confidence is quickly replaced by genuine shock. For standing before her is Priscilla, but not the glamorous, relaxed beauty of the Crème de la Crème club. No: to Eve's astonishment, she is facing Priscilla dressed in a stunning French maid's costume – a gorgeous black silk and satin dress, with a very short, heavily petticoat-laden skirt and a plunging, frilled neckline that reveals a pair of astonishingly realistic and very large breasts. Around her slender waist is a pretty cream-coloured silk apron whose only function is erotic decoration. Her long, beautifully shaped legs are sheathed in very sheer black nylon stockings, the red satin garter-wrapped tops of which are clearly visible through the mist of petticoating. She is also wearing five-inch-high, stiletto-heeled mules of a very shiny black patent leather and white glacé gloves. Her striking red head is bound in a tight bun held in place with a diamond-studded clasp. She looks at Eve, smiles very slightly and then performs a very deep curtsey, revealing heavily frilled white silk panties.

'Please come in, madame.'

At first, Eve is too startled to move, but eventually she enters the hallway, unable to keep her eyes away from the luscious sado-erotic package that is Priscilla.

With a slightly knowing smile, Priscilla removes Eve's coat and hangs it up in the entrance foyer. She then conducts the beautiful, bemused she-male into a long, brightly lit hallway that leads through to a very large, beautifully decorated living room. As Eve follows this gloriously erotic apparition, her wide, aroused eyes are drawn to the elegant, exact seams of the stockings, lines of erotic direction that trace precisely the near-perfect shape of Priscilla's long legs. She feels her sex stir helplessly within the padded warmth of the body-shaper and takes the deepest of breaths. Then she is in the living room, standing nervously before two striking women.

'Eve, madame.'

Priscilla announces Eve's arrival to the taller of the two women and then performs another elaborate and incredibly sexy curtsey.

The woman steps forward, a wide, warm smile on blood-red lips, and holds out a beautifully shaped hand whose long fingernails match exactly the crimson paint decorating her sensual mouth.

'At last we meet. I'm Helen Bliss.'

Eve takes Helen's hand. There is no shake, just a brief and charged touching of fingers.

Eve smiles nervously and mumbles a weak 'Hello', stunned by this striking woman and her surroundings, and still shocked by the transformation of the beautiful Priscilla.

'Yes, it all must seem rather odd,' Helen continues. 'But you'll get used to it. '

Helen is a formidable beauty. A woman in her late forties dressed in a rather gorgeous pink cashmere sweater with a wide polo neck, a knee-length Prince of Wales check skirt, very sheer black nylon tights and modestly heeled, leather pumps. Her honey-blonde hair is cut short, but remains strikingly feminine and her ice-blue eyes radiate a paradoxically and definitely erotic warmth. She is both tall (at least six feet in the heels) and plump. Her height ensures she could never be fat, but she has a distinctly buxom frame, with very large breasts, wide hips and a rather substantial bottom. Her pretty face is undoubtedly chubby, but this only adds to a highly attractive aura of ampleness. Eve is immediately and very significantly attracted to her. Not only her buxom beauty, but also her confident and easy-going manner and the way it disguises something much harder and tougher.

'Get Eve a drink, Pris. I suggest a glass of the Australian Chardonnay.'

Priscilla curtsies again, her eyes filled with an adoring and utterly submissive love. She then minces off to a large dinner table at the end of the room, her high-heeled steps tiny, her pert bottom wiggling invitingly.

'Pris warned us you were a stunner, but I must say you've exceeded even our expectations.'

Eve blushes and tries to hold Helen's piercing, appraising gaze. Her voice is crisp and light and edged with culture and breeding. There is something inescapably aristocratic about her that Eve finds both utterly charming and deeply exciting.

It is at this point that the second woman steps forward. She is also tall, but with a more slender build. A redhead with dark green eyes, her thick hair bound in a rather severe bun, she is dressed in a grey pinstripe trouser suit, with an open-neck white silk blouse. The suit adds to an air of focus that is supported by a steely gaze. Eve notices that she is wearing very high-heeled ankle boots and that, in fact, she is much shorter than Helen.

'Yes, he's really quite something. I think it's the lack of masculine size in the usually problematic areas – the head, the hands. The femininity is very physical. The artificial shaping is more an enhancement than a pretence.'

Helen smiles with slight irritation at this intervention. 'Thank you for the scientific analysis, Sam.'

Pris returns with a glass of gold-tinged Chardonnay and performs another deep curtsey. Eve thanks her and takes the glass, still astonished by this outrageous change in the confident, powerful TV that she had encountered in the Crème de la Crème club.

'You'll have to forgive Samantha, Eve. She can be a little clinical sometimes. But she is a doctor, and I suppose it becomes instinctive after a while.'

Eve stares nervously at Samantha. Despite her height, she is far from slight in form; indeed, her figure is full and shapely, especially her chest. Yet there remains something fundamentally cold and pinched about her personality that completely undermines her physical attractiveness.

Eve's eyes move from Samantha to the spectacle that is Priscilla, and Helen's smile broadens.

'Yes, she really is quite something. Probably not what you were expecting either. I'm sure Pris was her usual impressive self at the club. But here, with me, she is something else, something a little less assured. And this, I think, is much more the real Pris. The Pris I love. My sweet, sexy slave girl.'

Pris smiles with helpless pleasure and curtsies her agreement.

'She can be a little naughty now and again. But a sound spanking and prolonged periods of strict bondage soon sort that out.'

Helen laughs lightly, but also cruelly. She asks Eve about her history, about the history of a desire and a secret. At first the lovely she-male is reluctant, in front of these strange and disturbing, yet also beautiful and fascinating people, to reveal any more of herself. The idea of attending the dinner party as Eve was testing enough, but now to be confronted by maid Priscilla and the cold eyes of Samantha: she is beginning to feel distinctly overwhelmed.

Yet, despite her nerves and doubts, she finds herself telling them everything. Revealing her history with a hesitation that dissolves into a flowing confession. Beneath the warm, almost maternal gaze of Helen and the cooler, analytical eyes of Samantha, she even reveals the erotic tale of her aunt and the fundamental role Debra has played in the creation and maintenance of Eve. And as she spills her history around the room, she cannot help being aware of Priscilla setting the table for dinner and, increasingly, of the savoury smells of the meal that someone unseen appears to be preparing.

'Your aunt sounds like a very interesting person; particularly given that you haven't seen her for so many years,' Helen says. 'An influence over time and space.'

There is something in Samantha's eyes when Helen says this that disturbs Eve. Some kind of subtle secret amusement; a hint of conspiracy.

'She obviously saw something in you,' Samantha says.

Then Priscilla is back among them, submissive, elegant and desperately beautiful.

'Dinner is ready, mistress.'

Helen smiles. 'Serve it now. I'm starving, and I'm sure our guests could eat.'

The group makes its way towards the large dinner table that fills a conservatory-like space at the end of the living room.

Priscilla carefully ensures that her mistress and each of the guests are seated and then minces off eagerly to the kitchen.

It is only when she has left the room that Eve finally plucks up the courage to ask the question that has been testing her since Priscilla first invited her to meet her wife.

'Why am I here?'

It is a surprisingly direct question, and one that the lovely she-male says with a frankness that fractures the slightly false tone of the conversation.

Helen smiles quizzically. Eve manages to meet her beautiful, piercing gaze, but only for a few seconds.

'Because Pris knew I'd want to meet you.'

'But why . . . why do *you* want to meet me?'

Samantha coughs slightly, seeming to stifle a laugh.

Helen's smile fades. A seriousness comes into her gaze that is both intimidating and reassuring.

'Pris isn't actually the manager of the club or the website, or any of the other services we provide. I am. I own the club and all the related business activities. Pris acts

114

on my behalf, but she has no control whatsoever. Crème de la Crème is one of the most successful TV clubs in the world. Not necessarily in terms of its members. No, that would be defeating the object. But in terms of the website – well, we have over twenty thousand individual subscriptions. That's £20 a month each. That's £400,000 a month . . . nearly £5 million a year. Then there's the other services. It's a significant business in an expanding market.'

Eve recalls the exotic and beautifully maintained picture galleries. She has only seen those open to non-members. She knows there are thousands more photos and streamed videos in the member sections, most featuring the gorgeous club members. The élite cross-dressing beauties of the Crème de la Crème club.

'And as the market expands, so do we,' Samantha adds. 'And that means diversification. New products to meet not so new needs.'

Helen laughs. 'Yes, it's all variations on a theme. Ultimately.'

'New products?'

Helen's gaze intensifies slightly at Eve's question.

'Pris tells me you have certain administrative skills.'

Eve is much more confident now: business is one thing she understands well.

'Yes. I'm a senior manager in a finance company.'

Helen nods, considering this. Eve suspects she is already well aware of Adam's background and also its relevance to whatever it is that she wants Eve to do.

It is at this point that the door to the kitchen opens and Priscilla reappears, carrying a large silver tray. On the tray are two bowls of hot, steaming soup. Yet it is not the spectacle of Priscilla in her dark, elegant maid's costume that Eve is drawn to, but rather the astonishing figure that follows her out of the kitchen. For behind Priscilla is the gorgeous, buxom Cherry, dressed in a stunning white costume that inspires a moan of shocked arousal followed by immediate embarrassment.

Cherry's costume is essentially a variation of the uniform worn by Priscilla, but rather than the various shades of

115

black that dominate Priscilla's attire, Cherry is sealed totally in pure white silk and nylon. A white silk maid's dress, complete with high, frilled neck (rather than Priscilla's plunging neckline) and elegantly puffed sleeves; a cream-coloured pinafore of white silk, also heavily frilled; sheer white nylon tights and pumps of white leather with fierce six-inch heels. A mass of creamy frou-frou petticoating fitted beneath the skirt of the already short dress causes it to rise up at almost a 90-degree angle and reveal white silk panties. Cherry's thick, wavy hair is bound in a tight bun and topped off with a dainty French maid's cap, also of white silk.

Cherry's eyes automatically seek out Eve's and the look of deep sexual attraction is immediate and unnerving. Eve remembers the way the beautiful she-male had looked at her in the Crème de la Crème club, with a terrible, simple frankness that inspired both fear and potent sexual excitement. But now the excitement is mutual, for Cherry looks absolutely astonishing, a fact made even more apparent by the tightness of the beautiful silk dress and the impact it has on her buxom figure. Then there is the exact and highly erotic contrast of the pure white of the uniform against her lovely, flawless, chocolate-coloured skin. Her large brown eyes seem to emit beams of raw need straight into Eve's body. Eve feels her sex stir helplessly and her heart pound desperately against the elegant artifice of the body-shaper.

'I think Eve is in love,' Samantha says, her voice filled with cruel amusement.

Helen laughs lightly and Eve finds herself looking briefly into the cold, hard eyes of Samantha. Her desire turns to fear, and then fear and desire are mixed together in a dizzying spiral of masochistic pleasure. She knows this woman wants to do dark, strange things to her, that in her brutal gaze there is imagination of sadistic intent, and this only excites her more.

Cherry is carrying a second tray laden with two more bowls of soup. The two TV maids mince forward and, with an impressive elegance, place the bowls before the four diners. It is Cherry who presents Eve with her bowl. She leans in close towards Eve and presses her body against the younger TV. An electric shock of intense physical pleasure passes through Eve's delicately feminised form and Cherry whispers, 'You look lovely, petal.' Eve turns and looks at her, at her large, straining bosom, at her so long, white nylon-sheathed legs. 'And so do you,' she whispers back.

'I suggest you save the love talk for later,' Helen snaps.

A look of genuine fear enters Cherry's beautiful eyes. She performs a sweet bob curtsey and minces back into the kitchen, closely followed by Priscilla.

The soup is superb and Eve finds herself fighting to maintain her feminine composure as she ladles it into her mouth.

'Cherry is a rather gifted cook, among other things. She used to be a professional musician, so I assume she had plenty of time to practise her recipes.'

'The soup is delicious,' Eve says.

'Yes, when Cherry visits we always eat well. There is love in her cooking.'

'And desire,' Samantha adds, aiming a particularly suggestive look towards Eve.

Eve blushes and Helen continues the earlier discussion.

'Anyway, the simple fact is, we'd like you to join us.'

Eve stops eating and looks up at this gorgeous, ample female with quizzical eyes.

'But I already have. Priscilla admitted me on Wednesday.'

Helen smiles weakly, a hint of irritation in her beautiful, ice-blue eyes.

'Yes. You are now a member of the Crème de la Crème club. There's no doubt about that. But I was thinking of something a bit more substantial. We'd like you to work for us.'

Eve's eyes widen with surprise. 'Work? What sort of work?'

'We employ a small group of the more impressive members to help us with the website. You'll have seen some of the preview galleries. But the member archives are a little more ... specialised; and they require a more

117

professional approach. We refer to these members as the Elect.'

'You want me to model?'

Helen considers the word 'model' as if she has been asked a particularly difficult philosophical question. 'Yes ... in a way. And act. And also to provide some much-needed administrative support. And then there's a new service we are planning to provide, a service you'd be an ideal candidate for, I must say.'

'What sort of service?'

Helen's smile fades and a harder edge fills her eyes. 'We can talk about that when we've tested your other skills.'

Eve ponders this surprising development with a sense of mounting excitement. She remembers the elaborate and deliberately erotic pictures that filled the preview galleries, many of them leaning towards the sado-erotic. Like so many TVs, Eve has always longed to photograph and display herself. To look into the mirror, to send photo attachments to her aunt – these have been poor substitutes for the constant urge to be seen, an urge that has flowered so powerfully and wonderfully over the last few days, but which remains constant and growing.

'Can I think about it?' she asks, avoiding Samantha's gaze.

'Of course,' Helen responds, her tone much harder now. 'You can tell us before you leave.'

Eve is about to say she was thinking in terms of a few days, but there is a look in Helen's eyes which is more akin to the one she sees in Samantha's, a forceful, dominant and utterly unyielding look that Eve finds both frightening and dreadfully exciting. She nods slightly and then returns her attentions to the rest of the excellent soup.

As she eats, she ponders the bizarre and highly erotic developments of the past hour. Every now and again she looks up at Helen, who is talking to Samantha in virtually a whisper. There is no doubt that Helen is a stunningly beautiful woman and that Eve is attracted to her. There is also no doubt that her relationship with Priscilla is based on a genuine love. Despite the harshness of some of her commands, there is always softness at their centre, and her tone – even at its coolest – is maternal, caring, even compassionate. Yet Helen is also the secret force behind the Crème de la Crème club. Eve is surprised by the size of the club, but not stunned. Adam is responsible for a 30-million-pound budget, and is already pondering the significant business potential of the club and its offshoots. Helen and her colleagues have clearly made a handsome living from the internet site alone; but Eve can envisage a much wider potential, and she knows that anything she has thought of in just a few minutes has already been carefully considered and discussed by Helen and Samantha. Eve looks again at Samantha, this haughty, cold-eyed beauty. Helen described her as a doctor. She wonders what type of doctor and why, besides her relationship with Helen – which appears more than a little close – she is interested in the beautiful cross-dressers of the Crème de la Crème club.

Then there is her own role. Eve cannot help admitting that the thought of modelling for the internet site is very exciting. To be one of the élite transvestite beauties featured on the site panders to her inescapable narcissism. So many hours spent in lonely self-regard before many mirrors over the last decade have prepared her for the dramatic exhibition of the model. She will find it hard to deny Helen's offer on this basis alone. But now there is the mysterious reference to the new service. The fascinating hint regarding her suitability appeals to her vanity and to her increasing sense of adventure. Indeed, if there is one thing that attracts her to Helen's proposition, it is the potential for new and exciting challenges that are far beyond anything offered by Adam's job, challenges that will allow her to express her true nature without question or guilt.

'Do you have a girlfriend, Eve?'

Helen's voice breaks through Eve's deep thoughts like an alarm bell in a submarine. She looks up with slightly surprised eyes and tries to smile politely. But the smile appears only as a worried frown scarring a particularly beautiful face.

'No, but I think I have a . . . friend.'

'Another TV?' Samantha asks.

'No. A . . . man.'

Helen and Samantha smile and nod.

'And he knows about Eve?'

'Yes.'

'And he doesn't mind?'

'No. In fact, it's why we're together. He seems to like TVs. That's his . . . thing.'

Samantha's smile widens. 'Richard perhaps?'

Eve blushes and nods weakly. 'How did you know?'

Helen's gentle smile broadens. 'He made his interest very clear to Pris. And she tells me everything. I must remember to talk to him. He can be rather . . . imaginative.'

Eve finds herself irritated by Helen's condescending tone. 'No, please. He's really nice. I like his . . . imagination.'

Helen and Samantha exchange another knowing look.

Over the next hour, there is more discussion and more excellent food. There is also a lot of drink. After four glasses of superb wine, Eve is both much more relaxed and also clearly tipsy, a state that loosens her tongue considerably. Indeed, Helen is soon able to get the lovely she-male to talk freely about her past and about the pivotal role her aunt has played in her development. Both women appear particularly keen to extract as much information as possible from Eve about her Aunt Debra, a fact that would have made the sober Eve suspicious. But now she answers every question with a reckless indifference, in the process confessing her helpless sexual desire and the way this has added a distinctly sado-masochistic tinge to their relationship.

'It seems inevitable that male cross-dressers exhibit some form of masochism,' Samantha says, addressing Helen as if Eve weren't in the room.

Helen smiles patiently and turns a warm, understanding gaze upon a slightly disoriented Eve. 'Well, it's perfectly understandable. The world of men is all about power and control over others, about assertion and aggression. Many

TVs are fleeing from that – seeking an alternative means of expressing themselves and their needs. I often feel it isn't just about being feminine, as much as being consumed and overwhelmed by the feminine. Don't you agree, Eve?'

Eve looks into Helen's gorgeous eyes and feels delightfully helpless. 'Yes,' she mumbles. 'Yes, that's definitely part of it.'

By the time they finish the marvellous strawberry cheesecake dessert, it is nearly eleven p.m. and Eve is quite drunk and very aroused. There is no doubt that the close proximity of Cherry has added to her state of sexual disturbance; the gorgeous TV, so carefully adorned in the elegant, erotic maid's costume, has served Eve with a close attention that has left the younger she-male startled and violently hard. By the time Helen motions them from the table to the lush white leather armchairs that are positioned in a semi-circle before the glowing fireplace of the living room, poor Eve cannot take her mind off her painfully rigid member.

Then she finds herself sinking into one of the expensive armchairs and being served a glass of sherry by the very same, stunning TV. Now she can see the wondrous creature via an exciting full-frontal view. Cherry stands before Eve, her white nylon-wrapped legs close together, her frou-frou petticoating and the white silk panties revealed in erotic detail. Eve stares up at the panties with a desperate, shocked, unforgiving need, her eyes widened by the outline of a very big, hard male sex traversing the shimmering, silken material. She looks up at the buxom beauty and sees a beautiful, milk-chocolate face peering down at her over a large, straining chest.

'I think it's time for us to play,' Helen says suddenly, her voice soft, calm, yet filled with a delicious and highly exciting wickedness.

Then Priscilla is back in the room. She performs a deep curtsey before the two women, who are sitting side by side on the sofa.

'I'm afraid Sam's a little upset with you, Pris,' Helen says, her eyes lit by the ironic but very real cruelty that has

121

risen suddenly to the surface on more than one occasion during the eventful evening.

'You spilt gravy on me,' the haughty redhead snaps.

Eve looks at this developing scene with a hazy curiosity, striving to remember if she had witnessed an incident of the nature Helen is describing. But before she can confirm or deny, Priscilla has stepped forward and dramatically knelt down in a shower of elegant frills and petticoating before Samantha.

'Punish me as you see fit,' the lovely TV whispers, clearly very aroused.

A slight smile crosses Samantha's hard mouth. She then holds out one of her feet and Priscilla presses her red lips against gleaming black-patent leather.

'A spanking, I think. Get the brush.'

Priscilla gracefully climbs back on to her high-heeled feet and minces into the kitchen, returning a few seconds later carrying a white hairbrush. She curtsies once again before Samantha – her deepest and most submissive curtsey yet, her eyes filled with sex need and anticipation. She presents the hairbrush to Samantha.

'Tie her hands.'

Cherry suddenly turns towards Samantha, performs her own deep curtsey and takes a length of thick white silk ribbon from a pocket in her dainty white silk pinafore. She uses this to bind Priscilla's hands tightly behind her back. Priscilla moans with a deep, dark pleasure as she is secured and Eve tries to hide her own considerable arousal, now very aware that Helen is watching her closely.

'Is this exciting you, Eve? I would have thought so ... given what you said earlier.'

Eve looks at Helen, a direct, yet frightened look; but also a look of helpless confession.

'I can't help it,' she whispers.

Helen smiles softly, leans forward and places a reassuring hand on Eve's black nylon-sheathed knee. 'Don't worry, petal. None of us can.'

Once bound, Priscilla is made to totter forward until she is just a few inches from the stern, beautiful Samantha.

Then Cherry returns her attentions to Eve, moving closer, so that the tips of her stiletto-heeled mules are touching Eve's own exotic footwear.

Samantha moves quickly, suddenly grabbing Priscilla around the waist and pulling her down across her wide, strong lap. As this happens, Cherry leans forward and takes Eve's right hand. The lovely, startled she-male does not resist, but allows her hand to be guided on to Cherry's white nylon-sealed right thigh. Eve feels the heat of her body through the sheer, soft material and gasps with pleasure, a gasp accidentally timed to coincide with the first crack of the ivory-handled hairbrush against Priscilla's tightly pantied backside and her own cry of pain, a cry that quickly transforms into an equally powerful and helpless moan of pleasure.

Samantha administers twelve hard smacks of the hairbrush, reducing the lovely Priscilla to a moaning, crying, wriggling wreck. And as the blows rain down, Cherry allows Eve to lean forward and edge her hand further up her nyloned thigh until it reaches the edge of her tight panties. And as the last blow is delivered, Eve's hand slips on to the panties' soft, electric material and she finds herself seeking out the hard, long, thick cock that is imprisoned beneath. Then Priscilla's cries of discomfort are suddenly augmented with Cherry's cry of intense and angry pleasure.

All the time, Helen watches Eve and her smile increases, a smile that betrays her own significant sexual arousal. Yet this smile is also a very obvious smile of triumph.

Eventually, poor Priscilla is thrown off Samantha's knees, her eyes red, her body shaking. Despite her bondage, she manages to clamber to her heeled feet and perform a deep, elegant curtsey before whispering a hoarse, sex-tinged 'thank you, mistress'.

Helen then orders Priscilla to kneel before her. Still bound, the beautiful TV maid obeys, lowering her form with a striking grace. Helen kicks off her stylish, sexy shoes and raises a beautifully formed, black nylon-sheathed foot. Priscilla leans forward and kisses her toes before the foot slips deep into her mouth.

Eve watches this act with some astonishment as her drink-hazed mind is being tormented by the feel of Cherry's substantial, silk-sheathed member. She feels this fundamentally male organ with a new and dark desire. She measures its length and finds herself wondering what it would be like to be fucked as a woman by this precision sex tool. She remembers the highly erotic tease of the vibrator and imagines this magnified by a factor of ten.

Then Priscilla finishes worshipping the buxom beauty's feet and her head is quickly forced deep beneath Helen's skirt and firmly lodged between her mistress's nylon-sheathed thighs. Helen's eyes are closed and a smile of sexual pleasure is spreading across her face like the shadow of the darkest desire. Cherry moans angrily as Eve increases her caress and her sex strains against the younger she-male's eager, teasing hand.

'So, Eve,' Helen says, an edge of unavoidable physical pleasure in her elegant, husky voice as Priscilla sets to her task. 'Will you be joining us?'

Eve looks at the clock. It is after midnight and she is now beginning to feel very tired.

'Yes,' she mumbles, only barely aware of what she is saying, her face inches from Cherry's silken bulge. 'Yes.'

Helen smiles. 'Good girl.'

The buxom beauty then releases a tiny cry of pleasure before continuing. 'We're really looking forward to working with such a gifted young she-male.'

Then Helen eases a stunned, extremely aroused Priscilla from beneath her long, elegant skirt.

'Sam, I suggest you take charge of Pris for the rest of the evening. I'm sure you can keep her entertained.'

Priscilla rises to her feet and straightens her pretty maid's attire. Her make-up is smudged and there is a look of wild sexual passion in her beautiful emerald eyes. Her wrists still bound behind her back, she performs a somewhat ragged curtsey before Helen and then wiggle-minces over to Samantha, where she quickly performs a more confident, deeper curtsey and looks up at her with desire and fear. Samantha smiles, her eyes filled with an ambivalent passion. Eve knows that poor Priscilla will suffer at her hands, but that there is also a profound sado-erotic desire here, a desire that Priscilla clearly shares.

Samantha climbs somewhat unsteadily from the chair, takes Priscilla by the hand and leads her from the room, turning briefly to Eve as she does so.

'I will see you again soon, Eve. Then we can get to know each other a little better.'

Her words are filled with dark promise and the lovely, intoxicated she-male feels a wave of electric anticipation flow over her feminine form.

As Samantha leaves, Eve's eyes fall once gain upon the redhead's long, finely hosed legs and her already tormented sex presses with a terrible frustration against the silken padding of the body-shaper.

'Come here, Eve.'

Helen's tone is hard and determined. She is now Eve's mistress. Suddenly feeling very tired, Eve removes her hand from Cherry's secret delights. The two TVs exchange a hungry, knowing smile. Eve then walks over to Helen. This beautiful, mature and erotically ample female is without doubt one of the most striking women Eve has ever encountered.

'Kneel before me,' she orders.

Eve obeys without hesitation, falling into exactly the same position as Priscilla. Her eyes rest on Helen's long, black nylon-sheathed ankles. She is a vision of female power and Eve is her willing subject.

'I met Pris, when she was a he,' Helen says, her tone softening, her body relaxing. 'Maybe ten years ago. He was just out of university – about twenty-one. I was in my late thirties. Strangely enough, I was the secretary to his boss. I'd just gone through a pretty nasty divorce, and the last thing I wanted was another demanding, neurotic, self-obsessed man. But Pris . . . well, let's just say that as a man he was very kind, considerate and also very interested in me. He made me feel important, powerful, attractive. He pursued me in a way that I had never experienced, in a way that I really couldn't believe. I was startled and aroused.

He made love to me on our first date and it was like I was being worshipped, like my body was a temple to him. I found out he was a transvestite after about six months, just before we got married. By this point, it had already become apparent that he wanted nothing more than to be my complete slave. His masochism was present in every respectful gesture. The harsher I was with him, the more attentive he seemed to become. And this excited me terribly. And then, in a moment of supremely erotic humiliation, he knelt before me and confessed his passion for knickers and tights. Then, at my command, he dressed for me. And when I saw Priscilla for the first time . . . well, to be quite honest, I was rather jealous. She was a beautiful young woman, a strikingly convincing and rather gorgeous girl. There had always been something inherently feminine about him, but as soon as I saw my lovely young man dressed as Priscilla, I knew this femininity was a profound and very fundamental aspect of his true identify, an identity that was more she than he.

'This is what really inspired me to develop Pris, to investigate cross-dressing – to create and build up the Crème de la Crème club. All of it really came from that first exposure. Driven by that first, startling encounter, I went from being a secretary to a self-made business woman. Along the way, we made refinements and changes. She has been Pris permanently ever since she first revealed herself to me. She resigned her job within a week and we were working on the Crème de la Crème project within a month. We sought out equally beautiful TVs. I'm afraid they weren't that easy to find. But then there was Cherry, a sexy bolt out of the blue. An established figure in the local scene and someone able to plug us into wider networks. And Cherry had a friend who worked in computers. That's how the website started. Cherry's friend had a transsexual girlfriend who was undergoing gender reassignment and knew a rather excellent plastic surgeon. And that's how things went to the next level. That's when we really began to develop the concept of the she-males at the heart of the Crème de la Crème club. The Elect.'

Eve listens to this detailed personal history fighting exhaustion and the elated shock of teasing Cherry. The mention of the plastic surgeon brings her back from the edge of an embarrassing slumber. She remembers the girls in the club, the pneumatic figures of Priscilla and Cherry. She recalls the stunning authenticity of their buxom figures, especially their large, firm breasts. The 'concept of the she-male at the heart of the Crème de la Crème club'. She tries to review the pictures from the website. Yes, all the same; every single striking she-male has the same utterly convincing chest, a chest that isn't a clever illusion of padding, but a physical fact created by silicon and the hands of an expert and sympathetic plastic surgeon.

'Samantha,' Eve whispers and Helen's smile broadens.

'Yes, indeed, Eve. Samantha is a superb plastic surgeon; an expert in the field of gender reassignment – and a key figure in the development of our little venture.'

'And do I get . . . developed, as well?'

Helen's smile fades slightly, a coolness returns to her luminous blue eyes. 'That will be up to you, Eve.'

Helen holds one of her beautifully shaped feet before the lovely, drunk she-male. There is a brief moment of hesitation. Eve then leans forward, takes the warm, nylon-wrapped foot in her hands and places a kiss against the shapely, scented instep. She knows this is as good as signing a contract of absolute servitude.

'Help Eve up,' Helen says to Cherry, who obeys by stepping forward and taking Eve's right hand gently in her own.

Eve turns as she rises and finds her eyes travelling up the splendid, erotic spectacle of Cherry's carefully crafted and packaged form. Then she is looking directly into Cherry's stunning, dark eyes.

As Eve beholds this gorgeous, perfectly formed she-male sex bomb, her cock struggling desperately in the relentless confines of the body-shaper, she is conscious of Helen rising from the sofa and standing in her stockinged feet behind her.

'I suggest you show Eve some of the pleasures of being a full member of Crème de la Crème.'

A hungry smile slides across Cherry's full, blood-red lips. Eve, her eyes pulled deep into the sensuously promising gaze of the dark beauty, takes a deep, anticipatory breath. The smile fades from Cherry's lips and the fires of desire burn brighter in her huge black eyes.

Cherry then leans forward and gently kisses Eve on the lips. A first contact that sends a bolt of high-voltage sex electricity blasting through every vein of Eve's so carefully feminised body. She swoons as Cherry wraps her long, silk-encased arms around her and pulls her into a tight, unyielding embrace. Eve's carefully constructed bosom presses against the astonishing and considerable breasts that Samantha's expertise has given all the she-males of Crème de la Crème. The kiss becomes more passionate. Wider, harder. Their tongues intertwine. Eve feels Cherry's hand slip beneath her dress and press against her upper thigh. She cries into the tight gag of the kiss and allows Cherry's hands to work up to the crotch of the shaper and then beyond.

Then, finding the front panel, Cherry hesitates. Her eyes widen with cruel amusement. She releases Eve and tells her to take the dress off. Eve hesitates and Cherry's smile widens.

'Please, my angel. I can give you so much pleasure.'

Eve smiles and turns, so that her back is facing Cherry. The dusky she-male beauty gently lowers the zipper and eases it over Eve's shoulders. Eve turns back to face Cherry as the dress slips down her body to reveal the erotic detail of the shaper. Cherry's eyes widen and she whispers 'Very nice', her voice filled with sex need.

To Eve's surprise, Cherry steps back, her eyes drinking up the expert perfection of her body. She then stretches her arms behind her back and unclips the top button of the startling white maid's dress, which is set into the high, heavily frilled neck.

'Please, unbutton me.'

With these words, Cherry turns and Eve, her hands shaking, steps forward to help Cherry out of the dress. Each button is made from an expensive cream-coloured pearl shot through with strands of silver grey. Eve, her

128

fingers increasingly impatient, struggles to free each one, sweat on her painted lips, her heart pounding, her tiredness changing swiftly into an edgy sexual arousal fuelled by a real promise of relief.

As the back of the dress parts, Eve finds her teased eyes presented with a slender white silk bra-strap, the satin panel of a very tight waist-cincher, and a pair of heavily frilled white panties. Her cock screams out its violent demand for release and she gasps with a hard, bitter animal pleasure.

Once the bottom button is freed, Cherry eases the dress over her broad shoulders and allows it to cascade down her sumptuous body to the floor. She then turns and reveals the true erotic genius of her creation to a stunned Eve. Her very large, firm and beautifully shaped breasts, the result of Samantha's careful, kinky labours, strain helplessly against the gentle prison of a snow-white silk brassiere. Her surprisingly narrow waist is held firm and fast by the cream satin-panelled, leather-reinforced waist-cincher, and a pair of spectacularly frilled white silk panties add a final touch of cream clarity to this deliberate look of servitude and innocence. Against the length of the front of the panties runs the hard, metallic outline of Cherry's considerable sex, and Eve stares at it with a helpless and hungry fascination.

Long, elegant legs sheathed in sheer white tights run from beneath the lovely panties, sliding down to the simple, sexy white leather court shoes. She is a vision of pure sex, and Eve's eyes betray a terrible, irresistible sexual need.

Cherry, smiling, her eyes on the front panel of the shaper, then slowly unclips the bra and gently eases it away from her breasts. Eve gasps with admiration as the bra is allowed to fall to the floor and the large, milk-chocolate orbs are fully exposed to her deeply aroused vision.

'My God,' she whispers. 'Oh my God.'

Cherry's smile widens. She takes Eve's hands in hers and places one on each warm, perfect tit. She gasps as Eve begins to gently knead her breasts and then to tease her rock-hard nipples.

'They're so dreadfully sensitive,' Cherry whispers, 'there's something in the final chemical brew that Sam uses that makes them . . . extra reactive to the caresses of fabrics and other skin.'

Her words fade and her eyes close as Eve increases her erotic ministrations. Then she leans forward and places a gentler, loving, worshipful kiss on each large, soft, brown boob. She revels in their perfection. Cherry moans with pleasure and, as Eve pulls away from this helpless act of adoration, she notices that Cherry's large sex is rigid and desperate beneath the tight silk panties.

Eve lowers a hand to the front of the panties and begins to rub the painful hardness beneath. Cherry's moans merge into cries of tormented ecstasy. Eve, never taking her eyes away from Cherry's, slips the panties down over the black beauty's broad, womanly hips and lets the cock pop up for air. But what Eve discovers is not what her sex- and drink-addled mind was expecting. Instead of a huge, brown male sex, rampant and desperate, she finds herself staring down at a large, firmly erect penis sheathed in very tight white latex, with two gleaming silver rings fixed tightly about its teased length, at the base and the head.

Eve steps back, astonished and horrified.

'We're all restrained, Eve,' Cherry says, her eyes now filled with guilt and dark sex hunger. 'Once we become Helen's property. Once we become members of the Elect.'

As Eve continues to stare at Cherry's massive, imprisoned cock, the dusky she-male steps forward and begins to release the front panel of Eve's body-shaper. Eve, too shocked to speak, watches as Cherry proceeds to slip her hands inside the body-shaper, over the rim of her black nylon tights and then inside to seek out Eve's own hard, tormented sex. Eve squeals with girlish shock and arousal as Cherry takes firm hold of the much sought-after item and gently extracts it from the shaper. A brighter, more relaxed smile appears and she kneels down, almost as if she is seeking a better vantage point to view the newly exposed sex.

'Make the most of it, petal,' Cherry says, just before she slips Eve's sex deep into her dark, warm mouth.

Eve is in a state of helpless bliss within a few seconds: Cherry's lips and tongue are expert in the art of oral pleasuring. She explodes quickly with a scream that is halfway between a terrible, black despair and agonised ecstasy. Her hot cum erupts out of the fat, ripe head of her crimson cock and crashes against the roof of Cherry's mouth. She grabs the beautiful she-male's shoulders and begs for some form of impossible forgiveness. Yes: there is, at the heart of this furious coming, a sense of absolute and inescapable sin. Suddenly, Eve is Adam, and suddenly he sees that this, all of this obsession, the endless, irresistible urge towards absolute femininity, is part of a profound illness whose name is Being, yet it is an illness he or she can only embrace and glorify.

Eventually, Cherry releases Eve and she staggers backward, her spent cock waving before her like some startled, stunned snake wounded in jungle battle.

Cherry, wiping her mouth, her smile wider than ever, rises to her feet and minces over to Eve. She takes her by the arm and leads her over to the sofa. Within a few seconds, they are splayed out, tangled in each other's arms, kissing, cuddling, Cherry gently working Eve's cock back to a state of full excitement.

Then Eve becomes aware of someone standing over them. She looks up and finds herself staring into the ice-crystal eyes of Helen.

'That's enough for now, Cherry. You can play with Eve another time.'

Cherry nods weakly, pulls herself up from the sofa, then stands to attention before the divine mistress of her sissy soul.

'Go to my room and wait for me.'

Cherry nods, curtsies deeply, takes up her discarded clothes and leaves.

'Get up,' Helen orders Eve.

Stunned, exhausted, hard once again, Eve climbs up off the sofa, her sex rising erect from the body-shaper.

Helen regards it with something approaching contempt.

'I have learnt one key lesson since forming the Crème de la Crème: control the cock and you control the mind.'

Eve looks at this buxom, painfully beautiful woman with confused eyes.

'Put it away and get dressed. It's time for you to leave.'

Eve nods weakly. She slips her hard, aching sex back into the body-shaper and seals it up. She then climbs back into the dress. Helen helps her zip up.

'You will be at the club tomorrow evening at eight p.m. sharp. Then you will be inducted formally into the Crème de la Crème. Bring Richard.'

Eve nods weakly, upset by her new, harsh, almost indifferent tone.

'I've called a taxi. It'll be here in ten minutes. You can wait outside.'

Eve looks at Helen with big hurt eyes and the gorgeous, mature beauty smiles cruelly.

'You must learn to accept my orders without question, Eve. Whether you like them or not. Use the hallway mirror to adjust your make-up and hair.'

Stunned by this sudden, deliberate cruelty, Eve can only watch helplessly as Helen leaves the room. Suddenly she is completely alone. Upstairs she knows there is much erotic perversity, but down here, in this silent, hot room, there is only the powerful scent of various bodies and desires and the sound of her own desperately beating heart.

After sorting her make-up and hair, she steps out into the cold early morning. The hallway clock says it is just after two a.m. She stands in the driveway watching her hot, sex-driven breath transform into a cloud of damp white mist and tries to understand the bizarre and violently erotic events of the last few hours. But her thoughts are quickly cut short by the arrival of the taxi.

As she rides home in the darkness of the back seat, her dress rides carelessly up her thighs to reveal her long, hosed and tightly crossed legs and thus provide a terrible and unknown distraction for the taxi driver. She ponders the strange adventure that was her visit to meet Priscilla Rouge and her stunning wife. She is aware of forces beyond her control. She has fallen into a vortex powered by desire and cruelty, by the profound need to be someone hidden for so long and by an increasingly masochistic sexual energy burning with increasing intensity in the heart of this concealed, secret self, a self that is emerging at great speed from years of careful isolation.

Once home, she strips naked and falls into her bed with a gasp of absolute exhaustion. The vortex takes her completely then, dragging her down into a booze- and sex-fuelled unconsciousness. As she slips from this increasingly strange real world into the sensual madness of dreams, she finds her self briefly gripped by a dark, almost cowardly apprehension. Tomorrow, she knows a new and even more testing stage of this incredible adventure will begin. Then a river of sweet blackness envelops her.

7

The Space Between

She awakens to the sound of the telephone, dragged from a dream of Cherry and the nylon-wrapped feet of the mysterious and beautiful Helen. The first thing she feels is a painfully severe erection pressing against the bed-sheets. Then there is the headache and the dull sickness of a disabling hangover. She moans into the pungent darkness of the bed covers and surfaces for air. The phone is her mobile, placed at some point last night on the bedside table. Its persistence is painful and disturbing. As she picks it up, she notices it is nine a.m. exactly.

She mumbles a hoarse 'hello' and is immediately greeted by Richard's voice.

'Was it good?'

'Sorry?'

'Your evening out. Did you enjoy it?'

'It was interesting. You should have been there. Then it would have been even more . . . interesting.'

'I can imagine it was interesting enough without me.'

They both laugh, the intimate humour of lovers.

'What happened?' Richard says, persisting in his slightly over-eager interrogation.

'They invited me to the club. This evening. With you. They want me to become a member of the Elect.'

'Of course they do.'

'Will you come?'

'Of course. I wouldn't miss it for the world.'

There is a pause.

'Did you miss me?' Richard then continues.

'Very much.'

'I want to come over; I want to spend the day with you. Before we go out.'

'Yes, I'd really like that. But give me a few hours to straighten myself out.'

'I'll come at lunch time.'

Then the phone goes dead. Eve laughs gently and pulls the sheet back over her heavy head.

She finally hauls herself out of bed just before eleven a.m. and spends half an hour under a hot, steaming shower. Then she sits before the dressing-table mirror, still naked, and ponders her somewhat dishevelled reflection. Red eyes betray the ongoing trauma of hangover and the hand that reaches for her hairbrush is shaking visibly. As she combs out her short hair, she considers an appropriate outfit. Her sex remains uncomfortably hard. In the shower she was almost overwhelmed by the need to masturbate, but controlled the savage urge with thoughts of Richard and the need to guarantee she can perform properly in any sexual adventure the afternoon might bring. This sustained state of sexual excitation also ensures that she is able to focus carefully on her dress and its impact on her boyfriend. Yet even as her imagination stirs, she finds her thoughts travelling through time, backward to the night before and then forward to the forthcoming visit to the Crème de la Crème club.

At first, in the dark heart of the initial hangover, she had felt an overwhelming sense of guilt, the sort of terrible regret that many feel as they half remember the drunken antics of the night before. What a fool she had been. To expose herself, to reveal the truth of her history; to expose Aunt Debra. To confess her secret desires. And then to allow herself to be overwhelmed by them under the cruel eyes of Helen and Samantha. And finally to agree to become something more than just a simple member of the Crème de la Crème club. To become a slave object, to become a fully transformed she-male sex toy of some kind. To give up her job and to work in a variety of ways – some mysterious and disturbing – for Helen Bliss. Yet even as she guiltily ponders the drunken truths of the previous evening, she is becoming even more aroused. Yes, the thought of her forthcoming servitude is undeniably arousing. And then there is Richard. To add the gorgeous, perverse force of dark nature that is Richard to this already kinky mix.

She dries her hair and slips into the white satin-panelled body-shaper, white nylon tights, modest white silk panties, a red-and-black check skirt and a tight white nylon sweater with a pretty polo neck. She adds red patent-leather shoes to this gentle, girlish outfit and a short, strawberry-blonde pageboy wig. Again, there is modest make-up, but with the added touch of lipstick that more or less exactly matches the striking, sexy shoes.

She stands before the mirror and admires her perfect, convincing reflection and feels the familiar tingle of deeply narcissistic desire. Then she finds herself thinking of Aunt Debra.

She logs on to the Internet and discovers an e-mail from her beloved aunt. A detailed response to the massive letter she had sent as a file attachment. She reads it with eager, even desperate eyes, a smile of relief and helpless desire spreading across her beautiful face as the contents of the message become clear.

Aunt Debra's response is filled with joy and excitement, and something else: a darker, harder curiosity. She is very happy for Eve and congratulates her on the fundamental success of her public 'revealing'. She is clearly fascinated by the events leading up to and during her adventure at the Crème de la Crème club, particularly the expansion of Eve's identity and the confidence flowing so powerfully from this. Then there is Priscilla Rouge. Of course, Aunt Debra knows nothing about the revelations of the night before and considers the image of Priscilla very carefully within the confines of Eve's description of a strikingly confident, self-possessed and devastatingly beautiful transvestite. Indeed, as Eve reads Aunt Debra's flow of hungry discourse and recognises the truth behind it, she begins to realise the disturbing strangeness at the heart of the truth. The figure of Helen Bliss rises out of the gap in Debra's knowledge and appears much more clearly drawn and alive than Eve's drink-fuelled impressions of the night before. And then there is Richard. It is here that Aunt Debra's tone shifts slightly. Enthusiastic interest turns to a much more interrogatory analysis (she even asks for a detailed physical description). Indeed, hidden in this new tone is surely a hint of jealousy. She is clearly impressed that Eve has managed to attract a man, but she is also disturbed that Eve – perhaps – is taking things a little too fast. Debra counsels her, in a perfectly relaxed and careful way, to take care. 'He sounds like a particularly explosive personality. Make sure he doesn't overwhelm, you, Eve.' Yet even as she reads these words, which so effectively sum up Richard, Eve can only confess that – to a certain extent – she wants to be overwhelmed. In Richard's dominant personality, Eve finds a very real and darkly erotic excitement; just as she had found when she had kissed Helen's delicately hosed toes and pledged to become a fully fledged member of the Crème de la Crème Elect.

Richard arrives thirty minutes later, dressed in black attire very similar to the day before.

'Tell me all about it. Tell me everything while you cook lunch.'

As they stand in the kitchen, as Eve cooks them both a large Spanish omelette, she tells the story of her dinner at Priscilla's, a story that Richard consumes with the same passion that he applies to the omelette and wholemeal bread when they sit down at the dining table and Eve continues this strange, erotic narrative, sparing no detail.

'She sucked you off? In front of Helen? Good grief!'

She nods, almost proud of the tale she is telling, of her perverse and graphic exposure before the gorgeous Helen Bliss.

'Do you have a drink?' he asks suddenly. 'A glass of wine would really help here. This omelette is wonderful.'

Eve, the obedient maid, takes a bottle of Chardonnay from the fridge and pours two large glasses of golden-green liquid. Richard takes a long gulp and insists that Eve continue her story.

Then she tells him of her final act of compliance, her acceptance into the inner circle of Crème de la Crème girls, and Richard's slightly ironic smile widens considerably.

'I'm sure you've made the right decision. The thought of you with real breasts . . . beautiful real breasts. It would be the perfect affirmation.'

She smiles, agreeing, knowing he is right. Yes, this would be the final expression of the fundamental truth of Eve.

'And you'll do this. I mean . . . undergo the changes they want. The breasts?'

Eve smiles slightly and nods. 'Yes,' she says, her voice now without doubt.

Yes, to be like Cherry and Pris, to become fully the ambiguity she has always lived within and for: a fully fledged, completely realised she-male.

'It's the final part of the transformation,' she continues, much clearer now about the meaning of her acceptance. 'It's the purest expression for my true state . . . my real self.'

'The space between,' Richard responds, his voice filled with a sudden, cutting lucidity.

'Yes. Exactly.'

Richard then stands up from the table and takes Eve's pretty face in his long, elegant hands. They kiss. Eve tastes wine and an elemental sexual need.

Eve comes up for air, her cock harder than diamond, and allows herself to be consumed by Richard's commanding gaze.

'And I want you to be with me, my darling,' he says. 'As my lover, as my partner . . . as my slave.'

Eve feels her hosed knees buckle and she falls forward into his tight, possessive embrace. She looks up into his eyes and feels a dark, romantic sense of absolute submission, and a hint of something much deeper and profound.

'Yes, of course. That's what I want as well.'

Then they kiss again and Eve is lost in a pure, blistering, blinding bliss.

After the meal, they sit on the sofa and make gentle love. She sits on his knees. His hands slide over her nylon-sheathed thighs. She meows with feminine pleasure. A hand slips beneath the short skirt. She feels the warmth of his smooth skin through the film of nylon and her cock expands to its full, aching stiffness. He reiterates his love for hose and insists she always wear tights and the shortest of skirts to show off her beautiful, perfectly shaped legs. She sighs with feline pleasure as he complements her physical perfection and his hand reaches the edge of her silk panties. She slips into a whirlpool of utter erotic bliss and cries out her helpless and furious arousal. She feels a huge wave of feminine submission crash over her body and sighs. This is ecstasy; this is heaven.

Soon, she is on her knees, between his legs, working free the zip of his jeans, her heart pounding with elated anticipation, her eyes wide with desire. His heavy, hot, desperate breathing fills the room as she slips his rampant tool from his underpants and begins very gently to stroke it with tender, slender fingers. He moans and squirms. He is already very close to coming. She kneels forward and very carefully slips the enraged, dark-purple head between her cherry-red lips.

After he erupts into her, his body rising up from the sofa like a launching rocket, his cries of pleasure filling the room, she knows an afternoon of exciting and intricate perversion lies ahead. Soon, he will reinsert the teasing, dainty vibrator, bind her, gag her, leave her wriggling in uncontrollable physical arousal on the floor, then she will dress for him – as she promised – in the maid's uniform, and serve him as his obedient and devoted slave.

'Let me dress for you,' she whispers, wiping his come from her lips, her voice shaking with sex need. 'Let me be your servant this afternoon. Please. Oh please.'

'OK,' he mumbles, stunned, elated, overwhelmed by the power of his need and her desire to meet it. 'Yes . . .'

'But first, tie me up. Like you did yesterday. Like you promised to do today and every other day.'

His smile returns from the clouds of the stunned orgasm. 'Of course,' he says.

It is just after five p.m. when she steps naked into the shower. The first stage of her preparations for the night ahead. Richard is in her room. He has made it clear he will select the clothes she will wear tonight. For the last four hours they have explored the nature of their nascent relationship in a most rigorous and highly erotic manner. Her bottom is still cherry-red from the last, fierce spanking and red, raw rope marks still scar her wrists and ankles. He has just slipped the vibrator from her widened arse, and the aftershock of its wicked buzzing, plus the spreading heat from the spanking, ensures that her sex is still rock-hard.

Her heart feels as light as air. A strange, almost unnerving happiness is washing over her, as if some strange mood-enhancing chemical has been poured into the water supply.

Eventually, wrapped in a thick, pink towel, her body soft and scented, her aching cock pressing teasingly against the soft material, she steps out of the shower and into the bedroom. Here she finds herself staring at the clothes laid out on the bed and then up at the striking figure of Richard.

'I think this should impress,' he says, almost shyly.

It is clear that while she has showered, Richard has carefully trawled through the wardrobe and drawers to identify clothing that will have a maximum impact. Set out before her is the sexiest of the black body-shapers, panelled with patterned black satin and heavily frilled; a pair of very sheer and seamed black nylon tights, a shimmering black silk blouse and a black micro-mini. A pair of stunning black shoes have been placed on the floor by the bed, shoes she bought from a fetish website some years previously and which she would never have considered wearing outside of the house, shoes with awe-inspiring six-inch heels. Cut from very shiny black patent leather, and which, thanks to the most severe of curved insteps, always leave her feeling she is walking on tiptoe, and thus inspiring the tiniest of sissy totters.

'Wear the velvet choker and the black pageboy with the stud earrings.'

Eve looks at Richard with a new respect and then at the jewellery and wig set out on the dressing table.

She nods, knowing that Richard is determined to take control of her tonight, to be her master and to present himself as such to the Crème de la Crème. Indeed, since the sexual adventures of the last four hours, he has become much more defined in his dominance. He now has the strident air of a confident master and, knowing this, Eve feels an even deeper arousal whose core is a dizzying tingle of masochistic pleasure.

'Hurry up. We've got less than half an hour.'

Richard sits on the bed and watches with wide, sex-possessed eyes burning with a teasing cruelty in the soft electric light of the bedroom. Eve stands before him naked, her sex achingly firm.

Despite Richard's exhortation, Eve dresses carefully, with the feminine grace demanded by her true identity. Yet Richard doesn't complain. Indeed, the sex flame merely burns brighter in his deep, dark gaze as Eve slips into the beautiful, erotic attire, as the soft, glistening silk and nylon encloses her slender form in a glove of gently unyielding femininity.

And as she dresses, as Eve is created like a painting made more real with each careful brush-stroke, the sense of perfect harmony returns with a power she hasn't felt since her first visit to the Crème de la Crème club. And with this deeply arousing sense of rightness comes the slightly mind-bending confidence that had led to the very edge of exposure. She looks into Richard's dark, devouring eyes and releases a smile of serene desire.

Eventually, she is dressed and sitting before the dressing-table mirror. Richard, now standing over her, insists that Eve apply a thicker, more 'sluttish' make-up than she has

141

used previously. She nods, whispers an obedient 'Yes, of course', but actually applies very little in addition to her normal modest face paint; except for the lips. Here, with a deliberation that barely hides her ironic intention, she applies dark, bloody paint to the soft, ripe flesh of her full lips, her eyes moving rapidly between her reflection and the face of Richard, who has now taken up position directly behind her.

As she glides the red stick across her lips, she continues to hold Richard's fascinated, aroused gaze. The message that flows between them is the truth of a strangely fluid sado-masochistic desire.

'You're so beautiful,' he whispers. 'So very beautiful.'

Eve responds with a quiet, modest 'Thank you' and then slips the elegant, expensive velvet choker around her neck, which is deliberately exposed by the open neck of the shimmering black silk blouse.

She looks at her reflection and her smile widens. Again her striking and highly convincing feminine beauty is confirmed.

She rises from the leather-backed stool and gasps with a pleasure mixed with trepidation. She balances on the highest of heels with expert care, at the core of which will always be a highly erotic fear of falling. She totters forward, her mini-skirted bottom wiggling helplessly, the perfectly formed and tightly nylon-sheathed edges of her buttock globes just visible. Her steps are small and precise, each a deeply felt sado-erotic gesture.

Richard immediately moves behind the she-male beauty and slips his warm hands beneath the virtually non-existent skirt. Eve moans with a shocked pleasure and pressures her bottom against the teasing hands.

'A bum made for spanking,' he whispers. 'Should I spank you before we leave? To warm you up a bit?'

Richard lets one hand slip between Eve's legs and begins to tease her crotch through the film of nylon and the silk and satin walls of the body-shaper.

Eve's moans of pleasure increase in volume. 'Yes. Please.'

Richard pulls her towards the bed and then throws her firmly over his lap. He administers a hard and extended spanking that leaves Eve kicking her high-heeled feet and begging for mercy. Her nylon-sheathed bottom, fully revealed after Richard has rolled up the skirt and then pinned her wrists behind her back, wobbles like the sexiest jelly in the world under the repeated and harsh blows, and by the time he has finished, poor Eve is close to coming and thus creating a rather sticky situation seconds before they leave for the Crème de la Crème club.

The heels make driving impossible, so Eve is the passenger in Richard's expensive sports car.

The journey is made in a nervous silence. Eve's heart pumps with aroused anticipation. She has very little idea of what the night before her holds, but she knows that at the very least it will involve her total acceptance of a transformation that will change everything. With Eve there has always been the possibility of denial – the opportunity to return to the fundamental and simple fact of Adam. Yet, once she submits herself as a full member and adherent of the Crème de la Crème Elect, she knows this opportunity will disappear. And with it, the safe and very carefully constructed life of Adam. Indeed, as she reviews – yet again – the events of the last week, she begins to see a certain inevitability, a gradually increasing drive towards fundamental and inescapable change. The moment she stepped out of the door on that cool winter's evening dressed as Eve, she opened a doorway through her previous, easily controlled reality, a reality based on a clear dual identity, into the truth of Eve, a truth that will always demand full transformation and openness to the world.

They arrive at the club with two minutes to spare. The anonymous metal door is opened, to Eve's surprise, by Honey, the petite beauty so intimately and painfully displayed in the club a few nights before. She is dressed in a very short white silk dress, with matching nylon tights and white, high-heeled shoes. Her hair spills over her shoulders in thick, long curls, and her pale-blue eyes are filled with a haze of sexual excitement.

She says nothing, just smiles sweetly and then indicates that they should follow her.

And soon they are in the reception area, by the thick red velvet curtains. Cherry is sitting at the reception desk and the moment her dark eyes fall on Eve, a wicked yet deeply adoring smile crosses thick, cherry-coloured lips. She rises from the table and Eve feels a strange but elating dizziness wash over her. She smiles and blushes as the striking black beauty comes around the desk and embraces Eve.

'I'm sooo glad you came! I've been looking forward to this all day.'

Her manner is flamboyantly feminine, yet delicate and gentle. She is wearing a very tight red leather mini-skirt, black fishnet tights, high-heeled boots that reach up to just above her knees, plus a very tight black-nylon sweater. She is also wearing a striking wig of very thick, glossy black curls that spill over her broad shoulders. The sweater accentuates her considerable and perfectly formed breasts to such an extent that two very long and very hard nipples are clearly visible through the erotic second-skin material.

As she moves closer, Eve feels Cherry's sex press against her lower stomach and finds herself staring into two beautiful brown orbs of helpless desire. She remembers the black beauty's soft, bloody lips embracing her painfully hard cock and feels a sudden, deep love for this gorgeous she-male, a love that she can see returned with interest. Then there is a silence, a brief moment of mutual insight. The smiles fade, the eyes widen. A terrible, sensual and emotional truth has been made disturbingly apparent.

Richard coughs slightly. Eve is suddenly shocked out of the magnetic pull of Cherry's eyes. She turns, smiles slightly. Cherry smiles knowingly at Richard.

'Hi, Ricky,' she says, with a coy familiarity. 'You've certainly hit the jackpot this time.'

Richard smiles and nods. 'No doubt about it.'

Eve blushes, both proud and embarrassed.

Cherry leads them through the red curtain, followed by Honey.

The main club area is, to Eve's surprise and horror, packed and very noisy. Every table is taken and there are a number of erotically attired TV serving girls wiggling on painfully high heels serving drinks to surprisingly rowdy guests with glazed, sexed-up smiles. It is almost as if every member of the Crème de la Crème club has been drafted in to deal with the eager, desiring mob and that each is wallowing in the intense sexual pleasure induced by their intricate exposure in the outrageously sexy costumes. Each gorgeous servant girl is attired in the waitress uniform Eve had first pondered with deeply aroused eyes on the previous Wednesday night, and many of these sexy beauties are fending off advances from the loud, teasing men and women sitting at the tables. Most are lost in the shadows of the club and it is difficult to make out details, but one thing Eve notices almost immediately: a significant majority are men.

As she follows Cherry through the shadows cut periodically by blinding slashes of powerful white light exploding from spotlights hung from the ceiling above the long bar-front, Eve finds herself, despite her increasing nervousness, considering the startling physical presence of Cherry and remembering the kinky adventures of the previous evening. She has sucked my cock and I have teased hers through films of satin and nylon. Yes, she knows that much without question or doubt. Yet there is a deeper need for Cherry, a need she has felt for no one, not even her glorious Aunt Debra. And as Eve's eyes seek out the long legs of the dusky maiden, and as her mind submerges into a glistening vat of thick sex dreams in which her fingers walk across this nylon-sheath, on a journey of sensual discovery, she is again overwhelmed by the strangeness of it all, by the rapid descent into this astonishing world of sex mystery. She gazes into the shadow-wrapped crowd and for a minute, thanks to the flickering, changing lights, is convinced that she can see each pair of eyes burning like orange sodium in the darkness, enflamed by a violent animal desire, a possessive and unforgiving need; eyes that want her in the most fundamental and complete of ways;

145

eyes that ravish and overwhelm. She feels her cock press harder against the body-shaper and returns her gaze to Cherry's lovely, eagerly wiggling bottom.

They walk across the dance-floor area and then directly in front of the stage. Eve totters precariously on the hard wooden floor on her sky-high heels and looks up at the blood-red curtains. She remembers the sado-erotic performance played out with such dizzying commitment on Wednesday night. At first she is convinced they are to be paraded on the stage before this baying mob; indeed, ever since Cherry led them through the velvet-curtained doorway, she has been convinced that the evening will involve some kind of dark initiation undertaken beneath the unforgiving spotlights. But when they reach the end of the stage, Cherry gestures for them to follow her through a narrow doorway and down a dark hallway that stinks of petunia oil and seems to be lit by two very weak, pink-coloured, bare light bulbs.

The corridor is short and at its end are two doors – one on either side. Cherry raps on the right door and Helen's clear, elegant voice snaps a sharp, decisive 'Enter!'

And so Cherry leads Eve and Richard, still closely followed by Honey, into a surprisingly large room with red velvet-wallpapered walls covered in pictures of the Crème de la Crème membership. The room is much brighter than the corridor, its light clear white inducing a sense of momentary visual distortion that leaves all four of them briefly disoriented. But when Eve has adjusted her eyes, she finds herself facing a long, antique wooden desk, behind which sits Helen. Standing beside her is Priscilla, and sitting on a long red leather sofa in a darker corner is Samantha.

Despite the table's obvious age, it is littered with the tools and emblems of modern business: a black, flat-screen computer monitor, two phones, a palm-top device and a speaker to allow tele-conferencing. Off to the left of the desk is a row of very new-looking filing cabinets.

Helen's eyes have not left Eve's since she entered the room. The aristocratic dominatrix is dressed in a black silk jacket and a white silk blouse, with a large bow tied tightly at the neck. Her hair is worn in a very formal bun held in place with a diamond clasp. As she rises from the table to greet them, Eve notices that she is wearing a long black velvet skirt that reaches down to the edges of her ankles, together with very high-heeled black leather court shoes. Her ankles are sheathed in shimmering black nylon, and this tiny glimpse is, for a reason beyond Eve's imagining, fiercely erotic.

'You look utterly stunning, Eve. A vision of she-male sexual beauty.'

Eve smiles modestly and turns to her handsome, smiling partner. 'It was Richard's . . . selection.'

Helen turns her piercing crystal eyes upon Richard and they fill with a knowing amusement.

'Yes, Richard. How nice to see you again.'

Richard's smile hardens slightly, but he remains relaxed and clearly fascinated.

'Hello, Helen,' he says, his gaze firm, his manner demonstrating a simple fact: he is not intimidated by this strikingly robust (and busty) female.

Eve looks over at Priscilla. Gorgeous, rangy, mysterious Priscilla. A creation of careful deceit, whose own true self is locked in not just a male biology but a dual she-male identity as the nominal manager of the Crème de la Crème club and the servant of the stunning, imperial Helen. Tonight she is dressed in a short black silk dress, silk stockings and modestly heeled mules. Her striking red hair has been freed from the tight maid's bun and is once again exploding over her shoulders like a waterfall of gleaming autumn leaves dipped in liquid gold.

'We really must talk later,' Helen says to Richard, 'but now we need to focus on Eve.'

Richard nods with a careful indifference.

Helen, her buxom physique even more alluring in this black attire and heels, lowers her soul-crushing gaze upon the gorgeous she-male and Eve feels her heart skip a beat.

'Last night you agreed to become a full and true member of Crème de la Crème. You did so knowing full well what such an agreement entails and demands of you. You did so

147

knowing that the moment you formally join the Elect, you will surrender everything associated with the male life that currently sustains your physical existence. You did so knowing that you will become not just one of the Elect, but an employee, that you will work as my administrator, as one of our models and also as a key part of our new service. For this you will be paid a not ungenerous salary – certainly more than you are earning at the moment. You agreed knowing that membership of the Elect requires not just fundamental changes to your lifestyle, but also to your body; changes that will make it impossible for you ever to return to your male identity; changes that will firmly establish you as a transsexual who must live *her* life as a woman. But now there is only one question, one question you must answer without hesitation and with absolute certainty. For if you back out tomorrow or in two months' time, your association with us will be over forever.'

There is a moment of deeply unsettling silence. Eve meets Helen's firm, determined gaze and then looks back at Priscilla, who is now smiling at her with genuine affection and very obvious desire. Then she looks over at Samantha, who has remained silent since they arrived, her ironic smile hiding secrets Eve fears to know.

'So, do you still want to join?'

Eve feels surprisingly relaxed at this moment of highest tension. During the day, Eve has never questioned the decision she made last night, even though – at the time – she was very drunk. No: the drink had opened the door and now she knows the only way forward is to step through it without hesitation or fear. She is confident in her decision.

'Yes,' she replies. 'Very much.'

Helen nods and smiles. 'Good. We're all very happy you remain so confident in your decision, Eve. I'm sure you won't regret it. You will be given a month to wrap up the affairs of your previous male life. You will then begin work as my assistant. Between now and then, you will be expected to make yourself available as a model for the website and our range of videos. Most of the shooting takes place in the evenings and at weekends, so that shouldn't be a problem, especially as Richard is responsible for most of it.'

She looks over at Richard and they exchange cool, ironic smiles.

'We will also begin the hormone and associated drug therapies that are necessary for your full transformation into Eve. The final physical transformation will be completed in three months' time by Samantha at her private hospital. By that point, you will have already begun to see the impact of the drugs. I also wish you to begin our special training course as quickly as possible. This is run by Cherry, with help from Honey and Pris, and I think you will find it both instructive and very enjoyable. When you start working directly for me, you will also be required to join our new escort project.'

Eve listens in quiet astonishment, her life being re-engineered, her future being set out like the instruction manual for a new computer. Yes, I am being programmed to be the perfect Crème de la Crème she-male, she thinks. And this thought fills her with nothing but intense excitement. To surrender to the plans of Helen Bliss and her gorgeous associates is a prospect of almost unbearable anticipation. Yet in the heart of Helen's detailed and teasing descriptions is a new and slightly disturbing development. Despite her excitement, she finds herself wondering what on earth 'our new escort project' could be.

'Cherry, take Eve to the changing room and fit the restrainer. Then I think she can spend the rest of the evening serving at the tables. Yes, a very good introduction to her future duties, I think.'

'The restrainer?' Eve finds herself asking, despite having witnessed its wicked presence on Cherry.

Helen smiles coolly and nods.

'The restrainer is the heart of discipline. Restraint is the key to true understanding for our she-males. Without it, they would quickly descend into a totally useless and self-destructive sexual excess that would undermine both the club and themselves.'

'But who controls the . . . restrainer?'

'We do. You stopped being anything other than our property the moment you agreed to become a member of the Elect.'

'But what about . . . Richard?'

Helen's smile widens. 'Oh Richard knows all about the restrainer.'

Cherry steps forward and takes Eve by the hand. Cherry's smile is gentle and erotically reassuring. Then she is led from the room without another word.

As soon as Cherry has closed the door behind them, the black beauty runs a warm, elegant hand across Eve's pale cheek. 'Come on, petal. Let's get you ready for your new life.'

8

Bought and Sold

Cherry leads Eve through the opposite door into a small, cluttered dressing room, the kind seen in a million films of show-business life.

Set against a wall are three theatrical dressing tables, complete with mirrors framed by gleaming white bulbs. The tables are covered in make-up and the apparel of she-male transformation. Opposite the tables are mobile clothes racks from which hang a vast array of transvestite fetish wear and more conventional female attire.

'Sunday nights are very popular,' Cherry says, leaning down to open a draw beneath one of the tables and extracting a small wooden box. As she bends forward, her skirt rides up her fishnet-sheathed thighs to reveal a hint of red satin, heavily frilled panties. 'It's called Mistresses and Maids night. Basically, the wives/partners of the members ... well, they get to auction off their tranny mates. It's actually where Mistress Helen got the idea for the escort service.'

Eve stares at Cherry. In the somewhat dim, pink-tinged light of the dressing room, she appears even more beautiful, even more sexy. Cherry places the box on the dressing table and turns to face Eve.

'Auction off?' Eve mumbles, her eyes feasting on the splendid and incredibly erotic spectacle that is Cherry.

'Yes. That's why there's so many men. Most of them are well-off notables. They know they can trust Helen. They come here and buy themselves a pretty TV for the night.

It's really amazing how many men like transvestites in that way. I mean – look at Richard! That's why Helen wants to start the escort service. There's a real demand.'

Eve's eyes widen with shock. 'You mean they . . .'

Cherry bursts out laughing. 'Yes, they buy a TV to have sex. Nothing serious. Most just want a tranny to give them a blow-job. The whole idea of ambiguity seems to turn them on. And most of them are really nice.'

'And you've been auctioned?'

'Yep. Twice. By Helen. And tonight makes three times.'

'You're going out there tonight?'

Cherry's smile fades slightly. 'Stop asking silly questions.'

There is a moment of electric silence, a moment during which they look at each other with nervous, aroused eyes. Eve ponders being sold to the highest bidder, being with a strange man. She remembers the taste of Richard's large, harsh cock and feels her own sex react helplessly. Then, suddenly, Cherry steps forward and takes Eve's beautiful face in her large, graceful hands. Then they kiss. A long, soft, loving kiss that merges with a prolonged, erotic embrace. Cherry's hands slip beneath Eve's skirt and begin to ease it down her legs.

'I've never felt like this,' Cherry whispers, briefly detaching herself from Eve's mouth. 'Not with a girl, a man, or a TV.'

Eve feels her delicately hosed knees begin to buckle; she is gripped by a sudden, dizzying elation. 'Me neither,' she whispers.

Cherry's lovely face is illuminated by another beautiful smile. 'I wish we could be together tonight.'

Eve nods, her heart pounding, her stomach turning with nervous need.

Cherry then seems to shake off the sex madness gripping her splendid form. 'Maybe another night. Soon. When the training begins. But now, we've got to get the restrainer sorted out. You need to get undressed.'

There is a moment of hesitation, then Cherry begins slowly to unbutton the black blouse, whose translucent material shimmers under the soft lighting of the dressing room. Eve's lips part with helpless sexual abandon and she slowly runs her dark-pink tongue over glistening, blood-red lips. As Cherry releases each pearl button, her large, dark-brown eyes never leave Eve's. She feels her cock press desperately into the body-shaper and swallows down a terribly nervous, unforgiving need.

The buttons freed, Cherry slips the blouse over Eve's shoulders and down over the erotic structure and fabric of the body-shaper. She eases the tails of the blouse out of the mini-skirt and then pulls the wide, soft sleeves free. The blouse falls to the floor. Then Cherry kneels down in front of Eve, just as she did the night before. She slips her hands into the edge of the skirt and eases it over the shapely hips provided by the body-shaper's padding and down Eve's perfectly shaped, sheer nylon-encased legs. Eve moans with a dreadfully acute, mind-bending pleasure and her hands fall upon Cherry's shoulders. Cherry helps Eve step out of the skirt and then slowly, elegantly rises to her feet.

'Those heels look like trouble.'

Eve smiles and nods. 'They are. But I love them. The way they make me feel. The way they make me walk. It's an incredible feeling.'

Cherry then flicks a finger under the left silk shoulder strap of the body-shaper and eases it down Eve's arm. She repeats this with the second and Eve helps her slide the intricate, erotic foundation wear down her slender she-male body. As she does so, she feels her heart crash against the wall of her rib-cage and her sex burn into her stomach. Cherry pulls the shaper down over her stomach. Eve is wearing the tights beneath the shaper and the black silk panties over it. As she carefully lets her desperate, boiling sex pop up (still trapped fetishistically inside the tights), she manages to pull the shaper and the panties down over Eve's thighs and then over her knees. Then Eve is stepping out of the shaper. Now she is dressed in only the striking, demanding heels, the gorgeous, ultra-fine tights and the elegant, very pretty choker. Once again, Cherry straightens up as Eve steps out of the body-shaper. As she rises, she places a gentle kiss on each of Eve's pale-rose nipples.

Following Cherry's whispered instructions, Eve kicks off the stiletto-heeled shoes and wiggles out of the black tights. Cherry watches this deliberately erotic and deeply balletic display with wide, tormented eyes. A sense of acute frustration hangs in the air like a powerful sex perfume. Cherry faces a naked Eve, a she-male revealed to be physically so very male. The black beauty places a tentative but teasing hand on Eve's large, hard, burning cock and then removes it quickly, a playful smile lighting up her beautiful face.

'Ooo, it's so hot,' she says in a mock Marilyn Monroe-style voice.

Eve laughs lightly, but her heart is filled with the heavy weight of sexual need and helpless love.

'Can you cool it down?' Eve asks, her eyes filled with sexual suggestion.

'I think so.'

Cherry opens the small, pink wooden box. From inside she takes a narrow tube. She unscrews the silver lid and then presses a small amount of a clear, rosewood-perfumed gel on to the fingers of her left hand.

Her smile fades to a tight frown of concentration as she again kneels down. Then, with slow, infuriating precision, she begins to massage the gel into Eve's aching, steel-hard cock.

Eve squeals with a hellish, inescapable pleasure. She begs the stunning TV for release from this awful, ecstatic suffering.

'Let me come. Oh please, Cherry, my beautiful love . . . let me come!'

But Cherry doesn't let her come. Indeed, her mission is part of the discipline of controlling the urge for release and also part of the training regime of the Crème de la Crème. For as soon as she has thoroughly lubricated Eve's rigid, tormented sex, she steps back and extracts a small, pink rubber finger-like sheath from within the wooden box.

Eve looks down at the sheath and sees the fate that awaits her.

'No,' she whispers, her eyes wide with fear and need.

But no, in this case means, yes. This is a *no* riddled with melodramatic pretence. This is denial for effect.

Smiling, Cherry begins to roll the sheath very slowly over the engorged purple head of Eve's long-tormented, desperate sex. The poor she-male beauty cries out in an ecstatic agony and begins to wiggle uncontrollably.

'Keep still, you naughty girl,' Cherry chides. 'I could cut you with my nails.'

Eve looks down through tear-stained eyes and realises the potential for injury. She struggles to remain still, but as the sheath is progressed down the hot, hard meat of her cock, she finds herself truly tested.

Yet, perhaps amazingly, there is no injury, no pain, just unbearable pleasure. Then the sheath is stretched tightly over her bulging balls and snapped in place, and her hard cock is rising before her like a pink sex sword.

'The tip is lined with micro-filtering,' Cherry explains. 'This will allow you to answer the call of nature. However, the rubber and the rings make ejaculation impossible.'

Eve's eyes widen with genuine fear as Cherry proceeds to extract two slender, gold-coloured metal rings from the box. With a cruel light in her gorgeous dark eyes, she slips the wider of the two over Eve's aching, tormented sex and runs it down the gleaming rubberised surface. It fits tightly, but not too painfully over the base of Eve's sex. The smaller ring is less forgiving. Cherry has to fight to squeeze the fat head of Eve's cock through it, and this is both painful and strangely arousing. Then, as soon as it has traversed this obstacle, it snaps very tightly into place directly beneath the head. Now there is more than a mild discomfort and the lovely she-male moans with the pain created by a sudden and unrelenting pressure.

'Don't worry, Eve, you'll get used to it. We all do.'

Eve looks down at her tightly and perversely imprisoned sex in astonishment and horror.

'Must I wear this all the time?' she asks, in a muted, terror-streaked voice.

'As long as your mistress requires. Normally, it is

released only as a reward for good behaviour and as part of your training in pleasure giving and receiving.'

Cherry then runs a blood-red finger along Eve's enraged, but also tightly contained cock and the gorgeous, wide-eyed she-male beauty moans with a terrible, frustrated fury.

'I'm sure this will be let out when you behave, or when your mistress or master needs its services.'

'Master?' Eve whispers, her eyes closed, a gasp of infinite pleasure escaping her pretty mouth micro-seconds before the questioning word.

'Don't worry, I know all about Richard's tastes,' Cherry responds, removing her teasing fingers. 'Now, it's time to get you ready for the evening ahead.'

Cherry once again climbs elegantly to her feet. She places a soft, quick kiss on Eve's cheek and turns to the rack of TV clothing. Eve continues to stare down at her sensually and painfully restrained sex. She runs a curious hand over its rubberised surface and gasps with helpless pleasure.

Cherry holds up what appears to be a spectacularly sequinned, red basque, complete with generous padded bra-cups and a very tight waist.

'This should fit you,' she says, her eyes filled with arousal and conspiracy, her red tongue running across her soft, glistening lips.

She places the basque on the dressing table and takes a pair of bright-red silk panties from another drawer in the dressing table.

'Put these on.'

Eve obeys, drawing the sexy, skimpy panties up her silken legs and positioning them with obvious care over her hard, imprisoned cock.

Cherry covers Eve's slender, beautiful form in a mist of powerful rose-scented perfume. She extracts a shimmering pair of black, seamed and very fine nylon tights from the same drawer as the panties. As Cherry holds them before Eve, it becomes apparent that they are shot through with hundreds of very tiny silver stars that twinkle insanely under the soft dressing-room lights.

'They're gorgeous,' Eve whispers.

Cherry smiles and hands them to the fascinated, aroused and terribly frustrated she-male.

Eve rolls the left leg of the tights into a bowl shape and then gently pulls it up over her foot and long, perfectly shaped leg. She moans ever so slightly as the soft, sheer fabric covers the smooth, sensitive skin.

By the time she pulls the thick black waistband of the tights up around her slight waist, she is in a state of some considerable sexual excitement. This has an immediate and painful impact: as her sex expands helplessly, answering the fundamental call of a male's aggressively desiring nature, the cock rings tighten and press down. Cherry smiles almost sadistically when she notices the paradox of Eve's desire and discomfort. She then orders Eve to put on the basque.

Eve smiles weakly, her eyes torn between the gorgeous shimmering delight that is the basque and the erotically perfect vision of Cherry, her buxom she-male form almost unbearably delightful under the gentle pink lights.

She steps into the basque with a strange sense of inner peace. As she surrenders to this latest development, this further intensification of her grand sexual adventure, she feels at her most relaxed and content. Weirdly, despite all the madness and adventure of the past week, she is now more at one with herself than at any time since Aunt Debra placed her in soft, delicate, endlessly teasing panties and hose.

Cherry helps Eve draw the stunning basque over her thighs and then up her torso. A pair of slender, red silk shoulder straps hold the finally positioned piece of impressive fetish wear in place, and Cherry's hands linger lovingly upon Eve's shoulders as she gently slips them into position, causing a shiver of powerful, heart-stopping pleasure to cascade across her body.

Eve gasps with need and pain. The basque is much lighter than the body-shaper and the sense of control it brings is wonderful. She feels overwhelmingly feminine and utterly unhindered by doubt or, ironically, physical restriction.

Satisfied that the basque is properly positioned, Cherry retrieves the striking ultra-high-heeled mules that Eve had worn to the club and tells her to step back into them. Eve obeys with a half-smile of teased desire and is soon hovering a few inches above Cherry. Cherry looks up into Eve's stunned, aroused eyes and smiles.

'How do you feel?' she asks.

'Wonderful,' she whispers. 'Absolutely wonderful.'

Cherry smiles and extracts the final touch to this spectacular and deeply erotic dressing: a pair of shoulder-length white glacé gloves. She draws them over the silky arms of the younger she-male with a deliberate slowness that inspires more deep moans of intense physical and mental pleasure.

'I love the gloves. They're like stockings for the arms. You really do feel consumed by femininity.'

Eve can only nod helplessly at Cherry's sensually whispered words and lose herself in the infinitely soft caress of the gloves. She is submerged completely in wondrous feelings of submissive femininity. She is gripped completely by a womanly need. The sense of Eve, the erotic reality of the feminine personality that for so long has been at the very core of her being, is now burning with a fierce, erotic brightness. She feels her long, shapely legs so marvellously encased in the sheerest and most stylish of fine nylon and presses her thighs together. She wiggles her tightly sealed bottom with girlish delight and feels the restrainer demand absolute and eternal obedience to the spirit and power of dominant womanhood. She looks down at the buxom beauty of Cherry and feels, once again, a terrible love, a love bordering on pain, the same all-encompassing and deeply sexual pain that is now besieging her iron-hard sex.

Cherry takes a brush from the table and delicately combs the pretty pageboy wig. She then adds a touch of blood-red lipstick and another squirt of the expensive sex-mist perfume. 'You look good enough to eat.'

Eve looks at Cherry's incredible body with helpless longing. 'I want you so badly,' she virtually growls. 'So very badly.'

Cherry smiles weakly, shocked and aroused by this sudden, violent declaration. Then she steps forward and they kiss once again – longer, harder with the deep, deep passion of true lovers.

'I want to be with you forever,' Eve gasps between kisses. 'So that we can share it all – this ... wonderful feminine being.'

Cherry smiles and nods. 'Like true lesbian lovers,' she says.

Eve laughs and seconds later they are locked in another furious kiss.

But then Cherry very gently pushes the gorgeous, hungry Eve away.

'Come on,' she says, carefully adjusting her short, so terribly sexy skirt. 'There's work to be done.'

Cherry takes Eve by the hand and leads her from the dressing room. The dazzling she-male totters elegantly on the high, high heels, her bottom wiggling, her well-padded chest bouncing merrily before her. In seconds she knows she will be exposed to hundreds of people in this provocative costume. And the thought fills her with a terror-streaked, deeply sexualised elation.

Eve follows Cherry down the corridor and out on to the dance floor. The spotlights are blinding bright and momentarily Eve covers her eyes. She feels her precarious balance fail and a moment of sheer panic washes across her gorgeously feminine form.

Cherry steps forward and leads Eve directly into the unforgiving path of the lights. The crowd are even more animated now: there is much wild clapping and cheering and Eve becomes aware of a familiar female voice booming over a powerful public address system.

'For your pleasure, ladies, gentlemen and those somewhere in-between, lot number 39, Bethany Rose!'

There is a sudden ear-splitting deluge of clapping and cheering. Unbearable sound and light. A surreal nightmare which is only relieved when Cherry guides Eve beneath the light into a zone of deeply soothing darkness.

Cherry stops. 'Are you OK, Eve?'

Eve totters to a halt and lets her wide, shocked eyes adjust to the new semi-light. She is surrounded by tables packed with people. She feels a hand on her bottom and jumps with shock. She turns rapidly to find Richard staring at her with dark, powerful and highly excited eyes.

'Are you being auctioned tonight, my pretty?'

Eve smiles coyly, but before she can reply, she is dragged away by Cherry, who looks down at Richard with playfully angry eyes.

Cherry leads Eve through the tables and the crowd continues to respond passionately to unseen events on the stage.

Then they are standing by the bar. Eve notices that there are three other very pretty she-males in exactly the same costume as herself. Two are armed with silver trays, one is serving behind the bar.

Cherry leans over to the bartender, a very pretty blonde with a particularly large chest, and shouts, 'Brought you some help. This is Eve. A new member of the Elect.'

The blonde looks up at Eve and smiles warmly. 'We need all the help we can get tonight!' she shouts, just as another roar of dark pleasure fills the vast room.

Cherry turns to Eve. 'It's my turn soon, so make yourself useful. Daisy will show you the ropes. Pris will come and find you later.'

Cherry turns to leave, but Eve gently holds her back.

'When will we meet again?'

Cherry smiles sadly. 'When Mistress Helen allows us to.'

Then she is gone and Eve finds herself filled with a sudden, horribly powerful disappointment.

'Ever served drinks before, Eve?' Daisy shouts, pulling Cherry from her funk.

Eve looks at her with amazed, confused eyes. 'No. Well . . . yes. But just to my . . . boyfriend.'

Daisy laughs a loud, deeply male laugh and shouts 'Hilary!'

One of the uniformed she-males steps forward. She is a striking strawberry blonde, her thick, gold-flecked hair bound in a ponytail that runs down to the middle of her back. She has large, peach-coloured lips and slightly Asian, light-brown eyes. Her small, girlish ears hold large diamond-stud earrings. She smiles slightly at Eve and then gives Daisy a slightly bored, yet also mildly curious look.

'Eve's new. She's been sent over by Mistress Helen. Show her the ropes.'

Hilary nods and turns to face Eve. It is only now that this very pretty, rather petite she-male begins to take real stock of her new work-mate. Her eyes widen slightly as she takes in the full impact of Eve's beauty and her indifference is quickly washed away on a wave of powerful sexual attraction.

'I like the tights,' she says, her own hose simple seamed black nylon, yet still attractive and very sexy on her long, statuesque legs.

'Cherry chose them,' Eve responds.

Hilary smiles slightly. 'Good old Cherry.'

The clapping and cheering suddenly increases at this point.

'Take that tray and follow me,' Hilary says, leaning forward to shout over the noise.

On the bar before her is a silver tray laden with two tall glasses and a wine glass, all three filled.

Eve looks at the tray with genuine trepidation.

'Don't worry – just hold it before you. There's no need for anything fancy.'

Eve gingerly picks up the tray and Hilary minces into the jungle of tables. Eve totters after her, eyes locked fearfully on the alcohol sloshing about in the glasses.

As she moves between the crowded tables and the loud, almost angry din that is rising from them, she sees heads turn and eyes appraise her. There is no doubt she is a particularly impressive she-male specimen and quickly becomes the willing victim of numerous darkly suggestive shouts and clumsy, half-successful fondles. These boorish interventions are taken with a slight, nervous smile, but with no real displeasure. Indeed, in these words and gestures, Eve can see only a drink-fuelled, but deeply felt desire – a passion for Eve. A need for her splendid she-male sensuality.

161

Hilary comes up to her and ushers her over to a nearby table where she is shown how to curtsey deeply while holding the tray and serve the drinks to three older women. Still thinking of so many desiring eyes burning in the dark like bright sex-fire, she doesn't fully realise she is serving drinks to the city's most famous female MP, once a senior cabinet minister and now an outspoken advocate of sexual freedom.

It is only when the woman's penetrating gaze locks into her own, that Eve's consciousness finally tunes into reality. Suddenly she recognises the woman. Her pretty, blood-red lips stretch into an O of surprise and then, perhaps even more surprisingly, she performs another deep curtsey before placing the silver tray down on the table and serving the drinks to the women.

'This is a new one?'

The voice is familiar; deep, hard, yet not without compassion and certainly filled with a powerful sexual interest.

'I believe so. Helen told me she is one of the best for a long time. Real potential.'

The other woman, her voice partially distorted by the noise, is obscured by shadow.

'I take it she will be part of the escort service?'

'Yes. No doubt about that.'

Having served the drinks, Eve steps back and curtsies again, bathing in the hot sex-glow of the woman's eyes and knowing that they will meet again. Her sex struggles in its brutal prison and she is overwhelmed – again – by an intense masochistic arousal. She feels almost unbearably feminine, and thus utterly and delightfully subjugated.

It is then that a huge roar rocks the room. Eve turns to face the stage and, to her astonishment, finds herself looking at Cherry. A loud, bass-heavy electronic dance music suddenly fills the room. Harsh, clean Detroit techno. And Cherry is moving to it. No: she is *dancing* to it. An erotic, graceful, incredibly impressive dance. The clapping and cheering grows. The crowd, too, are impressed by the elegant and rhythmic gyrations of the lovely creature.

The black beauty has a wide, confident and aroused smile on her lovely face. As she dances in the high-heeled boots, her tight micro-mini skirt rides up to expose sensual glimpses of her red silk panties and this drives the crowd even wilder. Then, after a few incredible minutes, the music stops. Cherry performs a deep and elaborate curtsey and receives an agitated standing ovation.

Then the teasing female voice returns to boom across the public address system, cutting through the raucous enthusiasm of the crowd with an ear-splitting ease.

'How about that, ladies and gentlemen! A big hand for Cherry. Lot number 40!'

The clapping increases in volume and Eve, now pinned to the spot in amazement, watches Cherry take a bow.

'The bidding starts at £1,000.'

The voice has moved from the ersatz enthusiasm of a television presenter to the cool precision of an auction mistress in a split, disconcerting second.

It is then that the red cards begin to be held up, large rectangles with white numbers printed across laminated fronts.

'Table 15 – £1,500.'

Eve quickly realises that each bid is automatically for an extra £500. Then, to her amazement, the MP's assistant holds up a card.

'Table 20 – £2,000!'

Heads turn and Eve finds herself looking at faces filled with drunken admiration and envy.

And so it goes on. Up to £5,000 in under a minute, with the MP setting the pace. And soon the bidding has reached £7,500. It is then, to Eve's amazement and sudden, furious, sickening jealousy, she sees that Richard has held up a card.

'A double bid from table 19! £15,000!'

Eve stares at Richard in utter horror and amazement. His liquid eyes meet her gaze and he smiles with a cruel, almost contemptuous indifference. She feels her heart sink and her eyes begin to fill with tears.

The MP looks over at Richard with angry, bitter eyes. She says something to her assistant, who gets up from the table and walks towards the stage, edging carefully around the dance floor and then disappearing down the corridor that leads to Helen's office. She becomes aware that the MP is staring directly at her again, her cold blue eyes appraising the she-male beauty carefully.

There are no bids after Richard's spectacular intervention. The voice goes through the bidding motions rather half-heartedly: 'Going once, going twice . . . SOLD!' There is a round of surprisingly mild applause and Cherry steps down off the stage. Eve notices that she seems less than happy about her sale. She is only a few feet away from Eve. Their eyes meet and Eve's heart sinks as she sees tears welling in Cherry's gorgeous honey-brown orbs.

She curtsies quickly before Richard, her eyes avoiding his. A dark smile crosses his face as she bows her head in a gesture of absolute submission. Then he stands up, takes her by the hand and leads her from the room, winding slowly through the tables, his arms briefly brushing against Eve's. She finds herself looking directly into Cherry's stunned face. This is not what she had planned. Not at all. She shrugs and whispers 'Sorry'. Then Richard drags her into the darkness.

With the sale of Cherry, the auction is clearly over. There is an air of disappointment in the club, as if Richard's dramatic gesture has popped the balloon of erotic excitement that had previously made the atmosphere so electric. Hilary leads Eve back to the bar and she spends the rest of the evening coming to terms with her duties as a sexy waitress, a job she eventually takes to with ease, trying hard to forget Richard's bizarre cruelty and concentrate on the erotic caress of her provocative costume. She wiggles her hips and bottom with each tiny high-heeled step and tries to enjoy the light slaps and playful pinches that continue to follow her around the chaotic maze of tables.

But after about an hour and a half of tottering between the tables on her painfully high heels, she is tired, bored and her feet are aching terribly. Now she begins to understand the terrible sadistic demands of the stiletto-heeled mule and the suffering so many women endure in its name. At the same time her thighs and bottom are sore with the constant, teasing abuse dished out by male and female members of the crowd, which has slowly reduced to a core of loud drinkers entertained by TV dancing girls. Interestingly, the MP has remained, her table the focus of regular visits from a wide variety of the club's exotic clientele.

It must be well after eleven p.m. when Helen suddenly emerges from the door by the stage. She looks utterly ravishing in her long, black, sequinned dress. Eve stares at her with tired, hungry eyes, remembering the adventures of the night before and the strange events of their earlier meeting.

Helen works her way through the tables, smiling, shaking hands. It is clear she is well known by many of those present, a figure who commands respect and admiration. She comes within a few inches of Eve, but totally ignores her, making her way towards the politician's already very busy table with a cool determination, her stride elegant and sensual, her buxom physique an emblem of complete control and absolute authority.

As Eve watches her cross the floor, she feels her cock twitch painfully inside its tight, wicked, perverse restraint. Once again, she feels overwhelmed by desire – for her elaborate feminisation, for Cherry, for Helen. And even for the wicked betrayer, Richard.

Helen draws up a seat and sits by the MP. They talk for some time. Eve, while still serving drinks, tries to keep an eye on them, noting as she does that the MP's hand has rested in a familiar manner on Helen's knee.

Then Helen gestures for Eve to come over to the table. Her heart skips a shocked beat and she totters nervously forward.

Once at the table she curtsies.

'Teresa, this is Eve.'

Teresa March is a handsome, buxom woman in her mid-fifties. Tonight she is dressed in a knee-length grey skirt, a matching grey silk jacket and a shimmering white silk blouse with a high, almost Victorian neck holding a circular emerald that sparkles in the stroboscopic lights. Her thick, shoulder-length hair is a rather beautiful mosaic of grey and blonde streaks, and there is no doubt that she remains a striking vision of female authority.

Ms March looks up at Eve and smiles slightly.

'Very impressive. And you say she's pre-op?'

'Yes. Our newest recruit.'

Helen's tone is neutral, yet also very slightly deferential. It is clear that she, like most of the people present tonight, regards her with the respect and awe due the powerful.

Ms March smiles very slightly and nods. 'A suitable compromise.'

'The visiting room has been prepared.'

Ms March nods and then rises from the table. As she does so, she leans over to her assistant. 'Take Eve to the visiting room. Tell the driver I will be at least an hour.'

The assistant nods and gestures to Eve to follow her. As she totters forward, she notices that Ms March is smiling and shaking the hands of those around the table with a practised, weary diplomacy.

The assistant is in her late twenties. Eve's eyes widen with interest once her form is fully revealed. As she winds carefully through the maze of tables, it quickly becomes apparent that she is a very sexy young woman who has obviously been chosen carefully. She is wearing a black pinstripe jacket with a matching mini-skirt, sheer black nylon tights and stiletto-heeled court shoes. Her black hair is bound in a lose bun with a metal clip.

She walks with elegant purpose, and, as Eve wiggle-minces behind her, her eyes are drawn helplessly to the subtle vibrations of her thighs and buttocks. She feels her cock twitch painfully in the restrainer and her step falters. To desire is to be reminded of this most intimate and absolute control.

9

A Jewel in the Crown

They slip through the red curtain into the reception area, but instead of following the narrow hallway back to the main entrance, they turn left and Eve finds herself immediately negotiating a steep flight of stairs lit by a bright, bare bulb hanging from a slanted ceiling. Eve stares up at the assistant with helplessly male eyes. She can see the perfect globes of each plump buttock sheathed in black nylon and held tightly in the scented embrace of a pair of black silk panties. This intimate revelation is shockingly arousing, an awe-inspiring glimpse of feminine perfection. As always, Eve finds herself gripped by two conflicting passions: the simple fact of sexual desire, and the more complex one of wishing to emulate or become this desire, to be as beautiful and sexy as this striking woman. I wish to become that which I desire. And this evening, in the erotic madness of the Crème de la Crème club, this paradoxical fact – which is at the very core of her she-maleness – has never been more apparent.

At the top of the stairs is another door. Tall. White. With an ornate golden handle.

The assistant opens the door and enters the room beyond. Eve follows – aroused, curious, slightly frightened.

The room beyond is of medium size. Its walls are covered in an expensive white silk wallpaper that has been turned a light pink by soft electric lighting. In one corner of the room is a large, aged cherry-red leather sofa. Placed before it is a glass-topped coffee table, upon which has been placed a bottle of chilled Chablis and a single wine glass. A simple white wooden chair has been positioned in the centre of the room. The sofa, the table and the chair are the only furniture.

The walls are covered in artwork. All by the same artist. All depicting various sado-erotic fantasy scenes. Mostly feminised males (rather than fully blown she-males); all suffering exquisitely at the hands of beautiful, powerful women.

'Sit down on the chair, with your legs crossed tightly, toes pointed downward.'

Shocked by such sudden and explicit instruction, Eve hesitates.

'Now.'

There is a hateful fire burning in the assistant's eyes and Eve immediately complies with this second brutal order.

As she adjusts her position on the chair, she feels a wave of masochistic pleasure crash across her pretty she-male form and secretly wishes this attractive, fearsome woman would continue her verbal cruelty. But she merely inspects Eve's posture, nods with slight satisfaction and then leaves the room.

Eve finds herself sitting in this rather uncomfortable position for at least ten minutes, before the sound of stiletto heels striking the wooden stairs fills her with an instant sense of sexually arousing anticipation.

Then Ms March is in the doorway, her face slightly flushed by drink and the effort of climbing the stairs.

'Sorry to keep you, Eve. But there are certain duties someone in my position is always expected to perform.'

Eve looks at Ms March with wide, slightly awestruck eyes. It was one thing to be in her presence in the club, surrounded by so many other people. But now, here, in this warm, shadowy intimacy, she can only confess to being rather overcome.

Ms March walks over to Eve and studies her carefully. Up close, the MP is even more impressive and Eve finds herself desperate to please. Indeed, the dynamic here is one of power and identity. Ms March is the embodiment of female power, while Eve is the gorgeous symbol of feminine submission.

'You're very beautiful, Eve. And in a perfectly natural way. Yes, I think that is what makes you special. There is a distinct lack of artifice. Which is unusual in a transvestite.'

Her words have the clinical connotations of Samantha, yet they are delivered with warmth and curiosity, with a genuine concern and interest in what it is to be Eve.

Ms March, a careful, fascinated smile on her peach-coloured lips, steps back, as if to get a wider view of Eve. In her striking eyes is a very clear appraisal. Yet this is not the detached analysis of the clinician: in Ms March's eyes there is passion and desire.

'I've never liked men much,' she says, stepping around the table and pouring herself a glass of the honey-green and very expensive wine. 'Neither sexually or socially. Except gay men ... and transvestites. Men without the need to impress or control. Men who aspire to greater things.'

Eve smiles nervously and nods, not knowing where this strange confessional is going.

'Beth – my assistant – has been my lover for some time now. She puts up with my little kinks, but I know she is secretly infuriated by them. That's probably why she was rather mean to you, Eve. But please forgive her: she is cruel because she loves me – unconditionally. And that kind of love is rather priceless in this world. Is there someone you love ... unconditionally?'

Eve thinks of Aunt Debra. Yes, there is only her. She nods.

'Yes,' she says, almost unable to control herself.

Ms March's smile widens and Eve realises how very beautiful this woman is, and how very genuine.

'Tell me about her.'

So Eve does. Over the next half-hour she tells, again, the story of Aunt Debra. And as she tells her story, Eve retains her precise, feminine posture and is aware that Ms March, while listening, is visually devouring every inch of her pretty she-male form. In her sparkling blue eyes there is a terrible sexual arousal that is at odds with her relaxed posture. At one point she leans back and crosses her legs and the tight grey skirt rides up above her knees to reveal her firm, shapely, grey-hosed thighs. Eve finds her eyes drawn to this revelation and then back to Ms March's soft, desiring eyes. By the time she finishes her strange, highly erotic tale, her sex is writhing desperately in its fiendish restraint and her whole being is gripped by the most awful and exciting sense of physical arousal. She feels the fabrics of her elaborate waitress uniform tease her soft, silken body and smells her own perfume. She tastes her dark, strawberry-flavoured lipstick and thinks helplessly of the erotic, generous form of the gorgeous Cherry.

'You have beautiful legs, Eve,' Ms March continues. 'Strangely, quite a lot of men have very shapely legs. So many look good in tights. And you, I must say, look rather splendid.'

'Thank you.'

'Do you like your tights? The ones you are wearing? They look very special to me.'

Ms March's tone has shifted as the questions progress. It is now as if she were addressing a very young girl, trying to tease out a confession of naughtiness, and Eve finds this even more arousing than the nature of the questions.

'Yes, I like them very much. I love tights and stockings. It's my major ... thing. The part of the dressing I love most, in some ways. The feel of the nylon has always turned me on. The enveloping softness and the impact on my legs ... the way they make my legs look. It is so immediate. The feminising effect is quick and very power-ful. An instant transformation.'

Ms March nods and smiles. 'Yes, I love them too. These are by Falke. My favourite, I think. Expensive, but they have softness and body, and when I move, it's often like they're kissing my legs.'

She sits up and places the glass on the coffee table. She then uncrosses her legs and draws them together. Then, to Eve's delighted surprise, she pulls her skirt up to the tops of her thighs to reveal the full, beautiful length of her still very shapely legs.

'You've got very beautiful legs, too,' Eve whispers, her voice hoarse with sex need.

Ms March smiles softly and turns her powerful, sexual gaze full beam on Eve. 'That's very nice of you, Eve. Thank you. But I must admit they've had a rather demanding day. It would be lovely if you could come over here and give me a foot massage.'

Eve's eyes widen with arousal. She nods weakly and rises very carefully from the chair, her heart pounding in her head.

Ms March pushes the coffee table back to allow Eve to kneel down before her. The beautiful, nervous she-male does so with a grace that betrays her natural femininity and her eagerness to impress. As she takes her body weight on to her nylon-sheathed knees, she feels the restraining rings tighten and moans with a pain-streaked pleasure.

Ms March smiles sympathetically. 'The discipline of the restrainer can be rather testing at times. But I think it really does help focus the attention. Do you like it?'

Eve can only nod and stare down at Ms March's striking black leather court shoes. They are beautifully crafted and shaped, with a small diamond buckle that gleams in the soft light of the visiting room and cruel five-inch stiletto heels.

'Do you like my shoes?'

'Yes,' Eve replies, her eyes fixed on the sparkling diamond. 'They're Gucci . . . aren't they?'

'Yes. Yes, indeed,' Ms March says, clearly impressed by Eve's detailed knowledge of feminine footwear. 'You really are an expert, Eve. We should go shopping sometime. Would you like that?'

The thought of shopping with this beautiful and famous woman fills Eve with an intense and erotic joy and she moans a sexed 'Yes'.

'Good. I'll ask Beth to arrange something. Now . . . my feet.'

Eve nods obediently and gently slips the right shoe from Ms March's foot with a sigh of pleasure. She gently places

171

the shoe down on the carpet and repeats the process with the left shoe. Then she very carefully takes Ms March's right foot and places it on her black nylon-wrapped knees. It is a perfectly formed foot, if perhaps a bit large. But Ms March is a tall, firmly structured woman. Eve rests her hands on the warm, soft instep and feels a powerful electric shock of pleasure shoot through her body. This is fetishistic intimacy of the most sensual and electric kind. Eve's erection complains and her excitement increases. She feels her heart pound against her well-padded chest and fights to stifle a loud moan of bottomless pleasure.

'You have beautiful feet,' she whispers, her voice hoarse with desire.

Ms March smiles her gentle, maternal smile. 'Thank you Eve. I've always thought they were a bit too big.'

'No: they're perfect. You're perfect.'

Ms March laughs lightly and stretches her nylon-sheathed feet with a big cat's simple, sensual pleasure.

Eve then gently increases her expert ministrations, knowing this is an act of intense submission that the women of Crème de la Crème seem to demand of all their she-male slaves.

'I bet you can't wait until Samantha's special treatment begins. All the other TVs go wild with delight when they first get their boobs. Apparently, they're ultra-sensitive.'

'Yes, I'm ... really looking forward to it.'

Ms March nods, her smile broadening. 'Yes, of course you are. And so am I. In fact, I'm going to insist the first bra you wear will be bought by me. A special present for a very special she-male.'

Poor Eve swoons with a terrible delight. It is then that she leans forward and places a gentle kiss on Ms March's left foot and feels an orgasmic shudder of pleasure sweep across her handsome, buxom form.

'Yes,' she continues, her voice suddenly deeper, hoarse, filled with sex desperation. 'That's lovely, Keep kissing. Please. Everywhere. All over my legs. Right up to ... the top.'

And Eve eagerly obeys, covering Ms March's hosed feet in sissy kisses and then, after carefully adjusting her

172

position, very gradually and teasingly working her way up her long, firm legs. Ms March moans with a deep, fundamental pleasure. Her eyes close and her mouth falls open. She is clearly overwhelmed by this erotic attention. Her arms fall to her side and she slides almost drunkenly on to the sofa. The now empty wine glass slips from her hand and rolls across age-dulled red leather. Eve, her attention absolute, her arousal painfully intense, works her way from the elegant, mature beauty's calves, up across her knees and then sets to work on her outer and inner thighs. It is at this point that Ms March's moans begin to increase in volume, and then begin to fragment into hoarse cries of animal pleasure. Eve feels the heat of Ms March's nylon-sheathed skin against her lips, a heat that increases as she works her way to the edge of the mature beauty's grey skirt. Sensing that Eve is approaching a barrier, the tormented MP suddenly sits forward and rolls her skirt back over her thighs to expose her upper legs.

'Keep going,' she whispers between girlish cries of pleasure. 'Please.'

And, of course, Eve obliges, progressing closer to Ms March's most intimate secrets, guided by the increasingly powerful scent of her sex and by the dampness of her inner thigh. Eventually, Eve finds herself with her head lodged firmly between Ms March's muscular thighs, her face pressed against her nyloned and pantied crotch, her lips covering the approximate area of her sex in tiny, teasing kisses.

'Use your teeth,' Ms March cries. 'Nibble and bite. Oh God. Please!'

Eve obeys, carefully, even gently nibbling at the soaking, sheer grey nylon that lines Ms March's crotch area. Then there are a series of louder, darker cries and Eve finds her head squashed in the vice grip of Ms March's tightened thighs. Although her ears are covered by the thighs, she can still hear cries of 'Fuck! Oh fuck! Oh fuck yes!' as the beautiful, regal MP experiences an obviously very considerable orgasm.

Then the thigh embrace is loosened and Eve crawls free of a clearly devastated Ms March.

Eve carefully rises to her feet and returns to the chair, where she takes up the same carefully crafted, ultra-feminine posture. After a few minutes, Ms March manages to pull herself upright. She rolls down her skirt and wipes her brow. She looks up at Eve with a gaze of dark, brutal satisfaction and a slightly manic smile. Then she rises to her stiletto-heeled feet and adjusts the rest of her clothing.

For a moment, Eve thinks she will merely walk from the room without a word. But then Ms March walks over to Eve and regards her with a look of admiration.

'That really was quite wonderful, Eve. Thank you. I will talk to Helen about finding a time when you can spend the day with me. So that we can go shopping and get to know each other much better.'

Eve smiles nervously and nods. Ms March leans forward and kisses the lovely she-male full on the lips, an astonishing moment of passion that leaves Eve stunned and aroused. Then, without another word, she turns and leaves, Eve's eyes pinned with desperate hunger to her plump bottom and shapely legs, the taste and smell of her sex all-pervasive.

Eve retains her strictly ultra-feminine position for at least ten minutes before the sound of more high heels striking the stairs fills the room. A sense of real apprehension washes over her as the heels become louder. She assumes the heels' owner will be Pris, but it is, in fact, and to Eve's secret delight, Helen.

'Teresa loved you, Eve. Well done.'

Eve smiles and blushes. She stares at Helen and feels a sense of extraordinary and deeply erotic helplessness. Although she had found herself highly excited and impressed by Ms March, Helen's presence is, without a doubt, far more arousing. Yes, she is a startlingly beautiful woman who projects an aura of absolute assurance and real power. Before her Eve is gripped by a sense of awe.

'By the time we have finished your training and the physical changes . . . well, I think you'll be our jewel in the crown. Ms March has already booked a whole day and night with you. And I'm sure there will be plenty of others. The escort agency will make a fortune.'

'The escort agency?'

Helen smiles and sits down, crossing her legs. She takes the still intact glass from the sofa and fills it with Chablis.

'The new service I mentioned. Before you agreed to join the Elect.'

She looks at Eve with a much harder gaze now, a gaze that seems to be challenging her.

'You mean you want me to work as an escort?'

Helen nods and takes a sip from the glass. 'The latest Crème de la Crème service: TV escorts of the very highest quality.'

'You want to make money from sending me out with . . .'

'With men and with women. And with both. The other girls are all ready. The auctions have established a clear market. The new website is ready as well. And Ms March is our first customer. You will spend the whole of next Wednesday with her. She'll pay us £3,000, and you get to keep a third. Imagine that. Imagine three or four customers a week, Eve.'

Eve's eyes widen with shock and more than a little concern.

'But what do you want me to do? Just keep them company?'

Helen laughs loudly and bitterly. 'Oh come off it, Eve. You know it's more than that. Look at what just happened with Teresa!'

'You want me to . . . service them, for money. To be a prostitute for you?'

The word is harsh and clear and Helen's ironic smile fades as its unpleasant truth fills the alcohol-scented air of the visiting room.

Helen sits up and looks at Eve with clear, hard eyes.

'I don't want you to do anything, Eve. It's what you want. I'm talking about letting you be as you've always dreamed of being. To reveal, finally, the self you've hidden all these years – the secret self whose existence you have

175

never fully been able either to reveal or confess. I'm talking about finally, truly knowing yourself.'

Eve hesitates. Suddenly she can feel the tears welling up in her eyes. The smell of Ms March's cunt mingles with the remnants of her alcohol breath and Eve's own powerful French perfume. She imagines herself with a strange man, then she imagines Richard, Richard with Cherry, and feels a terrible sexual arousal, an arousal she fights to accept. For the first time in a long time she feels deeply uncomfortable with what she is. With Eve. With the strange adventures of the last two weeks. Suddenly, she feels she needs advice, the only advice she knows she can trust: the advice of her beloved Aunt Debra.

'I don't know. I'll have to think about it. I didn't . . .'

'There's no more thinking, Eve. You've accepted your position in the Elect. If you say no now, then it's all over. The journey's finished. And I'm afraid you will never reach the end.'

Tears begin to trickle down Eve's flushed, sex juice-stained cheeks. Yet even as this last struggle is waged, her sex burns with even greater darker force inside the wicked, sado-erotic restrainer. I am being dragged by my desire into the final dark room before the light, she thinks. I am fighting the thing that has always been so very obvious: my true self.

Then, with a helpless resignation, she nods. Slowly, wearily. Acknowledging the inescapable fact of her fate and the desire that has led her perhaps inevitably to this point.

Helen's ironic smile returns and she utters a decisive 'Good'. She then rises from the sofa and walks over to the now openly sobbing TV beauty.

'Don't worry, poppet. You're in shock. Acceptance is like that. Look at this little episode as a cathartic moment – the clearing away of final resistances.'

Eve looks up at Helen through tear-stained eyes.

Helen's smile turns a little more cruel. 'I think you need to go home now. But I don't think you should be alone.'

It is then that Cherry steps into the room, with Richard at her side.

10

A Plundered Soul

'We thought it would be best if you were with Cherry tonight,' Helen says, turning to Cherry and her handsome male companion. Teresa was very keen to have her, but Richard helped me out. And anyway, she got an even better treat.'

A weak, but elated smile passes over Eve's lovely face and all doubt fades. Now she sees the truth: Richard had bought Cherry for her! She smiles at him, divinely relieved and he seems genuinely moved.

'Tomorrow,' Helen continues, 'you'll go into work and tender your resignation, both from your job and from your male identity. You will cite mental health problems. Samantha will provide you with a doctor's note giving you at least a month's sick leave. You shouldn't have to return to work. I will come and pick you up at noon, so you'd better have made sure you've seen the necessary people by then. We'll leave immediately and return to your house. Cherry and Richard will stay with you until the evening. I'm having a little gathering at my house and I want you there.'

Eve can only respond with a look of helpless, happy confusion. She nods without understanding why.

Cherry then steps forward.

'She's a little upset, so be gentle with her,' Helen instructs.

Cherry smiles a warm, sensual smile and her large brown eyes lock with Eve's reddened, tear-logged orbs. It is then that the anger and confusion are brushed aside by the ever present and fundamental force of desire.

Noticing Eve's sudden change of heart, Helen nods with satisfaction and then leaves the room. Eve is so entranced by the spectacle of Cherry, that she hardly notices the woman who has changed her life forever depart.

Cherry holds out a long, elegant hand and Eve takes it, noticing that her long nails are now painted a sparkling silver.

'Come on, let's get you home.'

Cherry leads Eve from the room, over to Richard. He stands aside and whispers a teasing 'Enjoy yourself' before she is taken down the stairs and into the shadowy hallway that leads to the entrance.

Cherry takes a black leather sports bag from the reception table before they mince together down the hallway, down the damp alleyway and out into a cold, surprisingly clear night. It is now the early hours of the morning and the streets are deserted. Cherry, still holding Eve's hand, leads her quickly down a side street. And it is only as the sound of their heels ringing against hard concrete begins to echo loudly down the street, that Eve remembers she is still wearing the waitress costume. Yet she has little time to feel embarrassed; indeed, her primary feeling is one of sudden and intense cold, a fact made very clear by the plumes of steam that are flowing from their mouths as their breath quickens.

Eventually, Cherry totters to a halt by a small, red Nissan car. She opens the passenger door and tells Eve to get in. Eve obeys with enthusiasm, driven forward by the bitter cold and her desire for Cherry. Inside the car it is colder than outside and Cherry starts the motor with shaking hands.

'It's bloody cold!' she cries, a loud and desperate statement of the obvious.

She rubs her hands together and turns to face Eve.

'Cuddle me!' she suddenly snaps. 'It's the quickest way to warm up!'

Eve hesitates and then leans forward into Cherry's outstretched arms. Within seconds they are bound tightly together in more than a pragmatic means of warming each other. Indeed, as Cherry's large, soft bosom presses against Eve's own artificial chest, she quickly loses all self-control and seeks out Cherry's full, cherry lips with her own.

The kiss is long and hard. Their tongues quickly lock and the embrace collapses into a mutual fondling that discovers one simple, terrible truth: the restrainers they both now wear.

Eve's eyes fill with sudden, frustration-ridden sadness. Cherry senses Eve's despair and smiles weakly.

'Don't worry ... I've been told to look after you tonight, so I think we can dispense with the restrainers for a few hours.'

Eve looks at Cherry with a terrible, helpless gratitude. 'Really ... you can do that?'

'With a little KY jelly and some fortitude on your part, yes. The rings are very hard to get off when you're hard. But not impossible.'

They continue to kiss and cuddle for a few more minutes before Eve begs Cherry to take her home.

As they drive through the deserted streets, Cherry allows Eve to retain a hand on her fishnetted thigh.

'Did you enjoy Ms March?' Cherry eventually asks, her voice cut through with passion and need. 'You really smell of her sex.'

Eve blushes, but Cherry reassures her instantly. 'Oh don't worry ... it turns me on something rotten.'

Eve confesses the pleasure she took in servicing Ms March. She also confesses her fascination with the gorgeous, powerful woman.

'She's a real love,' Cherry continues. 'Very gentle. Very maternal. She likes to spank now and again and to dress you up like a little girl, but never violence or any nastiness. Always with this motherly love. Yeah, that's her big thing – the gentle mummy. One or two of the sisters don't like that. But I love it. And I think you will too.'

The thought fills Eve with genuine excitement and adds to her desperate need for some form of relief.

'What about Richard?'

Cherry's eyes darken. 'He'll find some way to keep himself entertained.'

'You don't seem to like him.'

She nods slightly. 'I used to like him a lot. And I thought he liked me. But what he really likes is playing games. It took me a while to figure that out.'

Eve feels a sudden, harsh pang of guilt. 'You mean he and you . . .'

'Yes. But a while before you came along. I'm really old news as far as he's concerned.'

She ponders the confusing pictures of Richard that her mind is painting.

'Take me home, *please*.'

Cherry smiles sympathetically and within a few minutes the car pulls into Eve's driveway.

Eve lets them into the house and within seconds of entering the living room, they are locked in a passionate embrace and covering each other in hungry, hard kisses. Eve gasps with desire as Cherry turns her back on the lovely she-male and asks her to unzip the striking dress. Eve's eyes widen and, with shaking hands and a pounding heart, she slowly lowers the zip down the elegant curve of Cherry's spinal column. Then the striking, dusky beauty turns back to face Eve, her gorgeous eyes gleaming with need, and slowly slips the dress over her shoulders. As it falls down her body and on to the floor, Eve lets out a moan of shocked pleasure. For Cherry is dressed in the most splendidly teasing and erotic of undies. A semi-transparent red silk bra holds her two large, expertly engineered breasts with long, hard nipples that threaten to tear through the delicate fabric. Her waist is sealed tightly in a red satin-panelled, boned mini-corset. A red, elastane-panelled panty girdle and red silk panties fill the gap between the corset and her long legs. The girdle's taut, perfectly flat surface suggests a real girl and for a moment a look of real surprise fills Eve's already startled eyes.

'Don't worry, Eve. It's tucked away nice and neatly.'

Eve smiles with embarrassment at Cherry, her eyes studying the way her fishnet-sheathed legs flow perfectly from the panty girdle down to the silk-enwrapped shoes.

'God, you're gorgeous,' Eve whispers, her head spinning with a breath-squeezing desire.

Cherry nods, as if Eve has made a statement of the obvious, and then slowly unclips her bra. Her teasing smile widens as she holds the unsupported bra-cups over her generous bosom, her eyes filled with daring intent.

'Oh please, Cherry. Please let me see again.'

Cherry laughs and then lets the cups go. Eve gasps as the flawless orbs are fully revealed.

Eve leans forward and places a soft, nervous kiss on Cherry's left breast. Cherry moans and unleashes a tiny squeal of pleasure. Eve then covers both breasts in girlish kisses and poor Cherry is soon a writhing wreck.

'Let's go up to your bedroom,' she manages to say, before pushing Eve gently away. 'Then I can help you get to sleep.'

'Sleep? I don't want to sleep. I want *you*.'

'It's nearly two-thirty a.m., Eve. You have to be up early. Remember you have a lot to do at work tomorrow.'

Eve is shaken from her heated ministrations and nods slowly, contemplating the morning with a sobering sense of dread, which is quickly dispelled when Cherry takes Eve by the hand and leads her from the room. Eve provides directions and soon the two gorgeous she-males are in her bedroom.

'Get undressed for me,' Cherry says. 'Everything ... right down to the restrainer.'

Cherry has brought the sports bag with her and dumps it on the bed. As Eve nervously undresses, Cherry inspects the room, complimenting Eve on her taste and on the intricacy of her imagination.

As she undresses (and fighting her way out of the waitress costume is not easy), her eyes remain pinned to Cherry's extraordinary breasts; her cock screams for release from the brutal prison of the restrainer and the cock rings.

Cherry returns to the bed and watches Eve finally slip out of the basque, then kick off the stunning stilettos and wiggle out of her tights and panties.

'Leave the gloves on,' Cherry says.

Eve obeys and faces the beautiful she-male, her rubber-and-steel-imprisoned cock straining angrily, her eyes filled with a painfully deep need.

'Sit down on the bed.'

Again, Eve obeys. As she does so, she knows that her physical image is now at its most exposed and, perhaps, problematic. Cherry rests her hands on Eve's shoulders and then gently guides her down on to her back. As her warm skin touches the smooth, cool silk bed sheets, she sighs with pleasure, a pleasure considerably enhanced as Cherry's breasts rest on her own, disappointingly flat chest.

Cherry lowers her face to Eve's and they kiss – soft, delicate, careful at first, and then hard, even brutal, mouths mashed together in harsh need. Eve screams into this inescapable flesh-gag as her cock presses against the front of Cherry's tight, all-encompassing panty girdle and she feels the hard, tormented length of her lover's own tightly imprisoned cock.

Eventually, Cherry pulls herself from Eve and sits up. She runs a cruel, teasing finger over Eve's tormented cock and Eve screams her terrible, inescapable frustration.

'You want to come so very badly,' Cherry whispers, her voice full of sadistic pleasure. 'There is nothing now but that fundamental urge. Your self has disappeared inside it completely. You've been truly consumed by desire.'

Cherry removes her finger and Eve gives her a terribly angry, outraged glare.

'Yep, you're angry with me. And so you should be, my pretty little flower. But anger never solved anything. You should know that by now.'

As Eve writhes on the bed, Cherry takes a tube of KY jelly from the bag and squirts a coil of the perfectly clear substance into the palm of her left hand. She then scoops a globular ball of the jelly on to her right index finger.

'Open your legs.'

Eve looks at her with pained, confused eyes.

'Now.'

The firmness in Cherry's voice is sudden and shocking and Eve obeys without question.

'Wider.'

Again, Eve obeys, knowing Richard has already paved the way for this erotic intrusion. Then, without further warning, she slips her index finger deep into Eve's backside, inspiring an instant squeal of pleasure. Eve instinctively tries to sit up, but Cherry places a surprisingly strong hand on Eve's chest, holds her firmly in position and pushes her finger further into Eve's most intimate region.

'Please,' Eve cries, tears now welling up in her beautiful sky-blue eyes. 'Oh, please . . .'

Cherry continues to work her finger inside Eve, driving her quite insane. And, within a few seconds, Eve's struggles lessen and her cries soften into longer moans. A look of surprise replaces the look of pain and fear and a knowing smile lights up Cherry's beautiful face.

'Richard told me it would be another week before you could be properly fucked,' she whispers. 'But I think we can probably bring that timetable forward a little.'

Eve looks up at Cherry and nods weakly. Yes, please, she thinks. With you, my dark-eyed beauty. Then Cherry presses a little harder and a kittenish meow of pleasure slips from Eve's cherry-red and very moist lips. Cherry stops pushing and begins very carefully to grease the walls of Eve's anus, a terribly arousing caress that adds new, tormenting pleasure and leaves her rigid penis protesting in a hard agony against its fiendish restraint.

After a few minutes of this infuriatingly exciting caress, Cherry gently extracts her finger and then smothers her hand in more of the gel. Then, as Eve watches with wide, desperate eyes, the beautiful she-male begins to cover her rubber-and-steel-encased cock in a thick, clear film. Eve begins to buck and squeal. Cherry is once again forced to restrain Eve.

'Lubrication is the key to getting the rings off,' she says. 'So try to keep still.'

Eve nods, gasping with pleasure, trying to control herself. Soon her cock is a glistening totem of helpless she-male need. Cherry takes the ring beneath the cock's bulging head and begins to work it gently upward. To do this, she must squash the edges of the head down and try to manoeuvre the ring over it. This is immediately very uncomfortable and quickly painful. Tears well up in Eve's big blue eyes and her gasps of pleasure become cries of pain, the two soon merging into another ambivalent middle space. Then there is a sudden give and the ring is free. Eve gasps with a furious relief. Yet her suffering is not over. As soon as the first ring is removed, there is the challenge of the second, a challenge Cherry is more than happy to meet. The second ring, fixed tightly to the base of the shaft, is eased free with relatively little discomfort, but then there is the same dreadful problem of manipulating it over the fat, angry head, and the same pain. But, after some more careful efforts, the ring is freed, and Eve is genuinely free of their wicked, cruel and relentless grip.

It is then a simple – and arousing matter – for Cherry to slip her long-nailed fingers under the thin rim of the rubber restrainer and ease it over Eve's bulging, aching balls and up the hot, hard length of her cock. And as Cherry slips the tight rubber glove off the head, Eve cries out her thanks and the released organ expands visibly, preparing, as always, for final, spectacular release.

Smiling coyly, Cherry then takes another handful of gel and begins to massage her own enflamed and still restrained weapon of desire. Poor Eve is left to wiggle and squeal and beg for release.

'Don't you dare come!' Cherry snaps, as she begins, with watering eyes, to work off her own restrainer. 'I'll spank your arse red raw if you do.'

This threat only serves to excite the beautiful she-male even more, and seeing that she is beginning to lose control, Cherry quickly leans forward and flips Eve over on to her stomach. Cherry gasps as she pulls the rings free and very quickly peels away the restrainer. Then she places her hands on the back of Eve's upper thighs and gently eases them apart.

Eve feels the gel-coated tip of Cherry's cock touch the edge of her arsehole and squeals with surprise and more than a little fear.

'Don't worry, Eve – I'll be gentle.'

And she is. Slowly, but surely, she eases her hard, slick sex inside Eve's back passage, a careful, ultra-erotic invasion that leaves Eve screaming with a new, terrible and blinding pleasure.

Cherry establishes a relaxed, regular rhythm and wiggles deep inside her prone, furiously aroused lover. Eve feels as if she is being split in two and fused back together again. This is nothing like the precise teasing of Richard's vibrator. This is an intimate and profound plundering of her very soul, and the pleasure it brings her is a dark revelation of the beauty of true she-male love. And as she cries her deep, deep pleasure out across the room, she realises this is the loss of her virginity, the first penetration.

Then Cherry comes, erupting her hot, thick cum into Eve's arse with a scream so very clearly the scream of a man, a vast, deep animal growl that shatters all illusions and pretence. There is at the heart of Cherry, as with all TVs, the truth of biological identity. As her body is beset by the seismic shudders of sex-quake orgasm, a dark biological truth inescapably makes itself known. Cherry screams her acknowledgement of this fact with a burst of serrated obscenities. Her body almost rises off the bed and nearly takes Eve with it!

Then, there is a gradual decline in the violence. A few aftershock ripples course through Cherry's buxom form, but the fundamental explosion is over. After a few more minutes, there is only the sound of Cherry's rapid breathing.

Cherry then releases her grip on Eve's thighs and sits back, a stunned smile on her face. She flips Eve on to her back and stares down hungrily at her hard, long cock.

'Feeling better?'

Eve smiles, stunned, her arse aflame, her desire at its most unbearable, her need absolute.

'That was amazing. I never knew . . .'

Cherry laughs, her large, perfect tits bouncing before her with the enthusiasm of absolute satisfaction.

'That's only the beginning, my love.'

She leans forward, resting her hands on the bed, and takes Eve's aching sex in her mouth. With her expert lips and tongue, she teases the lovely, shocked she-male to a quick and suitably fierce orgasm. And as Eve explodes, she knows this is Cherry's most intimate and simple gift, and also the purest expression of her truly feminine nature. In the height of this most natural of human pleasures, their eyes meet and there is a second of devastating realisation: they are lovers and they are, surely, in love.

11

A Goodbye

Eve is gently shaken from a dreamless sleep four hours later by a somewhat bleary-eyed and very tired Cherry.

'Come, sweetness, time for your big day.'

As consciousness is regained, Eve notices that Cherry is fully dressed and made up. Her strong, sensual rosewood perfume acts as an erotic smelling salt and Eve quickly becomes aware that she is – once again – violently erect.

'Oh God,' she mumbles. 'I'm so hard all the time now.'

Cherry smiles and then holds the rubber restrainer before her face. 'That's why you need this.'

Before Eve can say another word, Cherry throws back the bed sheets, and begins to work the restrainer over her massively engorged and tormented flesh. Eve is once again reduced to squealing like a baby as the fiendish rubber device is pulled very tightly and inescapably into position. Then, with the aid of more KY jelly, the cock rings are slid painfully back into position.

'Get a shower, then we'll get you ready for work.'

Tears of discomfort trickling down her pale cheeks, Eve nods and, with Cherry's assistance, manages to pull herself out of the bed.

She staggers into the shower feeling totally disconnected from reality. The sudden explosion of hot water against her head is like a brutal, reviving blow. The glass of exhaustion is shattered into a million pieces and she cries out with purifying shock.

By the time she returns to the bedroom, she is feeling considerably better and Cherry has set out her clothes for the morning ahead.

Eve is wrapped in a thick pink towel. The smell of scented soap and talcum powder fills the room, and as Eve stares down at the bed, Cherry steps forward and presses her hand softly against the tell-tale bulge raising from the bottom of the towel.

Eve moans and they embrace. After a long, passionate, almost painful kiss, Cherry returns Eve's attention to the bed.

'You'll wear suitably feminine undies beneath the suit today, Eve. Helen's instructions. You will be expected to have sorted out your resignation by midday. Helen will pick you up personally at noon from the office and bring you back here.'

Eve accepts these instructions with a sense of helpless resignation, then slips into a pair of black nylon tights and a white silk teddy. A heavily frilled pair of white silk panties adds the final touch of ultra-femininity. Without the body-shaper, she feels surprisingly exposed. Now, she is most certainly a male in female clothes, a clear and strange paradox. She thinks of the promised physical transformation, the gifts of the Crème de la Crème. Then she thinks of their price and feels a deeply ambivalent quiver of arousal.

Chanel No. 5 is applied in generous quantities to her neck, chest and shoulders and then she is presented with one of Adam's simple, black cotton suits, a white cotton shirt and a red silk tie.

She dresses with an increasing sense of inner disturbance. She feels trapped and exposed. Yet also masochistically excited. Now, more than ever, she is held tightly in the silken embrace of Helen. Now, more than ever, she is being forced to accept a fate that is both completely out of her control and also a perfect expression of her true, long-hidden self.

Despite having dressed like this on many previous occasions, the suit feels distinctly odd when placed over the

188

soft, constantly caressing feminine underwear. The trousers particularly emphasise the terribly erotic reality of the lovely, ultra-sheer hose, each step now a reminder of a pulsating, unbearably exciting sexual static.

'I feel so strange,' she whispers to a fascinated and clearly stirred Cherry. 'And I don't really know why.'

'You look really sexy,' Cherry says. 'Like a woman dressed as a man.'

Circles within circles. The ambivalent whirlpool of identity, the whirlpool that has sucked Eve into this strange, erotic adventure of final and irreversible transformation.

Cherry tells Eve to slip her black nylon-wrapped feet into a pair of Adam's black leather work shoes. She then sits on the bed and rather awkwardly attempts to tie their narrow black laces.

'I'm sorry,' she mumbles, clearly struggling. 'I can't do this any more.'

Cherry smiles sympathetically, kneels down before a helpless Eve become Adam and begins to tie her shoes.

'You really can't pretend any more, my love. The truth has overwhelmed you, I'm afraid. The moment you applied to join us, you knew that. And that's why you've given yourself completely to the Elect. That's why you must see this final change through to the amazing end.'

Eve nods, knowing that every word is true. Cherry finishes tying the shoes and then rises to her feet.

'There,' she teases. 'All ready for work.'

She takes Eve by the hand and leads her to the full-length wardrobe mirror. Here, the gorgeous she-male finds herself confronting a shocking and disturbing image. Before her is Adam. The male persona. The external face of Eve for twenty-eight years. A face she no longer recognises.

'Maybe this will be the last time you will confront him,' Cherry says, standing by Eve's side.

Eve looks at her male self and then at Cherry. As she does so, she becomes aware of the contrast and its meaning: my male self and my female self. And me? I am always somewhere in between. Yet what is perhaps most interesting about the image Eve 'confronts' is that, even in this male form, Eve is obvious. Before, it had been a relatively simple process to disguise her true, secret self beneath the trappings of formal male attire. But now, every movement, every gesture has become Eve's; now, she cannot escape the fundamental reality of Eve's revealed and powerful presence. The change is immediate, clear and quite remarkable.

Cherry leads her from the bedroom down to the kitchen. As she walks, her male clothes rub against the feminine frillies beneath and she is both aroused and embarrassed. Each step is a restatement of the absolute victory of Eve over Adam. Now she feels only uncomfortable when forced to become the vaguely defined male self that has served her as a pragmatic device of disguise for the last twenty years.

To Eve's surprise, Cherry has already prepared a breakfast of muesli and fruit juice.

'You must have been up all night,' Eve says.

The lovely, elegant she-male smiles. 'I managed to grab a few hours sleep on the sofa.'

After breakfast, they leave for Adam's office. Before dropping him outside the tall, glass-fronted building that houses the UK headquarters of the company, Cherry gives Eve a hard, passionate kiss and wishes her good luck. By this point, Eve's heart is beating with a nervous speed and a cool film of sweat is glistening on her forehead.

'Don't worry, Eve,' Cherry whispers. 'Everything will be fine. Just keep thinking about the future. About truly becoming your self. Think about what you've always secretly desired. And imagine that becoming a reality. A reality that begins today.'

Eve nods weakly and climbs from the car. Cherry waves, but Eve does not respond.

She rides the lift to the twelfth floor, her head spinning, her stomach turning.

She walks through the open-plan office that houses Adam's section, mumbling weak 'good mornings' to the virtually all-female staff. She looks at her secretary with a sense of utter despair and asks her if Adam can see the Managing Director before nine a.m. Adam's secretary, the handsome Angela, looks at Eve as if she is looking at a different person, which – of course – she is.

The MD agrees to see him for five minutes before the first meeting of the day. But this quickly becomes a twenty minute test of nerve when Eve as Adam announces her/his resignation. Adam tries to lie, to talk of stress and boredom, and then promises a full doctor's report. The MD is both furious and baffled, totally unconvinced by Adam's excuse of a nervous breakdown. And then, at the height of the heated discussion, Adam finally finds the courage to tell him the truth.

'It's not the work that's causing the stress. It's me. I don't want to be me any more. Me is a lie. It's been a lie since I was sixteen. I want to be the person I've always wanted to be. I want to be a woman, the woman I've been secretly for many years now.'

The MD's face freezes with a mixture of horror, disgust and utter disbelief. He then tells Adam to go back to his office, that they will meet later. That he is clearly unwell. That they can discuss special leave. To give him time to get over whatever it is that is upsetting him so much.

Adam nods and leaves without another word. He goes back down to his office and is quickly Eve again. She sits behind *his* desk. She stares into space for nearly an hour. Then she calls *his* secretary into the office and tells her everything. And, amazingly, she appears totally unsurprised. Indeed, her soft smile never falters once.

'I have to say,' she says eventually, 'I'm really not that surprised, Adam. You've always been a bit ... different. Most of the girls think you're gay.'

Eve smiles at this very typical response. Then she looks at Angela carefully, even coolly. She is in her mid-fifties, but without doubt an attractive woman. Eve has noticed this before, but has quite deliberately sought to detach Adam's professional life from anything to do with her desires or the truth of Eve. Before, when she had noticed what Angela wore, her rather prim, but always stylish attire, her impressively well-maintained physique, her obvious beauty, Eve had automatically deleted the inevitably sexual thoughts these observations inspired, a discipline she knew was the only way to survive, given her distinctly split consciousness.

Today Angela is wearing a knee-length tweed skirt and a matching jacket, beneath which is a high-neck silk blouse with a ruby centrepiece. Her tights are pearl grey and her shoes are three- or four-inch-heeled mules of gleaming black patent leather. Her hair, a slowly greying blonde, is bound in a tight bun by a simple wooden clasp. Her eyes are a light, limpid green and her lips are a thick strawberry. Eve feels her cock struggle with an almost surprised excitement in the restrainer and smiles ironically.

'It's been a real pleasure working with you, Angie.'

Her smile widens slightly. 'Thank you, Adam. I think I can say the same with some conviction.'

Eve laughs. Then the laugh fades and a darkness fills her slightly stunned gaze. 'Call me Eve. My name is Eve.'

Angela nods. 'OK. Eve.'

Angela then leaves Eve to her haunted speculations. She sits for a long time finally and fully contemplating what is about to happen. Driven by desire and a terrible need to experience the full reality of Eve, she has finally found the courage and conviction to be the person she has always secretly wanted to be. The person discovered by Aunt Debra. The person she had extracted from the torment of a repressed consciousness. A person that had been developed out of Eve's profound love for her aunt, a love that has survived the terrible fact of their long-term separation. A person she so desperately wished she could now reveal to Debra in person. This thought inspires a moment of genuine elation. Yes: as soon as she – Eve – is fully and properly changed, she will arrange a visit to America and Aunt Debra. But this elation is short-lived. She – Eve – the secret self made known – will require a passport, and thus – surely – a fully recognised social identity. It isn't just a matter of physically changing: it is a matter of a complete transformation of identity. And then she begins to realise the true cost of surrendering Adam so completely. Adam wasn't only a convenient social façade behind which to hide: he was a way into the machinery of modern existence. Without him, she will be both totally exposed and profoundly reliant on whatever infrastructure of identity the Crème de la Crème might decide to provide. This is surely the ultimate submission: the true and complete destruction of a personality. And Eve knows this is what they are demanding of her. To become Eve, she must utterly destroy the safety net that is Adam.

The sound of the phone ringing shakes her out of these rather gloomy considerations. She picks up the handset and is confronted by the soft, mildly ironic voice of Angela.

'Eve, a Ms Bliss is here to see you.'

Eve mumbles a nervous instruction to send her in.

A few seconds later, the door to Adam's office opens and the stunning, imperious and deeply intimidating Helen enters. Eve stares at her with a sense of absolute defeat and an intense and terrible need. As she stands to acknowledge the entrance, she realises Eve can only ever truly exist through the will of a woman, of a mistress, of a powerful female facilitator; a fact that excites her in a profound and absolute manner, a fact that brings a smile of helpless masochistic pleasure to her girlish face.

'I hear you found the courage to do what was necessary.'

Her words inspire a look of confusion and a slightly cruel smile crosses Helen's face.

'Angie told me all about it.'

It is then that Angela walks in behind Helen, her eyes beholding Eve with a calm, slightly detached look that betrays the same confidence and control Eve has seen in all the women associated with the Crème de la Crème.

'You knew . . . you . . .'

Eve's eyes dart angrily and nervously between the two women.

'Let's just say that Angie has been keeping an eye on you for us.'

Her mind races as she tries to grasp the meaning of Helen's words.

'We can talk about all this later,' Helen says. 'Now it's time for you to say goodbye to Adam and this little, meaningless office forever. Get that horrible suit off and put these on.'

Helen throws a sports bag down at Eve's feet. Eve looks down at it and then up at Helen.

'Hurry up!'

Her tone, filled with sharp, brutal power, is an electric sex charge that crashes through Eve's she-male soul. Instinctively she performs a tiny bob curtsey and Angela bursts out laughing. The smile on Helen's perfect lips is less cruel, but not mocking.

'This will be so easy,' she whispers and Angela nods, the older woman's eyes filled with dark amusement and erotic fascination.

Eve opens the bag. Inside she finds a white nylon sweater, a pair of black leather court shoes, and a black cotton micro-mini. There is also a pink rubber make-up bag.

With a sense of relief, Eve removes the shirt, tie and suit. As she undresses before Helen and Angela, her heart pounds and she ponders the disturbing truth of Angela's association with the Crème de la Crème.

Eve stands before Helen and Angela in the teddy, tights and panties. She is utterly exposed and deeply aroused. To be so intimately revealed before these two very beautiful women inspires a deep, intensely masochistic sexual pleasure.

She then slips into the sweater and micro-mini with a grace that has become, over the years, natural. Angela watches all of this with increasingly astonished and excited eyes.

'You're right,' she whispers to Helen. 'He ... she is absolutely gorgeous. The transformation is amazing.'

Helen smiles. 'This is nothing. Wait until she's all properly padded and wigged. She's by far the most physically convincing. She'll make us a fortune.'

Eventually, Eve is dressed in the soft, sexy feminine clothes and stands with her hands at her side before the women.

Helen steps forward and tells Eve to pull the chair out into the middle of the office. She is then ordered to sit on it and Helen carefully applies a surprisingly generous amount of make-up to her face, using a thick pale foundation, blusher, pale-blue eye-shadow and a thick, cherry-red lipstick to produce a look of doll-like glamour.

Helen steps back and admires her handiwork with a cruel, conspiratorial smile. She then takes two white pearl clip-on earrings from the make-up bag and attaches them to Eve's small, girlish ears.

'Perfect.'

Eve looks up at Helen with a sudden panic. 'But the wig,' she gasps. 'Where's the wig, and the padding?'

Helen snorts a dismissive contempt. 'It's important everyone knows the truth about Adam. You'll leave this office as Adam feminised. As Adam in the process of changing.'

Eve's eyes widen in sudden anger. 'No, please. Everyone will see! I look ridiculous. This is unnecessary!'

Angela steps forward. 'You look beautiful, Eve. A perfect representation of the ambiguity at the heart of transvestism. I want the other girls to see you as you really are: gorgeously feminine, yet incomplete.'

'No!' Eve cries. 'I won't do it!'

Helen laughs and suddenly takes Eve's face in her hands. 'Yes you will, Eve. You know you will. You know this is just Adam speaking. His last desperate attempt to protect himself. He knows the moment you step out of that door, Eve will be in complete control. Forever.'

There is a painful extended silence. Her sex is burning like a molten ember of desire inside the fiendish restrainer. She knows, even as she protests, that the thought of being exposed in this strange half-state excites her in almost exactly the same proportion as it appals and terrifies her. Then, she very slowly nods her agreement as tears of confused defeat and acceptance trickle over her pale-rose cheeks.

'Time to go,' Helen says.

She turns to Angela and smiles warmly. 'We'll see you at my place later.'

Angela nods, allows Helen to kiss her on the cheek, then helps Eve to her unsteady feet. 'Don't worry, princess. They'll love you.'

Angela's teasing words ring in her ears as she totters to the door in the high-heeled court shoes. Already the ultra-feminine walk of Eve has taken complete control. Yet the collision of the sense of Eve with the deliberate inadequacy of this transformation is jarring and disturbing. As she walks into the open-plan office area, she feels twenty sets of eyes turn on her, all female and all wide with a mixture of shock, malicious amusement and sadistic pleasure. Helen makes a point of addressing her as Adam and asks her to say goodbye to the 'ladies' as sweetly as possible. Yet despite this cruelty, and despite the ultra-humiliation she is being subjected to, there is a strange sense of theatre within Eve, a sense of the ultimate occasion. In the heat of her terrible exposure, she finds the same dangerous confidence that informed her first real public display of Eve. She knows she must look odd – a man, even a very pretty man, dressed and made up as a rather sluttish young woman, with no attempt to address issues of hairstyle and figure. But in this deliberate statement of falsification there is a motor for masochistic excitement, and it is this that drives her to perform a deep, dainty curtsey before Adam's staff, flashing her shapely, black nylon-enveloped thighs and frilled panties with an abandon that is suddenly and deeply arousing. The women's response is to clap and cheer, and to jeer. They mock Adam: their eyes burn into the spectacle of Adam feminised with a bitterness that is both shocking and – bizarrely – amusing. Eve adjusts her virtually non-existent skirt and follows a wildly amused Helen from the office. As they pass between the tables, she endures more verbal abuse and much slapping of her pretty, hosed and perfectly formed thighs and bottom.

Then, as if walking from a violent snowstorm into an empty room, they are in the lift, descending through the building, leaving the memory of Adam to fill the exaggerated stories of the disillusioned and embittered for years to come.

'You handled that very well, Eve. I'm very impressed.'

Eve remains silent.

'You have a particularly appropriate sense of occasion, my pretty sissy petal. That will serve you very well in your new role.'

They ride the lift to the basement car park. As Eve follows Helen across the large, shadow-infested underground, the sound of their heels crashes across an emptiness which seems to be as much inside Eve as inside the car park.

Once in the beautiful, expensive Mercedes, Eve cannot resist articulating the feeling coursing through her ambivalent form.

'I thought Eve was created. In the world. That I had finished the work of becoming when I came to you. But I haven't even started.'

Helen smiles and nods. 'You've started today.'

12

Secret Selves

They drive back to Eve's house. She tries to understand what has been happening, but Helen is coolly evasive.

'You know Angie?' she asks.

'Yes. I've known her for quite a while actually.'

'So she was planted. To watch me. Even before Crème de la Crème? But how would you . . . could you know that I would be contacting you?'

'Enough questions for now, Eve. Leave the questions until tonight. Things will become clearer then.'

'But . . .'

'Be quiet or you'll have to be gagged.'

She falls silent, aroused by Helen's domineering tone, but also deeply perplexed and disturbed by the fact that she seems to be the victim of an elaborate plot.

When they arrive back at the house, Richard and Cherry are waiting. Eve follows Helen into the living room to discover a bizarre and deeply sado-erotic image. Richard, dressed from head to foot in black, is standing over the prone form of Cherry. Poor, lovely Cherry is lying face down on the carpet. She is dressed in semi-opaque white nylon tights, bra and panties – and nothing else. Her arms have been lashed tightly behind her back at wrists and elbows with layers of white nylon cord. Her ankles and knees have been secured in exactly the same manner, and her ankles have in turn been tied tightly by means of another length of cording to her tethered wrists, thus leaving the beautiful she-male in a painful, rigid hog-tie. A thick strip of white duct tape has been stretched over her lips and, judging from her desperately bulging cheeks, is holding in place a particularly fat and testing gag.

Eve looks down at Cherry's gorgeous, bound form. The black beauty looks up at her with wide, sex-starved eyes, and Eve realises she is enjoying every second of her intricate, deeply kinky bondage.

'Get Eve ready. We need to be at the club by two p.m.'

Richard nods, acknowledging Helen's terse order.

He turns dark, hard eyes on Eve and she feels a quiver of masochistic pleasure.

'Strip down to your undies,' he orders, his voice filled with a terrible masculine power that makes her feel deliciously helpless and possessed.

Helen leaves the room and Eve hears her march upstairs. She begins to undress once more, pondering what this beautiful, powerful woman is planning.

Eve removes the sweater, skirt and high heels and stands before him, hands at her side, her tightly restrained cock bulging desperately through the teddy and the panties.

'It's not only your cock that needs to understand the meaning of restraint, my pretty little sissy pet,' he says, his voice filled with a new authority. 'Bondage will be a key part of your training as a member of the Crème de la Crème Elect. Put your arms behind your back and cross your wrists.'

Eve looks at him with a mixture of genuine fear and helpless sexual excitement. Again she looks down at Cherry and the thought she is about to share her fate inspires a dreadful sense of masochistic elation.

At the foot of the sofa is another black sports bag. From inside, Richard extracts the lengths of cord that are to secure her delicate she-male form. She squirms with a terrible pleasure as he winds the first length tightly around her crossed wrists, forcing her shoulders back and pushing her perfectly flat chest forward. He secures the cord with a tight, unyielding knot and then, using a second length of the cording, binds her elbows together in a tight, painful cinch that inspires a gasp of shock.

'Please,' she pleads, her voice weak, feminine, 'it's hurting.'

Richard laughs and pulls the cinch tighter, then secures it with another fat, inescapable knot.

Cherry watches Eve's developing bondage with heavily aroused eyes. Eve hears Cherry's muffled moans of delight as her bondage progresses and knows she will very soon be joining Cherry on the floor, a thought that fills her with a powerful joy.

Once her elbows are secured, Richard spends some time enjoying her ambiguous she-male form. She squeals with pleasure as he begins very gently to caress her bottom through the silk panties, teddy and tights. His hand slips between her buttocks and fingers press against her anus. Her squeals become deep moans of fierce pleasure and her wrists strain uselessly against the cording that secures them so very tightly together.

'I'll be out for about three or four hours. Then I'll be back to enjoy you, my pretty trannie slut,' he whispers.

Eve moans with desperation, begging him to begin his no doubt deeply perverse ravishment much sooner.

But no: she is to be tightly tied, gagged and left for the rest of the afternoon with the gorgeous Cherry.

He binds her ankles and legs just below and above her knees. Then he orders her to kneel down. From the sports bag he extracts a pair of black silk panties.

'A little present from Ms March, to remind you of the challenges to come.'

He carefully rolls up the panties into a ball, so that the gusset area is fully exposed. He orders her to 'open wide' and then stuffs the panties deep into her mouth. Eve gasps and gags and immediately tastes the sweet flavour of Ms March's sex: she is being gagged with her still warm, freshly soiled panties.

More white duct tape is used to hold the panties firmly in place. Eve's eyes widen with a fierce masochistic joy as he stretches the thick strip of tape across her dark strawberry lips and then uses the flat of his hand to press the tape tightly in place. She squeals and moans and he laughs. Her eyes plead in bad faith for an impossible release. His response is to lower her on to my stomach and set to work on the hog-tie.

He attaches a longer length of the cord to the cord tightly securing her ankles together and then attaches the free end to the cord binding her wrists. As he does so, he pulls her ankles up so that they are within a few inches of her wrists and leaves her bound in a painfully tight and deeply exciting hog-tie. She has never felt so absolutely helpless, so utterly in the power of another person. A definite sense of sado-erotic submission binds her soul as tightly as these fiendish, expertly secured ropes bind her body. She squeals into the fat, pungent gag with a supremely ambiguous mixture of pain and pleasure. She wiggles her pantied bottom with girlish trepidation framed by helpless and savage desire. She delights in this act of distress, this classic performance of femininity tethered and teased. She roles on to her side so that Richard can see her violently erect and painfully restrained cock. He laughs at this desperate display, kneels down and begins gently to tease her imprisoned member with long, elegant hands.

'You really are a little tart,' he whispers. 'I'm going to enjoy taming you.'

She widens her eyes, nods furiously and squeals her desire: how much she is looking forward to being tamed!

He rolls Eve on to her right side and she finds herself facing Cherry, the she-male with whom she has developed the deepest emotional attachment. Cherry looks at Eve and moans her need into her own very fat gag. Her dark-brown eyes fill with a helpless love and her squeals become sissy mews of adoration.

Helen returns from her mysterious investigation a few minutes later and she and Richard leave without another word. Cherry and Eve are left hog-tied and helpless, wiggling and moaning with a deep sexual arousal. Eve looks down at Cherry's panties and sees the huge, hard length of her sex strain against the shimmering silk material. Their eyes meet again and exchange a look of mutual intoxication. Yes: they are both drunk on a powerful potion of masochistic desire. They strain with wild abandon against their bonds, knowing that if they were to break free, they would be bitterly disappointed. The sense of absolute and precise constriction is over-whelmingly sexual. Yet the possibility of their bonds loosening is virtually zero: Richard is a true rope expert and they are truly and wonderfully immobilised.

Cherry manages to wiggle a little closer to Eve, and as she does so, her brassiere loosens slightly and one of her large, milk-chocolate-coloured breasts pops out of its pretty silk prison. Eve squeals with sissy pleasure at this hyper-erotic spectacle and Cherry's eyes widen with her own furious excitement. She moves close enough for Eve to wriggle her body into a position where their restrained cocks can touch and she can press her exposed breast against Eve's silk-sheathed chest. And this is where they stay, helpless and ecstatic for the next three hours, lost in a mutable sado-masochistic arousal built around a terribly dark and immediate intimacy, and also a very terrible frustration. As their tightly restrained cocks rub through nylon, silk, rubber and steel, they are, despite their exciting closeness, very far apart. Yet this frustration of true desire only adds to the pleasure the bondage ordeal brings. Communicating only with helpless looks of brutal she-male need, they are lost in a brilliant universe of ultimate and extended submission, willing damsels in distress.

During this splendid ordeal, Eve finds time to reconsider the strangeness of the events of the past few hours, and the more she ponders, the more certain she is that there is some unseen force behind what has happened to her, a force that spans more than the last seven days. Angela made that fact very clear.

Richard returns after more than three hours, by which time they are both very tired and terribly aroused. Yet, for the first half-hour he does nothing. It is dark and he flicks on the living-room light. They squeal into their fat gags and he steps over them with a deliberate indifference. He goes into the kitchen and makes a call on his mobile phone. His voice is inaudible and they can only stare at each other with longing and confusion and wiggle with melodramatic delight in their sissy bondage.

Eventually he returns and begins, Eve thinks, to untie her. But all he actually does is free the cord securing the hog-tie. Then, to Eve's amazement and horror, he slips his hard, powerful arms beneath her armpits and pulls her to her feet. She sways precariously before him and he smiles with real affection. Then he picks her up and in one shockingly powerful move throws her over his shoulder. She squeals with a melodramatic fear and a dark, dark pleasure and he slaps her pantied behind, a quick, stinging blow that is genuinely painful.

'Be quiet,' he snaps, and, her bottom stinging, her heart beating with an almost crazed excitement, she obeys.

Then she is carried from the room and upstairs to her bedroom. Here, she is flung on to the bed, a terrifying experience that leaves her squealing with something approaching a genuine outrage.

He ignores her protests, protests that try, with little conviction, to communicate that he has gone too far. Then she notices that the sinister, apparently bottomless, black sports bag has been placed at the end of the bed.

He sits down and begins to search through the bag's strange, worrying contents.

'I trust you found Cherry's company pleasant,' he says, his tone one of regal contempt. 'She certainly likes you. Which is actually very helpful, as Helen wants her to play a crucial part in your education.'

Then, to Eve's genuine horror, he extracts from the bag what looks like a pink rubber dildo. He turns and crawls across the bed to where she is lying, helpless, wide-eyed with real, heart-stilling fear.

He holds the dildo directly before her eyes and she manages a low, desperate moan.

'Say hello to the plug. You'll wear it permanently as part of your training. Except, of course, when you're being fucked. It's not that big, really. It's certainly not as big as Cherry's cock.'

Slowly, carefully, he unties her, but leaves the gag in place. Then he grabs her waist and turns her on to her stomach. She squeals and wiggles. He slaps her silk-pantied bottom hard two more times and she feels her rock-hard, rubber-sealed sex press angrily into her stomach as he pulls her up on to her knees and forces her head down, so that her bottom is jutting upward helplessly before him. In one swift tug, he pulls down the panties. He then gently slips his free hand between her legs and frees the crotch clips that hold the teddy in place. Once these are removed, he pulls the crotch area of the teddy out and rolls the rear section up over her back, thus exposing her black nylon-sealed bottom to full view and his no doubt perverse attentions.

The tights are hauled down over her backside with a speed that betrays an impatient desire. His need is also apparent in his increasingly laboured and desperate breathing.

Then she feels his finger begin to work inside her, just like before, but harder, crueller.

'Cherry told me about last night. I know I don't have to do this, but I want you to know I can.'

She squeals a confession of helpless pleasure as Richard works his finger deep inside her. He laughs and slaps her desperately wiggling backside again, inspiring an even greater pleasure. Again, she is overwhelmed by a dizzying sensation of sweet feminine submission and she knows she can never ever return to the drab, bleak universe of Adam.

Then the finger is being pulled out, slowly, teasingly, even gently. She gasps with a dreadful, mind-bending pleasure that inspires a grunt of dark satisfaction from Richard.

'This is only the beginning, my little sissy slut,' he says, his voice now filled with an aggressive, determined desire.

There is a strange, unsettling pause – a moment of erotic suspension. She can feel the sex electricity crackling in the air around her, feeding on anticipation and frustration. And then suddenly, and with some force, the tip of the dildo is being pushed against the edge of her anus and

204

worked inside. Very quickly she is moaning through the fat, inescapable gag, locked in the grip of a deeply ambivalent pleasure which is always only seconds away from becoming pain.

She squeals and writhes. Richard grips her waist with his free hand and holds her firm as he completes this deeply erotic insertion. Then there is a sudden give, as if a barrier has been broken, and the dildo appears to be lodged firmly and inescapably inside her. She gasps with shock. She feels filled to bursting point, yet also oddly comfortable. Richard releases his grip and allows her to sit up. As she lowers her buttocks on to the silk sheets of the bed, she feels the dildo press deeper into her and she moans with helpless, electric pleasure. Her tightly restrained cock rears up before her, its pink rubber-sealed head bulging with a vast animal frustration.

Richard helps her off the bed and, in one rough tug, pulls the tape from her mouth and extracts the damp, pungent panties. Then he tells her to undress.

'Ms March has sent you a special costume for the party.'

He points towards the wardrobe doors. As she adjusts to the constant teasing of the dildo, as she adds its weight to her own being, as she begins to feel the heightened sense of absolute femininity its presence imparts, her eyes fall upon a startling homage to ultra-sissified femininity. Hanging from one of the bronze door handles is a dress, a dress she now realises was delivered by Helen earlier in the day. She sighs with pleasure and steps towards this shockingly fetishistic masterpiece. And as she takes that first dainty step, she feels the plug move inside her, and as it moves it caresses her anus, and the sigh turns into a helpless cry of sex joy, of pure pleasure.

'Oh my God,' she whispers, turning to look at Richard with wide, stunned eyes.

'Don't worry, you'll get used to the impact. After a while, you'll come to terms with the fact that to walk is to be teased.'

She nods weakly and turns her attentions back to the wondrous dress.

The dress is made from a hot pink satin. An adult version of a little girl's party dress, with a very high, button-up and heavily frilled neck. The bodice area is covered in a truly beautiful pattern of carefully embroidered white silk roses, and the wide, ruffled skirt supports an explosion of multi-layered frou-frou petticoating of alternating white and pink. The long sleeves are puffed spectacularly at the shoulders and frilled sleeves, and there is a thick pink ribbon belt around the waist tied at the back in a huge, flowery bow.

Eve stares at the dress in awe, her lips parted into a cherry circle of astonishment and desire.

'Put it on,' Richard orders, 'and the other stuff on the table.'

On the dressing table are a pile of equally dainty and lovely undies: a pair of white nylon tights covered in hundreds of sparkling silver stars, a pair of heavily frilled white silk panties and a white rubber mini-corset. At the foot of the table are a pair of white patent ankle boots with pink silk-ribbon laces and striking six-inch stiletto heels. And then there is the wig: a beautiful concoction of strawberry-blonde ringlet-style curls, a vast homage to the sweet delights of ultra-sissification.

Still divinely tormented by the perverse and constant caress of the dildo, she struggles out of the remaining underwear and soon stands naked before the dress, stunned, elated, stilled by a heart-stopping fascination and an animal craving that seems to have frozen her consciousness in a state of pure arousal.

Richard snaps an impatient 'Hurry up', his dark eyes feeding on Eve's freshly revealed and disturbingly male form. She sees him looking at her cock, at her arse, at her shallow, flat chest, and she sees something else in him: an obvious, but no less surprising homosexuality. She smiles at him and turns to the dressing table. She looks down at the underwear and then asks him why there is no bra or body-shaper – something to give her the illusion of the chest that Samantha's kinky genius promises.

'Ms March wants you to look like a little girl, Eve. Not

a pretty, busty she-male. In a way, there's a certain irony here that I'm sure you can appreciate.'

She nods, disappointed in one way, but also darkly amused and aroused in another. After everything she has done, after all the work that has gone into the illusion of Eve and thus made her the prime possession of the Crème de la Crème Elect, the first client wants her to look like nothing else than a pretty boy in petticoats.

She slips into the tights, which are almost unbearably soft, and turn her long legs into sparkling, erotic jewels. Richard's eyes betray his increasing sexual excitement. Once again the power dynamic is shifting. Now Eve controls the desire. And that means she is – inevitably – in charge. For the time being.

After the tights, she steps into the silk panties, with their hooped layers of thick frills, extremely, excessively feminine. As she pulls them up her freshly hosed legs, she knows she is performing an erotic dance for her master, a teasing inversion of the striptease that is both the creation of an illusion and its destruction. As the thicker, elasticated edge of the panties traverse the rigid outline of her cock, she watches his mouth open slightly and a glaze of helpless need cover his eyes.

After the panties, she takes up the rubber mini-corset. Richard climbs from the bed and walks over.

'I think you'll need a hand with this.'

He takes the corset from her and tells her to turn around. As she does so, she feels his hot hands wrap around her narrow waist and his lips brush against her neck. She moans with deep sensual pleasure and falls willingly into his embrace.

Then, trapped in his arms, he carefully slips the corset around her waist. She sighs with delight as he begins to pull the two sides of the corset together, as they press against her lower torso and erotically constrict her waist.

He binds the corset in place and turns her round. She faces him with wide, desire-streaked eyes. He leans down and kisses her, a kiss she accepts with a desperate surrender. Her knees turn to jelly. Her hard, tormented sex presses into his thigh.

'Take me,' Eve whispers, 'please take me.'

His hungry smile widens. 'Soon, my sissy petal. But not now. We have a very special party to attend, and if you don't hurry up, we'll be late.'

She nods, disappointed, but also sure he is right. She sits down on the dressing table stool and feels the plug sink deeper into her arsehole. She moans helplessly and leans forward to put on the striking white boots. Then she is back on her feet, mincing across the room to the dress, the boots inspiring the most feminine of walks via sweet sissy totters and an outrageously erotic wiggling of her pert bottom, a wiggle which captures Richard's gaze and refuses to let it go.

She takes the dress from the hanger and holds it against her body. Instead of a zipper, it has a line of white pearl buttons that run from the neck down to the edge of the billowing skirt. She slowly releases the buttons and pulls this grand, beauteous creation open. Then she takes a nervous, excited step into the unknown, a step into the dress's quivering ocean of frou-frou petticoating and a step into a new stage in the story of Eve. She pulls the dress up her sparkling, hosed legs and then over her waist. Eventually, she manages to wiggle the dress up the rest of her body and over her shoulders.

'Help me,' she whispers, overcome by the sissy beauty and softness of the dress.

Richard steps forward and buttons up the rear of the dress. The bodice section tightens around her already tightly constricted waist and against her perfectly flat chest. She turns to face him again and his eyes say all there is to know.

Eve wiggles back over to the dressing table and applies a blood-red lipstick to her pale lips. She uses a powder puff to add a touch of colour to her exhaustion-drained cheeks. Then she takes the wig from its stand and carefully slips it over her head. As she pulls it into position, Eve notices that Richard is again fiddling about in the sports bag, but she is more interested in her reflection. So she totters back to the wardrobe and the full-size, built-in mirror.

She stares at the reflection with something approaching genuine elation. Without the carefully constructed and generous bust provided by the body-shaper, there is a strange, yet beautiful androgyny at the heart of Eve, a perfect, clear expression of the swirling ambivalence that has always been at the very core of the true she-male being. I am not whole, she thinks, but I am. In this erotically sissifed state she is pure enforced femininity accepted. She feels the vital narcissistic thrill that the most intense moments of self-observation have brought her. She stares at her round face and her large, sky-blue eyes, at her bloody, perfectly shaped lips, at the aroused blush lighting up her cheeks. A face perfectly framed by the mass of carefully sculpted curls that is the sissy wig. She beholds the intricacy of the dress and its tight grip on her slender, petite form. She feels a wave of helpless sexual excitement consume her as she ponders the beauty of her long, flawlessly formed legs wrapped softy and tightly in the sheer embrace of the sparkling white tights, legs that lead to small, dainty feet bound tightly in the fetishistic and erotically elegant ankle boots.

Then she is aware of Richard standing directly behind her. She turns and, without any warning, he shoves a fat, pink rubber-ball gag deep into her mouth. Her eyes widen with shock, she squeals and tries to escape. He wraps a free arm around her waist and holds her firmly. The ball gag is fitted with a single, elasticated, white rubber strap, which he manages to pull over her heavily wigged head and snap in place. She looks at him with betrayed, angry and terrified eyes. He smiles at her with a heart-stopping cruelness. She feels her sex stretch even harder against the painful restrainer. And before she can do anything else, he has lifted her off her heeled feet and bound her wrists tightly behind her back with a length of pink silk ribbon. Then she is carried over to the bed and thrown on to it.

She releases a series of well-muffled pleas, her panic melodramatic, part of the game he now so obviously wants to play, the game that will let him recover the power that was lost during her dressing. He smiles and shakes his head as she wiggles her hips and kicks her feet.

'You look so good in bondage, Eve. You should be tied up all the time.'

He grabs her ankles and uses another length of ribbon to bind them tightly together. He then drags her up from the bed and throws her over his shoulders. She squeals with genuine fear and he unleashes another harsh, stilling slap to her exposed, pantied bottom. He holds her like a sack of potatoes, like a thing. An object. An object of someone else's desire.

He carries Eve down the stairs and into the living room. Here, she discovers a still tightly tethered Cherry. Poor Cherry is now obviously very agitated. She is wiggling furiously in her painfully rigid bondage and obviously very annoyed that Richard has not untied her.

'I'll be back for you in a sec,' he says to Cherry.

Then, to Eve's horror, Richard carries her from the living room, through the front door and out into the cool, dark winter's evening. Once outside, Eve notices that a large, dark-grey transit van has been parked in the driveway. Its wide back doors are open and Richard quickly deposits his pretty sissy package inside. Eve finds herself on her stomach, lying on a thick black rubber mat. Richard jumps into the van and very quickly uses a length of white rope to secure poor Eve in another tight, painful hog-tie. He then disappears, leaving Eve feeling frightened and terribly exposed. There is the sound of angry squealing and poor Cherry is deposited in the van next to Eve. She too is quickly re-hog-tied and the doors are closed. They lie in virtual darkness, Cherry furious and Eve now more frightened. Eve ponders the possibility that this is the final part of the strange plot she has seen hints of over the last few weeks. Now, finally, the terrible truth is revealed: she is being abducted, perhaps to be sold into she-male slavery. The escort agency is a front. She and Cherry have been tricked. They are being taken to a port and shipped abroad!

This elaborate fantasy exposes one undeniable truth: Eve remains darkly aroused by all aspects of this strange adventure, even her apparent kidnapping.

Richard climbs into the front of the van and starts the engine.

The van pulls out of the drive. Cherry wiggles over to Eve and presses against her body. In the dark it is impossible to see her eyes, but from her laboured breathing and intermittent squeals of protest, it is clear she has been tricked into a bondage ordeal somewhat more extensive than originally planned.

The journey is less than twenty minutes. And when Eve, freed from the hog-tie, is carried from the van, she discovers, not to her entire surprise, that she is back at Helen's large and exclusive residence. The front door is opened before they reach it and Richard gently carries a stunned, uneasy Eve past a smiling, clearly aroused Priscilla, once again dressed in her beautiful, elegant maid's costume.

Richard gently lowers Eve to her feet and unties her ankles. He tells her to walk ahead of him into the living room. She obeys with a sense of weird elation. Now she is here, she is sure things are about to change yet again, but not in the way her dark, masochistic fantasies predict. She totters on the spiked heels into a room filled with women. Some she recognises from the club, others are unknown. There is Samantha and Helen, the formidable Ms March, and Angela. All turn as she enters. And as their eyes fall upon the sissy vision that is Eve, she instinctively performs a deep curtsey, exposing her beautiful panties and her delicately hosed thighs. A ripple of affirming whispers pass among the women. Then Helen steps forward.

'You look utterly divine, Eve. I'm sure you agree, Teresa.'

Teresa March, dressed in a black evening dress and matching hose and heels, observes the gorgeous spectacle that is Eve with hungry, suitably impressed eyes. Eve stares at her with a sense of sweet doom. She knows this woman is intent upon realising all her dark, kinky fantasies of maternal control with Eve and there is nothing she can do to stop it. A thought that inspires her hard, angry cock to protest even more vigorously in its rubber-and-steel restraint.

Teresa March smiles and nods, her eyes betraying her perverse designs. Eve recalls the musky taste of her sex and her propensity for sissy she-males. For a moment she is sick with frustrated desire. But then the group of women parts slightly and all thoughts of the illness of desire are replaced by genuine astonishment and deep, deep love. For emerging from the group is a beloved figure from the past (yet also from the present), the guiding light of Eve's existence. Yes, standing just a few feet from her is Aunt Debra!

If her mouth hadn't been tightly stopped by the ball gag, it would have fallen open in true amazement. Indeed, she finds herself unable to believe that this gorgeous image, this dream become reality, is in fact Aunt Debra. But a detailed analysis confirms the shocking truth. Dressed in a very tight red nylon sweater that perfectly displays her still firm and large bust, a black velvet skirt that reaches down over broad, curvaceous hips and firm, shapely thighs to just above her knees, sheer black nylon tights and three-inch-heeled, black leather court shoes, she is, as ever, a vision of mature sexual beauty.

Aunt Debra smiles warmly and holds out her arms. With her own hands still tethered behind her back, Eve totters forward eagerly and falls into her aunt's tight embrace. Debra presses her she-male niece's head deep into her warm, scented bosom and Eve sinks into a perfect world of total sensuality, barely holding back tears of joy.

Eventually, Aunt Debra very gently extracts Eve and looks down at her with love-filled eyes.

'You look absolutely gorgeous, Eve.'

The pretty she-male wants to announce her joy and love, but the gag is tight and highly effective, and all she can manage is a series of desperate, well-muffled squeals.

Debra smiles and runs a blood-red-nailed finger over the curved edge of the gag.

'You look so sweet gagged, Eve. Now you can tell me all your deepest desires with your eyes. Your voice will always be the greatest threat to Eve. That's why it's been so wonderful, in a way, to hear your true voice – the voice inside – the secret voice – in your letters and in our e-mail conversations. And now in your eyes. Yes, my darling, I can see Eve so clearly now. Let's keep you gagged for as long as possible, my pretty sissy dove. And your dress – isn't it utterly divine? Teresa has always been such a terrible tease when it comes to costumes for sissies.'

Poor Eve is lost in an ecstatic whirlpool of adoration and masochistic desire. She has forgotten everything but the glorious apparition that is Aunt Debra. Her aunt's powerful rose-scented perfume – the same perfume she wore on those two fateful days twelve years before – washes over Eve's sissified form and sends her hurtling back in time to Debra's elegant bedroom, that gorgeous garden of life-changing secrets. Her sex screams for release and a twinge of pain shoots through her dainty form, a pain that momentarily flickers across her eyes.

'Helen tells me you have finally been sealed in the restrainer and plugged. If I had remained here with you, after your mother died, I would have done it much sooner. Not only to keep you under control, but to ensure that all those pretty girls didn't get their hands on you. Luckily, you were far too shy ever to allow a girl near you, and you certainly listened very carefully to my counsel.'

Her aunt's voice has deepened with age and now has a distinctly American tinge; it is also huskier and thus much sexier. There are signs of age in her face, but this has only added a depth to her profound, maternal beauty.

But then, as Eve stares into her aunt's soul-consuming eyes, there is a question, a simple and obvious question: how did she get here?

'I can see you're curious about my sudden arrival. And here of all places.'

Eve nods eagerly.

'I'm afraid there has been a certain deception, my love. But a necessary deception. When I first came across the Crème de la Crème, I knew they were the perfect agency for your true self-realisation. I also knew they were an ideal business opportunity for me. An expansion of my existing interests. You see I have made a rather good living in

213

America in what is rather brutally described as the sex industry. My experience with you wasn't actually my first experience of male submissives or transvestites. I had already begun to explore the commercial potentialities of female domination after my marriage broke up. But this, plus my nascent career as a dominatrix ... well it really tested my ex-husband's patience. Unfortunately, he was a very powerful man and, soon after we parted company and your mother passed on, he began to make life rather difficult for me professionally. Especially with the police. So, with the money I made on the house and my professional profits, I moved to California, where there was a particularly strong market for the services of an English dominant.'

Eve listens in astonishment, amazed and excited. Now everything begins to make sense. The reason she had been so sympathetic, so expert, so informed. Adam's transformation into Eve had been initiated by a professional dominatrix.

'A client drew my attention to the Crème de la Crème website and club. He had travelled in England and attended a Sunday evening event. As he was a wealthy, powerful man in his own right, I was more than interested. I contacted Helen at a time when the club was planning a significant diversification. A fortuitous communication, as the club was looking for investors. I had always envisaged getting you to come to the States when the time was right, when Eve had fully matured, and when I could find the time to be with you. But Crème de la Crème came along and then everything seemed to have a perfect, unavoidable logic. You wouldn't come to California: I would return to the UK. Helen and I drew up a partnership agreement, I persuaded you to come to the club. We employed Angie to keep an eye on you. It was obvious to both of us that you would be a vital part of our future plans. This was proved as soon as Teresa laid eyes on you. There are many others who want you as well, my love. Many others who can see what we can see, what I have always seen: your feminine perfection and the erotic

214

ambiguity that comes with it. You really are the perfect she-male.'

Eve looks at her with a stunned gaze. All of this, everything that has happened in the last few weeks, has been driven by her aunt, her incredible Aunt Debra!

'So you see, Eve, we both have our secret selves. And yes, I admit I have, to a certain extent, misled you. But for a splendid cause and to help you finally realise your full potential.'

She releases Eve from her firm but gentle embrace and Eve moans with a terrible need into the fat ball gag, a need that has gone unfulfilled for twelve years. Eve looks at Debra's splendid, mature body, at her large, ample bosom, at her long, black nylon-sheathed legs, and then at her beautiful face. Debra's smile fades slightly and she laughs lightly.

'I think you and I need to spend a few hours alone, my pet. There's a lot of time to make up.'

Eve squeals with delight and again nods furiously. The rest of the women guests laugh.

'Don't work her too hard!' Ms March shouts, inspiring even greater laughter.

'You can use the second guest room,' Helen says. 'Richard is using the first. I believe he will be indulging himself with Cherry tonight.'

Aunt Debra nods. She leads Eve from the room and up a flight of long, winding stairs to a landing bordered by two rows of white doors, each with a gold-coloured handle.

During Eve's journey up the stairs, her eyes are fixed tightly on her aunt's elegantly hosed calves and her mind swims with this final chapter of her astonishing induction into the Crème de la Crème club.

Debra stops by a door at the end of the corridor and removes a small silver key from a pocket in her skirt. Smiling at Eve, she unlocks the door and pushes it open. The sound of angry squeals immediately fills the corridor. Eve gasps with even greater amazement into the fat ball gag. For before her is a small, somewhat anonymous room whose main focal point is a large double bed. On the bed is Cherry, still in the same sexy undies that had teased Eve's eyes so effectively during their joint bondage ordeal. She is still tightly bound and gagged and locked in a strict, taut hog-tie. She squeals with genuine fury when Eve and Aunt Debra appear in the doorway and, positioned close to the edge of the bed, sways precariously in her bondage.

Aunt Debra then turns to Eve. 'You both look so very lovely in bondage, and Richard is a keen exponent of disciplinary rope work.'

Cherry's eyes suddenly widen with anger and they fall upon Eve. Eve is instantly uncomfortable, yet also strangely aroused. And at the heart of this arousal is a sadistic pleasure. Yes: Eve is enjoying Cherry's predicament, and she quickly finds herself pressing her nylon-sheathed thighs tightly together to push the teasing dildo plug a little further into her arse.

'Cherry is clearly infatuated with you, Eve. And, over the next few weeks, you will get a chance to become the best of friends. But tonight, you are for me, and I have insisted that she be made physically aware of her overriding obligations. And Richard is more than happy to oblige.'

Eve remembers the afternoon, the deep pleasure of their mutual bondage adventure, and momentarily wishes she could join her on the bed.

'Now it's time to come with me.'

Eve nods, and after one more hungry glance at Cherry, follows her from the room.

'She's got a long night ahead of her,' Aunt Debra says, leading Eve to the next door down. 'And so have we.'

She opens the door and they enter a room that is almost exactly the same as the one holding Cherry. Debra shuts and locks the door, and then she sits down on the bed before a nervous, desire-tormented Eve.

'Over the next six months, you will achieve the final realisation of Eve. To do this, you will have to surrender to us completely, my love. I will personally oversee this final, vital changing. I have purchased a house nearby, and you will move in with me immediately. We will sell your house and the proceeds will go into a special bank account that will remain under my control, as will all your earnings from working for the Crème de la Crème as an escort and administrator. When not undergoing training or working, you will act as my personal maid. On weekends, Cherry will be allowed to visit. During these visits the restrainers will be removed to help progress your relationship.'

Eve nods, stunned and elated.

'Basically, you must give up everything you were. You must sacrifice your old self entirely to reveal what has until now been your secret self. This is the only way we can express the great, erotic truth of Eve.'

Aunt Debra then rises from the bed and slowly lowers the zip on her skirt. It falls away to reveal two perfectly shaped, very long legs sealed tightly in the sheerest and darkest of black nylon hose. Eve moans helplessly into her gag and watches as her beloved Aunt sits back down on the bed and parts her legs. Eve looks down at the soaking, dark patch spreading across the gusset of the tights and feels a sense of unbearable beauty and intense, mind-bending arousal. Her cock burns like a white-hot metal ember inside the erotically unyielding restrainer.

'Teresa was highly complimentary about your oral skills. I trust you will live up to her praise tonight. Now kneel before me.'

Eve obeys without a second's hesitation. Aunt Debra removes the gag. As she leans forward to do so, the powerful, arousing stink of her sex smashes into Eve's pale face and inspires a gasp of furious sexual need.

'I think you know what to do next, my pretty petal.'

Eve nods, runs her tongue over her blood-red lips and shuffles forward into the great sado-erotic darkness, knowing that now, finally, she is becoming what she has always known is her true self, that the secret hidden for so long, which has been so gradually and excitingly revealed over the last two weeks, is now – at last – being fully and spectacularly revealed. In a few months, she will have breasts, she will have male, female and she-male lovers and, most wonderfully, she will have a life of intricately and permanently feminised servitude under the gentle and absolute tyranny of her gorgeous and beloved Aunt Debra. As she leans forward, she knows she is truly looking into heaven.

nexus

The leading publisher of fetish and adult fiction

TELL US WHAT YOU THINK!

Readers' ideas and opinions matter to us. Take a few minutes to fill in the questionnaire below and you'll be entered into a prize draw to win a year's worth of Nexus books (36 titles)

Terms and conditions apply – see end of questionnaire.

1. Sex: Are you male ☐   female ☐   a couple ☐?

2. Age: Under 21 ☐   21–30 ☐   31–40 ☐   41–50 ☐   51–60 ☐   over 60 ☐

3. Where do you buy your Nexus books from?

☐ A chain book shop. If so, which one(s)?

_____

☐ An independent book shop. If so, which one(s)?

_____

☐ A used book shop/charity shop
☐ Online book store. If so, which one(s)?

_____

4. How did you find out about Nexus books?

☐ Browsing in a book shop
☐ A review in a magazine
☐ Online
☐ Recommendation
☐ Other _____

5. In terms of settings, which do you prefer? (Tick as many as you like.)

☐ Down to earth and as realistic as possible
☐ Historical settings. If so, which period do you prefer?

_____

☐ Fantasy settings – barbarian worlds

- ☐ Completely escapist/surreal fantasy
- ☐ Institutional or secret academy
- ☐ Futuristic/sci fi
- ☐ Escapist but still believable
- ☐ Any settings you dislike?

_____

- ☐ Where would you like to see an adult novel set?

_____

6. In terms of storylines, would you prefer:
- ☐ Simple stories that concentrate on adult interests?
- ☐ More plot and character-driven stories with less explicit adult activity?
- ☐ We value your ideas, so give us your opinion of this book:

_____

_____

_____

7. In terms of your adult interests, what do you like to read about? (Tick as many as you like.)
- ☐ Traditional corporal punishment (CP)
- ☐ Modern corporal punishment
- ☐ Spanking
- ☐ Restraint/bondage
- ☐ Rope bondage
- ☐ Latex/rubber
- ☐ Leather
- ☐ Female domination and male submission
- ☐ Female domination and female submission
- ☐ Male domination and female submission
- ☐ Willing captivity
- ☐ Uniforms
- ☐ Lingerie/underwear/hosiery/footwear (boots and high heels)
- ☐ Sex rituals
- ☐ Vanilla sex
- ☐ Swinging
- ☐ Cross-dressing/TV

☐ Enforced feminisation

☐ Others – tell us what you don't see enough of in adult fiction:

_____

_____

_____

8. Would you prefer books with a more specialised approach to your interests, i.e. a novel specifically about uniforms? If so, which subject(s) would you like to read a Nexus novel about?

_____

_____

_____

9. Would you like to read true stories in Nexus books? For instance, the true story of a submissive woman, or a male slave? Tell us which true revelations you would most like to read about:

_____

_____

_____

10. What do you like best about Nexus books?

_____

_____

11. What do you like least about Nexus books?

_____

_____

12. Which are your favourite titles?

_____

_____

13. Who are your favourite authors?

_____

_____

14. Which covers do you prefer? Those featuring:
(Tick as many as you like.)

☐ Fetish outfits
☐ More nudity
☐ Two models
☐ Unusual models or settings
☐ Classic erotic photography
☐ More contemporary images and poses
☐ A blank/non-erotic cover
☐ What would your ideal cover look like?

_____

15. Describe your ideal Nexus novel in the space provided:

_____
_____
_____
_____

16. Which celebrity would feature in one of your Nexus-style fantasies?
We'll post the best suggestions on our website – anonymously!

_____

THANKS FOR YOUR TIME

Now simply write the title of this book in the space below and cut out the
questionnaire pages. Post to: Nexus, Marketing Dept., Thames Wharf Studios,
Rainville Rd, London W6 9HA

Book title: _____

TERMS AND CONDITIONS

To be published in October 2006

BRUSH STROKES
Penny Birch

Amber Oakley is dominant and beautiful. But just a little too beautiful for her own good. As far from accepting her sexuality as she seeks to portray it, her fellow enthusiasts almost invariably want to get her knickers down, usually for spanking. In *Brush Strokes*, her attempts to resist the attentions of the firm and matronly Hannah Riley quickly come to nothing, and Amber is once more back over the knee, behind bared as a hairbrush is applied to her well-fleshed cheeks. Rather than give in, she tries to resist, but only manages to get herself into even deeper trouble.

£6.99   ISBN 0 352 34072 X

CORRUPTION
Virginia Crowley

The greater the degree of purity in a person, the darker the taint on their soul if they succumb to temptation. Not even the men and women of the holy orders are safe from corruption as Lady Stephanie Peabody and her host of greedy, voluptuous collaborators engage in the most sinister forms of seductive manipulation. Not even the Prior, the nuns at the convent, or Stephanie's principled stepdaughter, Laura, are safe from the threat of spiritual corruption.

With the aid of a powerful aphrodisiac, Stephanie's coven of cruel, demanding harlots tempt the righteous with the tawdry delights of the flesh – at the expense of their immortal souls.

£6.99   ISBN 0 352 34073 8

THE DOMINO QUEEN
Cyrian Amberlake

Wherever dark pleasure reigns, there the Domino Queen keeps her court.

Whether she's initiating a lonely peasant girl or training a trio of eager slaves, Josephine deals out tenderness and cruelty with an even, elegant hand.

Meanwhile Cadence Szathkowicz, the lover Josephine abandoned on Dominica, is searching for her. From pulsating Los Angeles to the strict discipline of Madame Suriko's house in Chicago, Cadence travels on an odyssey of pleasure and pain.

All she has to guide her is the sign Josephine wears between her breasts: the tattoo of the domino mask.

£6.99   ISBN 0 352 34074 6

If you would like more information about Nexus titles, please visit our website at www.nexus-books.co.uk, or send a large stamped addressed envelope to:

Nexus, Thames Wharf Studios,
Rainville Road, London W6 9HA